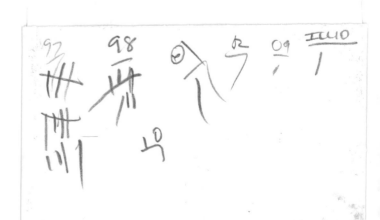

The *Fred Astaire*
and *Ginger Rogers*
Murder Case

The *Fred Astaire* and *Ginger Rogers* Murder Case

George Baxt

St. Martin's Press ⚓ New York

Production Editor: *David Stanford Burr*

Design: *Nancy Resnick*

Library of Congress Cataloging-in-Publication Data

Baxt, George.
    The Fred Astaire and Ginger Rogers murder case / George Baxt.
        p.   cm.
    ISBN 0-312-15129-2
    1. Astaire, Fred, 1898–1987—Fiction. 2. Rogers, Ginger,
1911–1995—Fiction. 3. Dancers—United States—Fiction. 4. Murder—
California—Los Angeles—
Fiction. 5. Espionage—California—Los   Angeles—Fiction. 6.
Hollywood (Los Angeles, Calif.)—Fiction. I. Title.
    PS3552.A8478F74   1997
    813'.54—dc21   96-48766
                                      CIP

First Edition: February 1997

10 9 8 7 6 5 4 3 2 1

*To Tom Toth—always a friend to me
and to the late Carole Lombard*

The *Fred Astaire*
and *Ginger Rogers*
Murder Case

One

*I*mpresario Sol Hurok's office on West 57th Street in New York City, snugly ensconced on an upper floor of an office building cosily situated near Carnegie Hall, was tastefully decorated, the walls festooned with placards advertising Hurok triumphs dating back to the early twenties. These triumphs included tours starring the legendary ballerina Anna Pavlova and the great Russian baritone Feodor Chaliapin (whom Hurok on occasion referred to as Charlie Chaliapin); they trumpeted the earliest glories of George Balanchine with the Ballets Russes de Monte Carlo and introducing three teenage dancers heralded as the "baby ballerinas—Tamara Toumanova, Irina Baronova, and Tatiana Riabouchinskaya. As violinist Yehudi Menuhin exclaimed once, "You are nobody until you have been presented by Sol Hurok."

S. HUROK PRESENTS on a billboard was usually a guarantee of sold-out houses. It wasn't always so, but now, in 1952, the last year of Harry S. Truman's presidency, Sol Hurok was riding higher than ever before in his long and lucrative career. There was 20th Century's movie about his life and career, *Tonight We Sing*, a tastefully packaged production of lies, legends, and myths in which the Jewish Hurok was impersonated by the gentile David Wayne and audiences stayed away in droves. There was a fanciful autobiography, *S. Hurok Presents*, which was ludicrous and laughable and soon won its place on the remainder tables of bookstores across the United States. Yes, Sol Hurok's star now blazed as it had never blazed before, and would never blaze again. He had captured the legendary Baronovitch Ballet for a long tour of the Americas, North, South, and Central, now that they were able to secure exit visas since the death that year of the despotic Soviet leader, Stalin.

("Poisoned, I'm sure," said Hurok, exhaling a smoke ring.

"If so, then there is a God," said Mae Frohman, who had been for over thirty years Hurok's trusted assistant and confidante.)

And then came an inspiration only the brilliant showman could conjure up. A television special for the Baronovitch Ballet (contracted by the National Broadcasting System, referred to by Mae as the National Broadchasing System), a two-hour special co-starring them with none other than the motion picture dancing legends Fred Astaire and Ginger Rogers. "The ratings," Hurok assured Mae, "will fly through the ceiling. And then through the roof and on to heaven and even past that!"

"Where to?" asked Mae, examining a fingernail.

"To wherever," said Hurok with a shrug. He got to his feet, cigar firmly clamped in his mouth, and began pacing the office, arms raised above his head like a victorious gladiator. He was warming up. "The public will clamor to see Fred and Ginger reunited after five years. You mock my words . . ."

"Mark," corrected Mae.

". . . it will be sensational! Fred and Ginger are very extinguished personalities!"

"Distinguished," corrected Mae.

"They are legends!" He sighed. "Now all I have to do is make a deal with them."

Mae's eyes rolled up in her head and then dropped down again. "You haven't got them?"

"I'll get them. I'll get them. Put your chips on the number marked S. Hurok. I'm on a roll, my darling Mae, a very big roll. What time is our flight to Los Angeles?"

"It leaves Idlewild at five P.M. sharp."

Hurok looked at his wristwatch. "My bag is here?"

"Outside, in the reception room."

"And your bag?"

"Also."

"Mae, you're not showing enthusiasm."

Mae managed a smile as she reminded her boss, "I hate flying. Do I have to keep reminding you?"

"You'd prefer perhaps a Greyhound Bus?" Hurok buzzed the outer office on his intercom. "Tessie, is that you?"

Mae's assistant, Tess Barrow, favored Hurok with her standard nasal response, "Yes, boss, it's me."

"When the car taking us to the airport arrives, tell me immediately."

"Yes, boss."

The office boy asked Tess, "They off to L.A.?"

"That's right."

"What time does the broom leave?"

Tess flashed him a withering look, little knowing that within the next decade he would open his own office, stealing stars from Hurok and hiring Tess, not because she was all that good but because she knew just about all of Sol Hurok's trade secrets.

It was three hours earlier—and sunnier—in Los Angeles, a smog-free Los Angeles where you could still see the sun and a beautiful cloudless sky and where cicadas chirruped in the Hollywood Hills above Sunset Boulevard. Dr. Igor Romanov's beautiful pink villa was situated on an acre that overlooked Sunset and Hollywood Boulevards, with rows of cedars of Lebanon trees towering over the driveway that led to the front door like a neat line of sentries on duty. The villa served as both office and residence. The front of the ground floor was the doctor's reception room and office, both spacious and sedately furnished. Alida Rimsky, in her neatly starched and ironed white uniform, was Romanov's assistant and the reception room was her domain.

It was late Friday afternoon and Alida was grateful the doctor was with his ultimate patient of the day. The patient in question was Ginger Rogers, glamorous movie star and one-time dancing partner of Fred Astaire, who had no use for psychiatry. When in need of advice, Fred would phone his sister, Adele, his first dancing partner and now the lady of a castle in Ireland, having wisely used her head over a decade earlier and snapped up Lord Carnarvon's offer of marriage and early retirement from the theater. He was of course rich and fairly attractive, the degree of his attractiveness being enhanced by the size of his wealth, which was sizable. Now that her baby brother Freddie was an international movie star, Adele capitalized on his fame and secured a solid niche for herself in Ireland's tightly knit social circles. She liked Ginger but did not care much for Ginger's ever-present mother, Lela, whom Adele had nicknamed "Lethal," a nickname that was even more appropriate as far as Adele was concerned since Lela had volunteered an appearance before the House Un-American Activities Committee (HUAC) in Washington, D.C., branding actors and writers and directors as communists ("Them rotten commies!"), which amazingly enough did not ruin her daughter's career. It was never known what Ginger thought of her mother's perfidy, as most of Hollywood assumed Ginger wasn't given much to thought. They were quite wrong, however, as at the age of forty-two, Ginger was constantly giving thought to her recently acquired younger husband, Jacques Bergerac, an actor by definition rather than by qualification. He was also gorgeous, and at forty-two that counted for a lot with Ginger.

Ginger was reclining on the doctor's well-upholstered couch, which he himself had designed, clutching the requisite tissue in her right hand, occasionally dabbing at her nose, her left hand artfully poised over her head. The doctor was staring out the window and stifling a yawn. He heard his patient say, "Sol Hurok wants Fred and me to do this TV special. You've heard of Sol Hurok, I'm sure. He's also from the Soviet Union but many years ago. Anyway, he wants us to do this two-hour special with some ballet company. With Hurok there's always some ballet company.

I sometimes wonder if he was born on his toes. Anyway, let me think . . ." She closed her eyes and rubbed her forehead with her left hand. Then her eyes flew open and she snapped her fingers. "Baronovitch?"

"Baronovitch?"

"Baronovitch. That's it. The Baronovitch Ballet. I've never heard of them, have you?"

"Actually, I have," he said smoothly, although he seemed to be having trouble controlling his voice. "Though they came into prominence after I fled the Soviet Union."

" 'Fled,' " repeated Ginger. "It sounds so exciting, so romantic. 'Fled the Soviet Union.' Boy, that's nothing to 'flying the coop,' which I have done on many an occasion. Now then, where was I?"

"Flying the coop."

"No no no no. Baronovitch, that's where I was, Baronovitch. Where is Baronovitch? Do you know?"

"North of Moscow. It was once a lovely little village."

"And now they're big enough to have their own ballet company. Think of that. And wouldn't you know Sol Hurok would snatch them out from under the noses of the other big booking companies."

"The company is coming to America?"

"They've been here touring for months. Don't you read *Variety*?"

"No, I don't."

"Of course you don't. Why should a psychiatrist give a damn how much a show grosses on tour unless he's invested in it. Have you ever invested—"

He interrupted her swiftly. "Miss Rogers, let's get back to the ballet company. It obviously disturbs you."

"It doesn't really disturb me. It's just that Hurok wants Fred and me to do a TV special with them."

"Do you want to do it?"

"Yes and no." The doctor looked with exasperation at the ceiling. In the year or more that she had been his patient, the doctor had come to recognize "yes and no" as the most common expression in Ginger's vocabulary.

("Do you want to marry Jacques Bergerac?"

"Yes and no."

"You wish your mother wouldn't get politically involved?"

"Yes and no," and so on ad infinitum.)

"Of course the prestige would be fantastic," he heard Ginger say. "I mean Fred and Ginger reunited again and dancing with a Russian ballet company. Wow!" Her eyes were sparkling. "It's going to be a lot of hard work. I'm not trained to dance on point. I'm a hoofer!" She sat up. "Fred wants me to do it. Jacques wants me to do it. My mother's all for it even though she hates communists."

"Not everyone in the Soviet Union belongs to the Communist party."

"They don't?" She struggled to a sitting position. "I thought they had to!"

"There are many noncommunists in the USSR. I fled from there. I'm not a communist."

"Thanks for telling me." She smiled. "That'll make Lela feel better. I mean she knows you're doing me a world of good but she worries you might be brainwashing me."

"My dear Miss Rogers, psychiatric treatment *is* a form of brainwashing. A very healthy form."

She thought it over for a moment. "Oh. I'll tell Lela."

"Why tell her anything?"

"If I don't, she gets suspicious and please don't ask me to explain *that*."

There was a knock at the door and Alida Rimsky entered.

"Is it time?" asked the doctor.

"Yes, doctor," said the nurse crisply.

"My," said Ginger, "how time flies when I'm with you, doctor." She went to the wall mirror and began fixing her luxurious mane of blond hair.

"Alida?"

"Yes?"

"Did you know the Baronovitch Ballet was in America?"

"The Baronovitch? Yes I think I read something about them not too long ago."

"Sol Hurok wants Miss Rogers and Fred Astaire to appear with them in a two-hour television special."

"On NBC," added Ginger.

"Well, isn't that something to look forward to?" Ginger found Alida's slight trace of a Russian accent charming.

Ginger asked, "Are you familiar with the company?"

"It's a long time since I left Russia."

The doctor spoke. "So now that Stalin is dead, Moscow is thawing. It sounds as though Gosconcert is being unusually free with their exit visas for artistes."

"Gos . . . what?" asked Ginger.

"Gosconcert. They decide which artists will be permitted to perform abroad and, of course, they control their fees."

"But that's communism!" exclaimed Ginger.

"That sure is," confirmed the doctor. "Gasconcert wields a lot of power from their shabby little office on Neglinnaya Street."

"You've been there?"

"In my youth, yes, I had occasion to apply for an exit visa. I wanted to go to Paris to study."

"Oh my. You wanted to paint."

"No, my dear. I wanted to be a concert pianist."

"No!"

"Yes, and now that you have pried a secret out of me, it is time to say *au revoir* until next we meet."

Alida said swiftly, "Monday at noon."

Ginger ignored both of them. "But here you are, so you got out at last."

"Yes," he said, leading her to the reception room, to which Alida held the door open.

"I'm so glad," said Ginger. "What would I do without you?" She moved her attention to Alida. "And here *you* are. Say, do either of you have friends with the Baronovitch company?"

Romanov said smoothly, "Who knows? I'm away from the Soviet such a long time, perhaps old friends are with them now. I doubt it. The few dancers I knew would be of an age where they would be of no value any longer as dancers."

"Ha! Don't I know that. Put them out to pasture or shoot them. Or put them in a Republic picture." She waved airily as she strolled toward the front door. "See you Monday!" She pulled the door shut behind her and walked to her automobile while rummaging in her handbag for the keys and wondering as she frequently had cause to what connection the doctor and his nurse might still have to the old country. She got into the car, put the key in the engine, revved the motor, and drove off to a date with Fred Astaire.

Mike Romanoff's restaurant in Beverly Hills was a very popular watering hole for the Hollywood community. Romanoff was a bogus prince who only kidded himself into thinking he was a scion of the Russian royal family. But his pose was great for business. Humphrey Bogart, for example, was there almost every night of the week either for cocktails or dinner or both, frequently escorting his glamorous wife, Lauren Bacall. Surprisingly, the food was good and for the stars he liked Romanoff's would deliver dinner to their homes on nights when they were either too tired after a day's filming or needed to stay home and memorize dialogue.

Ginger occupied a booth with Fred Astaire. She nursed a ginger ale with maraschino cherries, which she doted on, and he was working on a pot of tea with lemon. He explained to Ginger, "That's how the Russians prefer it. With lemon."

"I see. That's how the Russians prefer it."

"Stop sounding like your mother." Lela Rogers was one of Fred's unfavorite people. He wasn't a political animal but he disapproved of Lela's dedication to branding as communist anyone she disapproved of. He once started to ask Ginger how she could endure such a terrible woman as a mother but immediately thought better of it. Ginger knew her mother couldn't win any popularity contests and wasn't about to try to, but still Ginger didn't seem to make any effort to put a clamp on her mother's mouth. What the hell, he reminded himself, they'd been through hell together making Ginger a star without a father to help them. Lela had literally thrown herself on the altars of the gods bargaining for Ginger's success.

"Listen, Fred, Lela's worried we'll have HUAC on our tails if we work with Baronovitch."

"I've got news for HUAC if they don't already know, and I'm sure they do—this tour is approved and sponsored by the State Department."

"Is that good?"

"You couldn't ask for better. Hurok's no sap. He's been handling the U.S. and the Soviet for three decades. He's puppet master, ventriloquist, Machiavelli, and superb taste all wrapped up in one."

"Sounds like quite a catch."

"Now listen, Ginger, listen carefully. NBC is offering us both a small fortune to do this job."

"That's music to my ears," said Ginger, who in addition to supporting herself, her mother, an agent, a manager, and an impressive household staff, was now supporting her new husband.

"Here's more music. I'm to choreograph the show." Ginger smiled. She knew his ambition to choreograph. "Hermes will be there with me." Hermes Pan was the talented and highly respected choreographer who had done many of the Astaire and Rogers musicals and now worked with Fred at Metro-Goldwyn-Mayer where both were under contract. "You and I will do a few numbers together, I'll do a couple of solos, and of course you'll have some too," he added hastily. "But the big number will be my ballet, which will be the spectacular closing number."

Ginger folded her arms. "And what's the ballet?"

Fred said eagerly, *"Rasputin."*

"Rasputin? Wasn't he some crazy monk or something?"

"He was called the Mad Monk."

"Oh yes. I remember the movie with the three Barrymores . . ."

"Rasputin and the Empress."

"Right. I don't think it made any money."

"That's not important, Ginger. I'm going to dance Rasputin."

"And me?" She took a sip of ginger ale.

"The Czarina. The wife of Czar Nicholas the Second."

"Uh-oh."

"What's wrong".

"Didn't she have kids?"

Fred said weakly, "Five."

"Five kids? So what has she got to dance about? What kind of five kids?"

"Four daughters and a son. He was the youngest." There was a briefcase resting next to him and he opened it and found a photo of the Romanov family. "Here's a photo of the family taken a year before they were murdered."

"They were bad dancers?"

"Come on, Ginger. Be serious."

"I am being serious." She studied the photograph. Her eyes narrowed. "Fred."

"Yes?"

"These four daughters are four very large daughters. They are obviously in their teens." She leaned across the table and asked practically in a whisper, "You want me to be the mother of these *oversized* youngsters?"

"Ginger," said Fred seriously, "you'll be brilliant. A sensation. A *new* Ginger Rogers."

"As an *old* Russian mother." She put the photograph aside. "The hell with it. I'm no toe dancer and I don't plan to start practicing now."

"But Ginger," he said eagerly, "that's the novelty of it. While the others dance on point, we'll be tap dancing!"

Ginger sat back. "A tap-dancing empress? A tap-dancing Rasputin? Do you want the number of my psychiatrist?"

"Why? He can't dance."

"Fred Astaire. You have gone around the bend."

Fred said excitedly, "It's fresh! It's new! It's innovative! We'll knock them out of their socks!"

"I've got big news for you, you're knocking me out of my socks."

Fred said seriously, "Ginger, times are changing and we've got to change with them. I get older and my leading ladies get younger. It's ludicrous. Audiences aren't as dumb as we like to think they are."

"Go ahead. Say it."

"Say what?"

"I'm not the kid I used to be, that's what." She lowered her voice. "I'm forty-two, give or take a few hours, and how many parts are there for a woman of a certain age. I know it, Claudette Colbert and Irene Dunne know it."

"They've been playing mothers for years."

"They haven't been dancing for years." She reached into her handbag and dabbed at her nose with a tissue she pulled out of the bag.

"That's right. They haven't. But they've moved gracefully into more mature roles and they're still stars."

"Stop kidding me. The offers have dried up for them. I know. I keep in touch with all the ladies. And damn it, they're rich. I'm not rich!"

"You can be by opening up a whole new world for yourself. Ginger, I wasn't going to tell you, but Hurok wants to line up a grand tour for the ballet and us. We'll make hundreds of thousands of dollars and attract hundreds of thousands of new fans. For crying out loud, Ginger, he wants to bring us to New York. Think of it! Astaire and Rogers back on Broadway!"

Ginger sniffled. "In what theater?"

"The best the Schuberts have to offer, if I know Sol Hurok. Sol Hurok, Ginger. His name is synonymous with prestige, with impeccable good taste. A Sol Hurok presentation. The big time!"

"You nitwit! What the hell have we been in these past thirty years. The big time! The big time!"

Fred leaned across and took her hand. "Ginger, this will be the biggest time ever. Please sign your contract."

She took a sip of ginger ale and then said with a wicked grin, "I signed it this morning. But my, you do a real hard sell!"

*T*wo

*H*erb Villon was probably the movie crowd's most popular detective. He knew just about everybody in films and those who knew him treated him with respect. They also knew they could call on him for help when help was needed and he would offer his services with discretion. He never asked for or expected monetary rewards, he just wanted assistance when assistance was needed, which was frequently. He was a dab hand at covering up scandals, especially when he felt the victim or victims were being set up. He was instrumental, for example, in helping clear Errol Flynn when a couple of teenagers accused him of raping them on his yacht, the incident giving birth to the expression "in like Flynn." He was particularly helpful to powerful producers, especially when they were on the verge of being rendered powerless by accusations of infidelity.

Villon was a veteran of the L.A. police force, having served as a detective since the last days of silent films. With him in his office in his precinct in downtown Los Angeles was his partner, Jim Mallory, a few years Villon's junior and most often referred to, especially by actresses and gay actors, as "adorable." Neither man had ever married and neither Herb nor Jim thought they were missing anything. Herb had a steady girlfriend, Hazel Dickson, who sold gossip to columnists. She was a genius at picking up tips and following up on them. She knew just which items to peddle to the queen of Hollywood gossip, Louella Parsons and the lesser queen, Hedda Hopper. Both were equally vicious, dangerous, and feared. Hazel forgot when she gave up wondering if Herb would ever marry her, because one day she realized it wasn't important. She didn't want children, because she had no time to be a mother and she knew Herb had little taste for Little League or Boy Scouts. He didn't want to take any children to a football. game or to enjoy the rides on Venice Pier. His idea of a good time, besides the occasional roll in the hay with Hazel, was to spend some time in the peace and tranquility of such popular and populated cemeteries as Forest Lawn and Hollywood Cemetery behind Paramount Studios. There he enjoyed the Douglas Fairbanks Lagoon, an impressive waterway constructed to the silent film star's memory by his son Doug Jr. He liked visiting the mausoleum that held Rudolph Valentino's ashes and once saw the mysterious lady in black who honored Valentino's memory with a visit on each anniversary of his death.

Jim Mallory was wondering if his tuxedo would fit for the big do that night. Sol Hurok was throwing a lavish wingding in the ballroom of the Ambassador Hotel, situated in the downtown section on Wilshire Boulevard, and Jim, Herb, and Hazel had invitations. Hazel wangled her own as she usually had to do, but Herb and Jim were invited at the express request of the handsome young man sitting across from Herb Villon's desk. He was Don Magrew of the CIA, whom they had met several days earlier in Sol Hurok's suite at the Ambassador. Magrew, when apprised of Villon and Mallory's reputation, had asked Hurok to secure their services to which Hurok responded lavishly with "Anything for the CIO." Magrew learned that just about any mangled English would pop out of Hurok's mouth and wasn't surprised when Hurok asked him at lunch, "How long have you been with the COD?" When Magrew warned Villon that Hurok was a lot like the other mangler of the language, Sam Goldwyn, Villon said they were interchangeable, adding, "And besides, Sam's press agent writes most of his Goldwynisms for him. Hurok's are strictly his own."

Magrew asked, "You know Hurok?"

"Oh sure. We've crossed trails many times in the past. I helped clear one of his tenors, who was accused, in Sol's own words, of moral turpentine."

Magrew chuckled. Mallory had heard that one so often the best he could muster was a weak snicker.

"Anyway," said Herb, anxious to get on with the purpose of the meeting, "let's get going. Have you any positive makes on suspected spies in the Baronovitch company?"

"Just about anybody in the Soviet Union is a suspected spy, but not all that many are active. The State Department doesn't want anybody in the troupe hauled in, because that could cause a very big stink. If we get anything on anybody, the boys in Washington would prefer we wag a finger under their noses and tell them to lay off or they get sent home pronto. Unless, of course, we catch them red-handed—no pun intended—with a hand in the cookie jar and then we have every right to detain them. They're useful for exchange."

"What kind of exchange?" asked Mallory.

"We trade spies all the time. You know, we'll give you such and such for so and so and no questions asked. Of course often ours are returned slightly damaged. Cigarette burns unpleasantly made to nipples and/or genitals, you know, the sort of thing that brings a song to a sadist's lips."

Mallory was buying none of it. "You trying to tell me we don't torture theirs?"

"Never physically. Only subtly. You know, like putting a sex-starved bastard in a room with a couple of naked women, except they're separated by a thick glass partition."

Mallory said, "Yeah, that's torture."

Magrew asked Villon, "You've got the lists of the guests invited?"

Villon held up several sheets of paper. "Just about every Russian name in Hollywood. From Mischa Auer to Slavko Vorkapich."

Magrew asked, "Who's Vorkapich?"

"Hollywood's most expensive special-effects genius."

"I don't think we did a check on him."

"You don't have to. I'll vouch for him. Chances are he'll skip the evening. He spends most of his time in his workshop." He stopped talking while studying Magrew, who was torching a pipeful of tobacco. "You did a check on every guest invited tonight?"

"That's right."

"Including Jim and me?"

"That's right."

"What have you got on Hazel Dickson?"

"A very nosy yenta."

Villon smiled broadly. "That's my Hazel!"

"Now let me fill you in on the Baronovitch troupe." He had extracted typewritten pages from a briefcase and a pair of glasses from his inside jacket pocket. They were frameless. Very chic, thought Mallory. "Now let me see . . . You know, of course, Hurok didn't import the full complement of the company. Just the major stars and some of the muckalucks that run the troupe. The prima ballerina is Nina Valgorski, a very well preserved forty or more."

"She in a class with Maya Plisetskaya?"

Magrew said admiringly, "You've been doing your homework."

"Jim and I together. The past couple of nights I suspect Jim's fallen asleep counting ballerinas." Jim had a silly smirk on his face.

"Plisetskaya is in a class by herself," said Magrew, "the top pantheon. Nina's equivalent in the West would be Alicia Markova, Alicia Alonso, or Nora Kaye." He stared at the pipe bowl as though expecting to read something important in it.

Villon asked, "Who is Nina's rival?"

Magrew laughed. "There's always a rival. In this case it's Luba Nafka, though the ladies seem to get along amicably."

"You've met them before?"

"Oh yes. We do a constant check up on a gang like this. I saw them in Toronto, Portland, Seattle, etcetera etcetera."

"Haven't they gotten suspicious?"

"They never knew I was with them. This is the first date in which I'm surfacing. This is the big one."

Villon asked, "How many men will you have at the party?"

"A nice variety. Also ladies. You'll never guess who they are."

Villon responded, "I won't try unless I have to."

"Even if you try and you guess right, I'll deny everything."

Herb studied the guest list on his desk. "The company's leading male star is Gregor Sukov?"

"That's him. Very very Russian. Practically a stereotype."

Villon beat his chest and Mallory expected to hear a Tarzan yell. Villon said, "Very moody. Dostoevski and Chekhov with a lavish dash of Tolstoi."

"You got him. He also dotes on Shirley Temple."

"How?" asked Villon. "She hasn't made a film in years."

"Herb, the Soviet Union is years behind in distributing American features. I mean Fred and Ginger are a big deal with the company because their films only reached the Soviet Union about five years ago. I mean there are parts of the country where they go berserk when they hear 'Flying Down to Rio.' And let me tell you, it's no easy chore playing that one on a balalaika. Okay, let's proceed." He referred to his wristwatch. "I haven't that much time. Got to prepare for the big doings tonight. Now then, there's Theodore Varonsky, the *maître de ballet*—the ballet master—and his word is law, he thinks. And last but not least, Mikhail Bochno is the *régisseur général*, the overseer. Everybody seems to like him."

"Any distinguished physical characteristics about any of them?" asked Villon.

"Varonsky, that's the ballet master, has a lovely scar on his left cheek. Presumably nicked by a sword."

"War wound?"

"No. He got it in a duel."

"Aha! Defending the honor of a beautiful *cygnette*."

"Why no, as a matter of fact," said Magrew with a twinkle in his voice, "defending the honor of a beautiful cadet. Anyway, that's Hurok's explanation, and anything you hear from Hurok you take with a grain of salt."

"So Varonsky might have cut himself shaving."

"In this case, if he shaved with a saber, and you can't duel with a saber. Hurok is traveling light this trip. He usually has an entourage, but here he's only with his assistant, Mae Frohman."

"Aha!" said Villon.

"You can scrub the 'aha.' Mae's been with him for over thirty years. Very very loyal."

"And knows where all the bodies are buried," said Villon.

"Probably helped bury them," said Magrew. "To simplify matters, they're all booked into the Ambassador."

"Which explains the Ambassador ballroom tonight," said Villon.

"It's a package deal. The rooms, the ballroom, three meals a day for everyone. Hurok strikes a hard bargain but hotels are always glad to give him a break. He's a good, steady customer, even when he's broke."

"Is he broke now?"

"Let me put it to you this way, he maneuvered the network to pick up the tab. Well, my friends, that will have to cover it for now. I've got to report to our office and then get to the hotel and dress. I'm also at the Ambassador, by the way. I need to have a word with Astaire and Rogers, but that'll wait until tonight."

Villon said, "I wonder if they know what they might be letting themselves in for?"

"They're letting themselves in for some hefty fees, some heavy publicity, and lots of hot borscht with heavy dollops of sour cream." After shaking hands, and as Magrew was crossing to the door, Villon suddenly asked, "Do we know you?"

"What do you mean?" asked Magrew.

"At the party. Should people know you're CIA?"

"Herb, I can assure you. The press will know the ball will be crawling with CIA and the Russian secret police . . ."

"And Hazel Dickson, who will put them all to shame."

"*Ciao,*" said Magrew and was gone.

"Well," said Mallory, back in the chair he had deserted, his feet on Villon's desk. "He seems like a nice enough guy. Not what you'd imagine a CIA operative to be like."

"I'll let you in on a little secret. The chief says on a little assignment in Central America, Magrew personally oversaw the slaughter of a couple of dozen rebels."

Mallory digested the information rapidly. "If ever there was an example of don't judge a book by its cover . . ."

Villon was studying the guest list. "Varonsky, Bochno, Nina Valgorski . . ."

"Luba Nafka," interjected Mallory.

"You've seen her?"

"So did you. The film of *Coppélia.* She danced the doll." He sighed, "What a doll."

There was a tap at the door. It opened and Hazel Dickson stuck her head in. "Got any coffee?"

Villon and Mallory were dazzled. Villon finally asked, "What the hell have you done to your hair?"

She smiled lavishly. "You like it? It's special for tonight. Mr. Eloise outdid himself."

"If he isn't dying from henna poisoning."

Hazel looked as though her head had been torched. Her hair was a bizarre shade of henna, an indescribable flaming red. "And he didn't charge me! On the house!"

"On your head," grumbled Villon.

Hazel's hands flew to her hips after depositing her handbag on the desk and her eyes narrowed dangerously. Ominously, she said, "You don't like it."

Villon stormed, "It's certainly not you!"

"Well, if it's not me, who is it?"

Mallory said, "Looks like Rita Hayworth."

"There you go!" said Hazel, hand outstretched to pinch Mallory's cheek. "And wait till she sees me tonight. She'll piss!"

Villon knew better than to suggest that Hazel was hardly competition to the glorious Hayworth. "It'll grow on me," he mumbled. "Why aren't you home getting dressed? You've only got five hours until the party." He was familiar with the length of time it usually took Hazel to prepare her toilette, especially for an occasion like tonight's.

"I need advice," she said glumly, lowering herself into the chair Magrew had occupied while Mallory poured her a cup of coffee from the thermos that he always kept handy for himself and Villon. Mallory put the coffee on the desk within easy reach of Hazel, who suddenly whipped open her handbag and extracted a small mirror.

"What's the advice you need?" asked Villon, wishing she'd leave him to study the guest list and not distract him with that insane dye job.

"What do I do about Louella and Hedda tonight? I mean having them together under the same roof, they'll be driving me nuts expecting me to dance attendance on both of them. Jim, you'll help me, won't you, like get Louella her drinks and light Hedda's cigarettes and bring their food from the buffet."

Villon answered for Mallory. "He can't. He's on duty."

Hazel sat up. "On duty? This is a gala, not a stakeout. Say! What's going on? I caught that look between you two! "She snapped her fingers. "I've got it. International intrigue! Come on, Herb, give. Will the place be crawling with spies?"

Villon leaned back in his swivel chair and stared at his beloved. How she could put her finger on something without realizing what she was putting her finger on! He decided it was wiser to level with her. He didn't want her eavesdropping on every conversation possible or poking under wigs and toupees in search of what she imagined was the elusive.

"The CIA suspects there are spies in the Baronovitch troupe."

"Aha!"

"But realistically, the CIA suspects there are spies all over the place. This goddamned HUAC investigation is making it rough on everybody."

"My God, don't tell me every actor, writer, and director who attends tonight will be under investigation!"

"They've already been investigated." He told her about the meeting earlier with Dan Magrew. "You missed him by just a couple of minutes."

"I think I saw him leaving the building. Tall, good-looking—that is, by my standards—with a pipe clenched between his teeth making him look like an Arrow collar ad."

The pipe did it for Villon. "That's him. The Russians have their secret police out in full force."

"You mean the Soviets, darling. They stopped referring to themselves as Russians years ago." She rubbed her hands together eagerly. "Now tonight sounds like it's going to be fun. But just the same, Jim, you'll try to give me a hand if you see the monsters are swamping me."

"I'll do what I can." His mind was on Luba Nafka, pirouetting in his subconscious.

"What's that silly look on your face?" Herb asked Mallory.

"What silly look?" Mallory asked innocently.

"When you're preoccupied with the thought of some female."

Mallory shrugged and slumped in his chair. Villon could always read him and it made Mallory uncomfortable.

Hazel, uninvited as always, was now standing behind Villon and studying the guest list. "Is it alphabetical?" she asked.

"It's alphabetical."

"Is it complete?"

"It's the same list as the CIA's."

"What about last-minute additions? There are always some at these affairs."

She happened to be right but Villon wouldn't give her the satisfaction of telling her. "The CIA is prepared for any emergencies."

"Ginger's Jacques Bergerac won't be there. He's night-shooting at Metro." Villon had visions of the actor aiming a rifle at the sky to pop off some portions of the night. "And Phyllis Astaire hasn't gotten back from the East yet. I phoned Fred earlier to check on his wife. He didn't seem bothered that she'd made no special effort to get back for Mr. Hurok's gala. Anyway, he was too preoccupied with other things. He let slip he and Ginger had been rehearsing all morning in the ballroom so I'm sure that means they'll be doing a number tonight." She was back in her seat. She sipped her coffee. "Awful."

Villon snapped, "Next time, bring your own."

"Now don't you pick a fight with me. I've got enough to worry about without you getting testy. If you want me to go just say so."

"Go."

She was rouging her lips. "Damn. This is the wrong color for my hair." She looked at her wristwatch. "I just have time to stop off at Max Factor's and get myself a new lipstick."

"Don't be forever at it," cautioned Villon. "I'm picking you up at eight sharp."

"Don't sound so testy. Am I ever not ready on time?" She was on her feet. Villon did not respond to her question. Her mother had told him long ago that Hazel's was a delayed pregnancy and that she'd been late ever since. "See you later, fellers!" and she was out the door.

"That hair," groaned Villon, "that awful hair." His face was in his hands, his head shaking back and forth.

"You want a cup of coffee?" asked Mallory.

"I want a cup of hemlock." He took his hands from his face. "For Hazel." Then he resumed studying the list.

Mallory asked, "What's bothering you?"

"Does it show?"

"The veins are beginning to stick out on your neck."

"To quote our friend Bette Davis, something tells me this is going to be a bumpy night."

"There's a name there that bothers you?"

"There are several names here that bother me. There are several names I've collared on morals charges. There are some I've hauled in for petty theft. And there are two Romanovs, which is one too many. There's Mike Romanoff. Well, Hurok eats at his restaurant on the house. So he probably figured it was a good idea to ask him. And Igor Romanov."

"The shrink?"

"The shrink," echoed Villon. He sat back in his chair. "Jim, I could use a drink. Break out the bourbon."

Three

$\mathcal{L}$ela Rogers was a very pretty woman who frequently harbored unpretty thoughts. She sat on an easy chair in her daughter's bedroom, watching the respected costume designer Edith Head make final adjustments to the gown Ginger was to wear to the ball. Ginger stood on a wooden stool she had borrowed from Paramount Pictures years ago with no intention of ever returning it. Just about every star in Hollywood thought it their right to appropriate something from one of the sets of their pictures, though Greer Garson went too far when she "adopted" an antique spinet and harp from *Pride and Prejudice*. Edith was on her knees fussing with the hem of the gown, a tight, form-fitting number in blue lamé with a shocking-pink trim. The gown wasn't borrowed, fortunately. Ginger ordered it designed by Edith especially for the Baronovitch gala. Just like everybody who came in contact with Ginger's mother, Edith thoroughly disliked the woman, and the poisonous monologue she was now spouting made Edith like her even less.

"The idea of throwing a grand ball for them commies. Our boys dying on the battlefields of Korea, and Hollywood dances! God how I hate commies."

Edith asked dryly, "Why? You once ate a bad one?"

Ginger's eyes flashed a warning to Edith but the designer was in no position to make eye contact, bending over the hem while wondering if she jabbed Mrs. Rogers with her scissors, would that constitute homicide or a mercy killing.

"Say, Edith Head." Mrs. Rogers was leaning forward and briefly resembling a judge at the Spanish Inquisition. "You've been in Hollywood a real long time, haven't you."

"Ever since Adam and Eve."

Lela Rogers let the sally fly past her. "You must have met a hell of a lot of commies."

"Lela," and Edith spoke the name with exaggerated patience, "I wouldn't know a communist from a Seventh-day adventist. And even if I suspected someone was a communist I wouldn't stoop so low as to finger them."

"Really!" cried Lela while Ginger looked upward seeking help from heaven. There was no muzzling either Lela or Edith, two of Hollywood's most headstrong, no-nonsense women. "If you know any of them rotten commies, it's your patriotic duty to name them."

Edith ignored the statement. Her heart ached for the several friends who were suffering the blacklist, Marsha Hunt, Jean Muir, Karen Morley, Gale Sondergaard, and so on. Lela was back on track and flailing away. "I'm sure you're not a God-fearing woman and you don't read the Bible."

"My dear Lela, among other things, the Bible is famous for its bad weather. I read it as a child in Sunday school and I have loathed Sunday ever since. Ginger, have you read the Bible?"

"Only the racy parts," said Ginger.

"Ginger!" Lela was bristling.

"Lela," said Ginger wearily, "why don't you rustle us up some tea and some cakes."

"I'll ring for them," said Lela, rising.

"There are no servants, Lela. I gave them the day off. Jacques is working and I'm busy with the ball so I sent them off."

"Undoubtedly singing 'Let my people go,' " said Edith under her breath.

"Oh very well," said Lela, "I'll get them," sounding as though she had been sentenced to twenty strokes of the lash. She marched out of the room with a petulant look and a sniffle of the nose.

Said Ginger in a tired voice, "Let's take a break. I've been rehearsing for hours with Fred and boy, am I out of shape. Want a cigarette?"

With Lela Rogers in mind, Edith Head was more in the mood for a fly swatter but said, "Do you mind if I smoke my own?" Her bones creaked as she got to her feet with an effort. She was a small woman but always dressed smartly and looked even smarter. Ginger said, "Your purse is on the dressing table in case you've forgotten." Edith had been looking around for the handbag and thanked Ginger. Ginger lit up and stretched out on the chaise longue. Edith lit her cigarette and sat on the bed.

Edith surveyed the beautiful reclining figure and spoke. "Sorry if I can't take your mother seriously. She reminds me of that mother-in-law in the Edgar Kennedy comedies."

"Dot Farley."

"My God. How do you remember her name?"

"Knew her at RKO. Nice lady. If you care to, you get used to Lela. All my husbands did. Even when she's not angry, Lela sees red." After a few seconds of silence, Ginger asked, "How do you cope with it?"

"With what?"

"Growing old."

"Since it's inevitable, there's no use fighting it."

"I wish I could be like Dietrich. She takes it in her stride."

"That's what *you* think."

"She seems so nonchalant about it!"

"Honey, she works on her face and her body every day. She watches her diet and her only indulgence is champagne. She consumes bottle after bottle. If she thinks she's eaten too much, she forces herself to throw up. Dietrich has made a career of eternal youth. But with her it's a cinch. That magnificent bone structure. A work of art. And the ease with which she floats back and forth to lovers of either sex. You've got to hand it to her."

"You might as well, she'll take it anyway."

"Don't be mean."

"I'm not being mean, I'm being jealous." Ginger was at the dressing table looking for an ashtray and found several. "Oh God. The mother of five children!"

"Who?"

"Me, for crying out loud. The Czarina!"

"Well, at least you're royalty." Edith hopped off the bed and doused her cigarette in an ashtray. "The dumb things actresses do to give the impression they're ageless. Do you know Norma Shearer turned down *Mrs. Miniver*?"

"So did I, Edith, so did I."

"I didn't know that!"

"You know it now. Are we almost finished?"

"Almost." Ginger was back on the wooden stool, and Edith was back on her knees with a suppressed groan. "Where does Dr. Romanov stand on this problem of aging?"

"He hasn't committed himself and that's because I can't bring myself to discuss it."

"Then why pay his exorbitant fee?"

"I find those sessions very comforting. He doesn't say much but what he does is from the heart. I know it is."

"You call that hovel a heart?"

"Now really, Edith. That's no way to talk about the doctor."

"Ginger, let me let you in on a little secret at the risk of my reputation for keeping very closemouthed about myself. I was one of Romanov's first patients. Doris Nolan recommended him to me."

"But she's . . ."

". . . Blacklisted. And that's neither here nor there. I was going through a bad patch and I needed help desperately. I was suicidal."

"Not you!"

"Of course me. That's who I'm talking about."

"But to everybody you've always been the rock of Gibraltar!"

"Well, this rock was about to topple over. So I went to Dr. Romanov a mess. By the time he got through with me I was a wreck. I went to Palm Springs and had a nervous breakdown."

"Did Romanov know about it?"

"If he did, I never heard a peep out of him."

"But he's considered a paradigm among psychiatrists!"

"A paradigm a dozen."

Ginger stared down at the top of the designer's head, the jet black hair neatly combed and held in place by several beautiful black combs. "But he's helped so many others. It was Gail Patrick who recommended him to me."

Edith Head said solemnly, "I'm sure he has. Not me. Not Edith Head."

From the hallway they heard Lela Rogers yelling frantically, "Girls! Girls!"

"She can't find the tea bags," said Ginger, shoulders slumped.

Lela burst into the bedroom, cheeks flushed with excitement. "The most wonderful news! It just came over the radio. Ethel and Julius Rosenberg are guilty! The commie spies are guilty! They're going to fry!"

Edith looked up and said softly, "That's the one thing I admire about you, Lela. You're all heart."

Sam Goldwyn, the eminent producer of numberless brilliant films such as *The Little Foxes* and *The Best Years of Our Lives,* sat on the sofa in Sol Hurok's suite sipping a scotch and water. His wife, the very lovely and very clever former silent-screen star Frances Howard, had elected to skip the gala to play bridge with the "girls." Truth be told, she couldn't cope with the thought of being caught in a crossfire of fractured English between her husband and Sol Hurok. Hurok sat in an easy chair with a glass of red wine, rattling off the guest list, which, as always, he had committed to memory. As he neared the end of the recital, Goldwyn interrupted. "I know he's no longer a star but still he deserved an invitation."

"Who are you talking about?" Mae Frohman was offering Goldwyn some hors d'oeuvres.

"How could you forget Comrade Nagel?"

"Comrade? A Russian actor here in Hollywood?"

"Mr. Hurok," offered Mae, "I think he means Conrad Nagel."

"So that's what I said, Comrade Nagel. Nice fellow. He acted with Garbo and Shearer."

"You have his phone number? I'll call him up."

"I don't have his phone number." He selected an hors d'oeuvre greedily. "Aha! Trifles!"

"Truffles," Mae corrected patiently. "If Frances knew what she was missing, she'd make such a fuss." Mae averted her head as Goldwyn consigned the truffles to his cement mixer of a mouth. She crossed to Hurok who chose a cream cheese and smoked salmon concoction.

After a sip of his drink, Goldwyn asked Hurok, "So what's wrong, Sol?"

"It shows?"

"How many years do we know each other? Of course it shows. You need money as usual?"

"No, just right now I'm pretty flesh."

"Flush," corrected Mae, now sitting on the couch with Goldwyn and wondering why neither of the men had complimented her on her lovely Balmain gown, her very first Balmain gown.

"You're having trouble with Fred?"

"No, he's a doll."

"Ginger?"

"No, she's getting used to being the mother of five children. Fred says not to worry about Ginger, she'll come through with frying colors."

"Flying," corrected Mae.

Sol said solemnly, "A few hours ago, when I was trying to take a nap, the enormity of what I have undertaken finally began to sway heavenly on me."

"Weigh heavily," corrected Mae. She was beginning to feel like a judge at a tennis match, her head moving back and forth between both men.

"A ballet company and two screen legends. And the CIA and the Secret Service and OGPU, the Russian secret police."

"They're also in the show?" Goldwyn was kidding of course.

"Sam," said Hurok gravely, "the CIA says the Boronovitch is a hard bed of spies."

"Hotbed," corrected Mae as she went to a sideboard for the carafe of wine to replenish Hurok's glass. She also poured herself one, though she usually was not much of a drinker. Goldwyn refused another drink, glancing at his pocket watch and thinking it was time Hurok put in an appearance at the ball.

"Did you hear me, Sam?"

"I heard you. Well, it stands to reason the Russians have to protect their citizens and the CIA has to protect ours."

"I got frightened thinking what would happen if there was trouble and maybe somebody would get killed . . ."

Goldwyn's eyes were shining. "What a lucky break! Such publicity! Hmm. That could make a good movie. I could maybe bring Vera Zorina back as the Russian ballerina. You know I gave her her first movie, *The Goldwyn Follies.* George Balanchine was the choreographer. He was married to Zorina then." He sighed. "It was George Gershwin's last songwriting job before the brain tumor killed him." He shook his head from side to side. "Such an egotist."

"Worse than you?" asked Hurok. They both laughed. Then Hurok said, "Why do I feel so uneasy? Like something terrible might happen."

"Nothing terrible will happen," Mae assured him. She said to Goldwyn, "Mr. Hurok is such a pessimist, he always expects the worst and usually he gets the best."

Goldwyn said, "Mae, why don't you come work for me."

"Again!" stormed Hurok. "Again! Again you're trying to steal Mae away from me!"

Mae smiled. She was flattered. She had played this scene with them on many previous occasions. She knew she'd never leave Hurok's employ. He was so good to her, so generous, even though he overworked her shamelessly. Like the summer she went to Paris and the phone in her room rang and it was Hurok saying, "I happened to be in Europe so I thought I'd drop up."

Sam Goldwyn said generously, "Sol, tonight you're going to make show business history." Hurok sat with his hands folded on his lap. For the moment he looked like a schoolboy waiting to be offered a piece of cake, and Goldwyn didn't disappoint him, he offered him a big slice. "You listen carefully because this is Sam Goldwyn talking, the second-best showman in the business. Of course you're the first."

Hurok demurred, "Oh please no, Sam." Mae looked at her nails. Thank God the two monsters had never done a deal together or the ensuing explosion would have made the atomic bomb look like a tiny puff of smoke.

"Sol, I am jealous."

"Oh don't be silly . . ."

"I am not silly. Sam Goldwyn is never silly, and when he is giving it to you straight from the heart, Sam Goldwyn is being very sincere." Mae was tempted to correct him, "Insincere," but kept her mouth shut. "I am jealous, because who but you would think of bringing Fred Astaire and Ginger Rogers together with the Boronovitch Ballet? Who? Tell me who?" He was lighting a cigar and Mae hoped she wouldn't get nauseous. She detested cigars and cigar smoke. She wondered if he would be offended if she turned up the air conditioning. "And who but you would con . . . convince NBC to pick up the tab. Who? Maybe me? Never! What do I know about concerts and television. I mean I make some pretty colossal mistakes." He shook his head sadly from side to side. "Anna Sten! What I spent to make her a star and she was a damn good actress, but the public stayed away from her pictures in mops."

"Mobs," corrected Mae. She was at the air conditioner and looking out the window, the suite overlooking Wilshire Boulevard and the front of the hotel. There was a crush of people below being held back by a cordon of police. Limousines were drawing up, delivering what Mae assumed were the numerous luminaries Hurok would be thrilled to see assembled in the ballroom. Klieg lights swept the skies and there were newsreel trucks alongside television trucks, and the cameras mounted on the roofs of the trucks were indeed recording and transmitting show business history.

It seemed Goldwyn was being carried away by his own oratory. "Sol, there should be a statue of you erectioned"—Mae decided not to correct this one—"in Central Park. In Columbus Circle!"

"They've already got Columbus there," said Hurok.

"Remove him! You've done more for America than Columbus, and besides, he first landed in Cuba I read someplace."

They heard cheers from outside. Mae said from the window, "I think it's Fred and Ginger. Oh, how cute of them to arrive together." She said firmly, "Mr. Hurok, I'm going down to the ballroom. This is so exciting I don't want to miss a thing!"

Goldwyn said to Hurok, "Sol, I'd offer you my arm, but there won't be any cheers when we enter together. Instead, somebody'll be asking, 'So what the hell are those two bums up to now?' "

"Bums?" echoed Hurok, following Goldwyn into the hall, "What happened to the statue in Central Park?"

The ballroom, as Mae would later describe it, was like she always imagined fairyland would be. The cavernous room was sumptuously decorated. The Ambassador Hotel had outdone itself. The ceilings were festooned with twinkling stars, and revolving crystal balls had been installed for the occasion by the management. There were many tables that were groaning boards of carved turkeys, hams, and roast beef, in addition to grouse and Smyrna ducks for a Russian touch. There were iced bowls of caviar, both red and black, accompanied by bowls of sour cream and chopped egg white. Bowls of chopped eggplant decorated with lemon curlicues were cheek by jowl with huge blocks of Russian halvah of varied flavors. There were trays of the sickeningly sweet Russian pastry baklava, and of course a chopped liver sculpture that represented the czar and the czarina. Commented one Hollywood wag, "No equal time for Lenin and Stalin?"

At the far end of the ballroom Barry Ennis and his sixteen-piece orchestra were bombarding the eardrums with a medley of Astaire and Rogers song hits. The guests danced to and some sang to, "Cheek to Cheek," "Top Hat, White Tie and Tails," "I'm Putting All My Eggs in One Basket," and "Change Partners," and for some dizzying minutes, everybody in the room was an Astaire and Rogers clone.

Mae Frohman drank it all in, committing as much as possible to memory so she could regale the office staff back in New York with her memories of what she knew would be looked back upon as a historical moment in show business. She heard Goldwyn saying to Hurok, "See, Sol! This is a truly memorable, a truly hysterical evening."

And Sam Goldwyn said, "My God, I don't believe it." Anna Sten was coming at him with arms outstretched. The photographers wandering the floor spotted Sten heading for Goldwyn and flashlights popped like a barrage on a war field. Nobody ever dreamed they would see Anna Sten and Samuel Goldwyn reunited and dancing to "Let's Face the Music and Dance." They had faced the music almost two decades earlier, but now they could dance with carefree abandon. "My God, Anna, you make me light on my feet. Why didn't you ever tell me you were such a good dancer? We could have done a musical!"

Though she was smiling for the benefit of him and the cameramen, she said seriously, "Sam. There are Russian secret-service men all over the place. I recognize some from when I was a young girl in Russia."

"I know dear, I know. It's nothing to concern yourself with. There's also an equal number of our secret service and the CIA." They both waved at acquaintances, both personal and business, and off to one side Louella Parsons gushed to no one in particular, "Oh my dears it's Goldwyn and Sten together again after all these years. Where's Sam's wife? If she sees this she'll have a hemhorrage."

Hazel Dickson's flaming hennaed hair was, as Herb Villon predicted it would be, a conversation piece. "Looks like she rinsed it in blood," said Hedda Hopper to her escort, Franklin Pangborn, one of filmdom's most popular and perennial character actors.

Mae was in front of the bandstand, swaying slightly to the music while admiring the two staircases surrounding the orchestra shell. It was obvious some grand entrances would be made on them.

The Hollywood Russians were beginning to arrive. Actor-director Gregory Ratoff was with his occasional wife (as he called her), actress Eugenie Leontovich who had created the role of Grusinskaya in the 1930 Broadway production of *Grand Hotel*; Akim Tamiroff made an entrance with his wife, Tamara Shayne; Ivan Lebedeff was with his beautiful Wera Engels; also on hand with wives or lovers were Mischa Auer, Leonid Kinskey, and Adnia Kouznetzoff, and there was a huge burst of applause when one of the baby ballerinas, Tamara Toumanova, arrived with her husband, Casey Robinson. She seemed more beautiful and glamorous than ever. Later Ginger commented, "Why shouldn't she be more beautiful and glamorous than ever? She's only thirty-five!"

Mike Romanoff the restaurateur, was overdoing the hand kissing while Humphrey Bogart took a moment to ask him, "Who's minding the store?"

Herb Villon spotted Don Magrew and nodded to him. Magrew winked. Jim Mallory asked, "He winking at you or me?"

Villon chose to ignore the fatuous question. "Jesus," he said, "a monocle. I thought those went out with Erich von Stroheim."

"Who's the monocle?" asked Mallory. "You know him?"

Hazel had joined them in time to hear Mallory's question and supply the answer. "That's Romanov the shrink. The dish with him is his nurse, Alida Rimsky. I wonder if they're having it off after office hours." She said to Villon, "You haven't told me how gorgeous I look."

Villon said glumly, "You look gorgeous."

Hazel was staring at a section of a buffet table where Louella

Pardons was dipping her fingers into a dip. "Uh-oh," said Hazel, "Louella's got her fingers in what looks like a clam dip. Don't touch it. You don't know where those fingers have been. With any luck she'll pass out early. Well, it's quite a turnout. Hurok has outdone himself. There's only one thing missing."

"What?" asked Villon.

"The Baronovitch Ballet."

Four

 $\mathcal{T}$ he ballroom reverberated with thunderous applause when Fred and Ginger entered, an entrance delayed by reporters and cameramen who besieged the two stars. Ginger loved the attention, which she felt was due a queen, let alone a czarina, while Fred amiably shared the spotlight, wishing his wife was there. In the ballroom, Hedda put her arm around Ginger while Louella commandered Fred.

"My my," my-myed Ginger, wondering how to rid herself of the arm around her shoulder. Like a good soldier under fire Fred gave Louella a peck on her chubby cheek and was rewarded with the celebrated Parsons gurgle, which sounded like the water in an emptying bathtub. As the guests moved in on Fred and Ginger and their captor columnists Ginger commented airily, "Everybody's here except Garbo!"

Fred said, "You never can tell, she might be using the facility. Ah! Forgive me, Louella. There's Sol!" He pulled away from Louella, who almost fell over, having been using Fred as ballast. She was caught by Franklin Pangborn, who quipped, "Still falling for me, Louella?" She glared at him and said, "I only fall for men." Pangborn released his grip on her arm and with the haughty sniff associated with the effeminate characters in which he specialized, went in search of a drink.

Fred said to Hurok, "I'll introduce the stars of the ballet before Ginger and I do our number. By the way, where are they? Have you seen them?"

Mae answered for Hurok. "They're backstage bickering over who gets the first introduction."

Hurok said firmly, "First should come Luba Nafka, then should come Gregor Sukov, and last should be Nina Valgorski, because she's the biggest star of the three. But first you introduce Theodore and Mikhail. Nobody will know who they are or give a damn about them, but we must do it as a courtesy."

Behind the orchestra shell, separated from the ballroom by a huge white curtain on which was artfully painted the names of all the participants in the television special, the imperious Nina Valgorski stood with one hand on a shapely hip and the other holding a glass of champagne. Gregor Sukov leaned against a wall, arms folded in front of him and a Gauloises cigarette dangling from his lips, thinking of all the places he'd rather be than the one where he was standing now. He had enjoyed almost all the cities of the tour but Los Angeles was not to his taste. Los Angeles had much bigger and more famous stars than he was and he missed the adulation that he knew was his due. He missed the women falling all over him in the rush to give him their phone numbers. But he also realized he must be patient. Los Angeles had not yet seen him perform; Hurok had guaranteed the telecast would be seen by millions of viewers after which, Hurok assured him, "You will be a household name! Like Brillo!" For weeks Sukov wondered who was this celebrated Brillo and would not ask anyone for elucidation as he was loath to display what would certainly be considered his ignorance.

Luba Nafka was admiring herself in a floor-length mirror wisely installed by the hotel manager who was familiar with the egos of ballet stars. "If necessary, they'd look for their images in a toilet bowl," he explained to his assistant. Luba wore a simple outfit of a black skirt and white blouse with a wide black belt and a single strand of pearls. She knew better than to attempt to compete with the *soignée* Nina, who, being the older of the two and a prima ballerina for more than twenty years, wore around her neck a very classy-looking silver whistle, which Luba assumed contained an emergency jigger of vodka. Luba listened to the orchestra, which had segued from Astaire and Rogers to jazzed-up versions of Russian perennials.

"*Bordjamoy!*" exclaimed Nina, "is that 'The Volga Boatman'?"

"Seasick," said Sukov. He ground his cigarette under his heel and wondered aloud in Russian, "What is going on? How long do we remain sequestered here?"

Hurok and Fred Astaire appeared with Mae Frohman. "Well, my children, are we ready?" asked Hurok.

"Ready? Ready?" asked Nina. "We are weary, that's what we are, we are weary. How much longer do you plan to keep us in this isolation?"

"This, my dear Nina, is showmanship! Keep the people waiting! They will thirst for your appearance!"

"I thirst for more champagne," said Nina coldly, "which, I'm sad to see, is domestic California."

"I'm hungry," said Sukov. "It is past nine o'clock. I always eat by seven."

"There's plenty to eat, plenty," Hurok assured them. "Like a Jewish wedding. Wait till you see the famous celebrities that have come to pay homage to my three great stars!"

"They come to, how you say, freeload," said the wise and worldly Nina.

Fred interjected, "Love that thing around your neck."

"Oh yes?" said Nina with a smile that took an effort. "A gift from an old admirer. My father." Her eyes narrowed. "Who is that person who spies on us?" She pointed to a chunky gentleman whose ill-fitting suit identified him as Russian. He was clicking away with his camera; then before they knew it, he had disappeared out a side door.

"Looks like one of your secret police," said Fred. "Anyway, we have more important matters to discuss, such as how I plan to introduce you three sublime artists." Hurok had told him to pour it on, be lavish with admiration for the Russians, and the usually subtle dancer laid it on with a heavy hand. The three dancers seemed to be flattered and Hurok beamed with pleasure.

Out front, Ginger buttonholed Dr. Romanov. "Why didn't you tell me you were going to be here tonight?"

"Does it give you a problem to socialize with me?" Ginger thought he wasn't looking well.

"Hell no, I'm delighted to see you. I see Alida over there chinning with the *maître de ballet*. They act as though they might be old friends." What she really meant was old lovers, but she was quick to edit herself in case behind the scenes the doctor and his nurse were a possible item.

Romanov said suavely, "It is Varonsky and I who are the old friends. He invited us. I entertained Varonsky and his associates at dinner a few nights ago."

Ginger sparkled as she said, "See? Didn't I say you might find some old friends with the company? And I hope I've found some new friends. The only ballet dancer I've had truck with was Harriet Hoctor." Romanov had never heard of the former Ziegfeld star. "She was in *Shall We Dance?* with Fred and myself. Hate to say it but I'll say it anyway—she was very old hat, but a sweet disposition."

Mae Frohman descended on them. "I'm sorry to interrupt, but Fred wants you backstage, Ginger."

"Oh dear, now I'm a bundle of nerves. I haven't appeared in person since my wedding."

May refrained from asking, "Which one?" Instead she said, "I know you and Fred are going to be marvelous. I can hardly wait."

"Really? Well, point me in the right direction." May took the hand Ginger proffered and guided her backstage. Ginger's fingers were ice cold but May made no comment. She really was nervous. The life of a celebrity, Mae had decided years ago, was not to be envied. For example, she remembered opera star Lily Pons saying to Hurok with a tear in her voice, "I haven't had sex in over four months and that's not good for my voice."

Mikhail Bochno had joined Dr. Romanov, saying, "How sad Maria Ouspenskaya is not here." Romanov was suffering some intestinal discomfort but said nothing.

"You were a fan of hers?"

"She's an old friend of my mother's. They acted together with the Moscow Art Theatre."

"Didn't word reach Russia when she died?"

"Ouspenskaya is dead?" Bochno's eyes were wide with disbelief.

"Over four years ago."

"But how?"

"She smoked in bed. She was consumed by flames."

"How awful! Varonsky!" he called out to the *maître de ballet,* who miraculously heard him over the din. Varonsky and Alida Rimsky joined Bochno and the doctor. "Ouspenskaya is dead! Did you know this?"

Varonsky looked from Bochno to Romanov and finally to Alida Rimsky, who could see by the tiny beads of perspiration on his head that the doctor was in a state of discomfort. "Who was this Ouspenskaya?"

Bochno couldn't believe his ears. "She was a great actress! The Moscow Art Theatre. *The Cherry Orchard!*"

Alida said, "Also *The Wolf Man* for Universal Pictures."

There was a fanfare from the orchestra. Barry Ennis, the leader, spoke into a microphone. "Ladies and gentlemen! Your host, Mr. Sol Hurok."

A spotlight found Hurok at the top of the staircase to the left of the orchestra. The applause that greeted him was music to his egotistical ears. For many in attendance, this was the first and probably the last time they would ever see him in the flesh. With a warm smile he slowly descended the staircase and Mae Frohman prayed he wouldn't trip and break his neck. The orchestra accompanied his descent with a slightly ragged "For He's a Jolly Good Fellow." Mae was grateful they hadn't chosen "A Pretty Girl Is Like a Melody."

Hurok reached the microphone, which Ennis adjusted to his height, and Hurok clutched it nervously. The orchestra and the applause subsided while too many heard Hedda Hopper's nasty comment, "Commie lover!" Herb Villon flashed her a look which fortunately the columnist did not see. She might have fallen dead.

Hurok greeted his guests profusely and thanked them for coming to the gala to honor not only Fred and Ginger but the three Russian stars. He thanked them for helping launch the TV spectacular for MBC. Out front Mae corrected him, "NBC," but he didn't hear her. Some NBC executives, who of course were present, flinched and one removed his hand from an actress's backside to cover his eyes. "You shall now meet the stars of the Baronovitch Ballet," *Ballet* emerging from his mouth as "belly." "And our wonderful Fred and Ginger will introduce them!"

The orchestra struck up "Cheek to Cheek" as Fred appeared at the top of the stairs on the right and Ginger appeared at the top of the stairs to the left. So great was the applause that Fred and Ginger were overcome with emotion. Fred gulped back his tears but Ginger let them gush. "Oh God!" thought Mae Frohman. "Her mascara!" But Ginger was prepared. She held a beautiful blue handkerchief bordered with Chantilly lace and dabbed gracefully and gratefully at her eyes as she came down the stairs where Fred met her. With an arm around her he took her to the microphone. Ginger was thinking, Oh Lela, what you're missing! Fred and Ginger were greeted by Hurok, who shook Fred's hand and kissed Ginger's cheek and then departed the spotlight.

Fred said, "I'd like you to meet two people very important to the Baronovitch Ballet!" He called for Varonsky and Bochno, who hurried to the stage. Hedda Hopper commented to Hazel Dickson, "They look like a couple of Marx Brothers, but I doubt if they're half as funny."

Herb Villon and Don Magrew were standing with Doctor Romanov, who had removed his monocle and put it in a jacket pocket. His eye was too damp to hold the piece properly and he was dabbing at his face with a handkerchief.

"Spies?" Villon asked Magrew as Hurok and Mae stood next to them, listening to the two Russian men take turns thanking the audience and telling them how happy they were to be on American soil. Hedda said to Hazel Dickson, "I wish they were under it."

Alongside you, thought Hazel.

Hurok quietly asked Villon if he knew what was ailing the doctor. "Looks like the flu to me," said Villon, "or maybe he's diabetic."

"Diabetic!" gasped Hurok. "Then maybe he should have a shot of insolence."

Fred and Ginger applauded graciously as the two Russian men departed the stage. Again into the microphone Fred said, "And now, ladies and gentleman, Ginger and I take great pleasure in introducing the three great artistes we will be privileged to work with. First, the great prima ballerina *assoluta,* Miss Nina Valgorski!" Nina oozed glamour as she wafted down the stairs, drinking in the applause as if it were the champagne she would have preferred. She thanked the assemblage, then Fred quickly introduced Luba Nafka.

Jim Mallory dined on her with his eyes. Here was his dream girl in person at last and he was determined to wangle an invitation. But his reverie was interrupted by the chorus of female cheers that greeted Gregor Sukov's entrance. He literally slithered down the stairs and Hazel decided he was a snake who'd be welcome in anybody's garden of Eden. The five stars had joined hands to take a bow together and as they filed off the stage, Barry Ennis said into the microphone, "Patience, ladies and gentlemen, patience. There's a great treat in store for you in a few minutes!" Voices hummed as the room buzzed with anticipation. No doubt Fred and Ginger were going to dance for them. Several guests were wondering who the men with cameras were. They could not be the usually recognizable professionals because they didn't ask any of the guests to pose. Instead they took candid shots at random, and several of the guests correctly guessed that these were secret-service men.

Ginger was cautioning Hedda. "Behave yourself, Hedda!" She had no fear of either Hedda or Louella. "These people are our guests. There's no need to be so rude."

"They're commies and not to be trusted. It's a disgrace! I dread to think what your mother has to say about this!"

"I should think at this hour Lela is rolling over in her bed," said Ginger.

"Have you no shame?" persisted the columnist relentlessly. "How dare you and Fred agree to dance with them!"

"They are great artists," said Ginger hotly, hardly believing she was sincerely defending the Russians, "and what we are doing is art, not politics!"

Hedda warned her. "HUAC has their eyes on the two of you!"

"Let them have a good look! Fred and I have nothing to hide."

Steamed Hedda, "The FBI is here and they're taking names and pictures."

Ginger suggested something else the the FBI could take and Hedda blushed.

Hazel, who had been eavesdropping on the conversation, said, "There's several of them who are welcome to my phone number."

Ginger said, "Hazel! Your hair!"

Herb Villon, standing off to one side listening, checked a rising guffaw.

Hazel took Ginger's comment as a compliment and said to Villon, "Boy, you're certainly in the minority where my hair is concerned!" Villon ignored her, his mind on Romanov who had requested a Bromo. He'd been eating some of the buffet and Herb worried some anticommunist crackpot might have fiddled with some of the food. Hedda Hopper had gone in search of Franklin Pangborn, who was at the opposite end of the ballroom autographing programs for some of the FBI, who recognized him from films but weren't too sure of his name. A select few were rewarded with Pangborn's phone number.

Fred was now with Ginger. "I hear you and Hedda had a bit of a dustup. Too bad Lela wasn't here."

Ginger snapped, "You leave Lela out of it. Lela is a very sincere patriot."

"So was Nathan Hale and a fat lot of good it did him."

"Nathan *who?*"

"Well, you two, I've been looking all over this place for you." The stars greeted Edward Everett Horton, the character actor–comedian who had appeared in and stolen several films of theirs. "What a night! I wouldn't have missed it for the world. I love ballet. I'm a true balletomane. I've been one ever since I saw the great Anna Pavlova dance *The Dying Swan* in Philadelphia when I was just a child . . . recently. I must say, there are so many men who've been taking my photograph. They're really feeding my ego. Oops. Here goes another one!" He shouted to the Russian secret-service man, "I'd appreciate your sending me the proofs! I always have photo approval." He asked Fred, "Why's he scowling? He doesn't seem to have understood me."

Fred told him, "I think he's Russian secret service."

"Oh really? Oh really?" Horton was notorious for echoing himself. In films it drove the other actors crazy, which was exactly what Horton intended. Horton's eyes followed the secret-service man as he stealthily moved away, sizing him up favorably. "Well, I have a secret or two he's perfectly welcome to service."

"Eddie, behave yourself," cautioned Fred as he took Ginger's hand and led her to the bandstand. En route they were confronted by Sol Hurok. "The doctor asked for a Bromo-seltzer but I got him good old Seidlitz powders instead. Did you know the hotel's pharmacy stays open all night? How very convenient."

Ginger, concerned, asked, "How is the doctor feeling now?"

"There's a little more color in his cheeks. He wants to go home and the nurse—what's her name . . .

"Alida Rimsky," said Ginger.

"That's right. She's looking for their car and chauffeur. But in this crowd, it's like looking for a noodle in a haystack."

"You can do better than that," said Fred. He and Ginger continued on their way to the bandstand while Hurok wondered what Fred meant. "You can do better than that."

Fred had signaled Barry Ennis, and the bandleader asked for a drumroll.

Outside, Alida Rimsky was describing the doctor's limousine to a valet parker, who dutifully went in search of it. She heard a familiar voice say, "I've been looking all over for you." Theodore Varonsky pulled her behind some shrubbery and took her in his arms, and they kissed passionately. "My darling, it has been so long."

"Too long," said Alida. "If you hadn't arrived I might have exploded with anxiety. So many years without you, so many years." They kissed again.

The valet parker found the doctor's car, but discreetly waited for the couple in the front seat to complete their kiss. He then tapped on the window on the chauffeur's side. The chauffeur, Mordecai Pfenov, lowered the window and asked sharply, "What do you want?"

"You Dr. Romanov's chauffeur?"

"I am."

"The doctor wants the car. His nurse is looking for you."

"All right. Thank you."

The valet parker hurried away. Mordecai Pfenov said, "You heard him."

"I heard him but I wish I hadn't. One more kiss." The chauffeur obliged. Luba Nafka patted his cheek, got out of the car, and hurried back to the ballroom.

Five

"So, Igor Romanov, we meet again after all these years." Nina Valgorski spoke with a trace of a smile.

Romanov spoke with an effort. "You haven't changed."

"How kind of you, Igor. How is your wife? Is she here or still in Russia?"

"I'm sure she is still in her unmarked grave in Siberia."

"But how tragic." Her voice was cold and unemotional, the way it was when she congratulated a rival on a fine performance. "I had heard she escaped with you."

"That was the original scenario. But it was revised. Elena's escape from the gulag was aborted. She was shot. I heard the gunfire from outside the men's section where I hid, waiting for her to join me. I waited longer than I should have. I was almost caught."

"But you weren't. How happy I am for you. And now you are a successful psychiatrist in your adopted country. But you aren't looking too well. Let me get you some soda water."

"No thank you." But Nina was already on her way to a waiter carrying a tray of soda water and glasses. She commandeered the waiter imperiously, who stopped and poured soda into a glass. She looked past other guests and stood watching Dr. Romanov, wondering if her life would have been different had she married him when he beseeched her those many years ago, she a rising ballet dancer, he a promising concert pianist. She walked slowly back to Romanov, watched by Hurok and Mae Frohman, Hurok wondering why Fred and Ginger's dance hadn't begun.

Mae heard a click and turned on a Russian secret-service man. "You get away from us, you stupid spy. Shoo! Shoo!" She waved her hands so ineffectively she wouldn't have frightened an alley cat. "My God, Mr. Hurok, the ballroom is crawling with spies!"

"Mae," said Hurok solemnly, "everybody in the Soviet Republic is a spy. Spying is more popular and challenging than sex."

Mae said, "Sex is less complicated."

"Since when?"

Nina watched Romanov down the soda water. She took the empty glass and placed it on the tray of a passing waiter. Romanov thanked her and wondered where the hell were Alida and the chauffeur. The ballroom lights dimmed and Nina turned to look at the stage. Fred and Ginger stood at the microphone awash in a wave of applause, while behind them Bruce Ennis gave the downbeat. The orchestra blared away and Fed and Ginger began singing: " *'Flying down to Valparaiso, That's where all the gals and guys go . . .'* "

Alida and Mordecai Pfenov found Romanov and hurried him out of the ballroom.

" *'Where some of the dumb and some of the wise go, And lots of the lows and lots of the highs go, To Valparaiso . . .'* "

Sam Goldwyn beamed at Fred and Ginger. How he ached to do a film with them and wondered if there was a spot for them in his next production, *Porgy and Bess.*

Alone, Fred was singing: " *'Some may think it somewhat silly, To follow your heart way down to Chile . . .'* " And Ginger rejoined him: " *'But we went there willy-nilly, To Valparaiso!'* "

Actor Cesar Romero was having a difficult time steadying Louella Parsons. She kept tickling him under the chin and he told a waiter to bring a chair in a hurry. Louella Parsons was incontinent and all of Hollywood knew it, and Romero prayed she wouldn't embarrass him.

" *They taught us down in Valparaiso, To let our blues and let our sighs go, And then blink your flirty eyes so, And tell some white lies, though, It's Valparaiso . . . Valparaiso . . . Valparaiso hohoh!* " Fred and Ginger began tapping and the crowd went wild. Fred leapt from the bandstand to the dance floor and turned to catch Ginger as she gracefully leapt and pirouetted into his arms. The years turned back and they seemed twenty years younger. Their taps were like machine guns exploding and they circled the dance floor many times in a dazzling display of their artistry.

Luba Nafka stood with Gregor Sukov, both holding glasses of champagne, mesmerized by the Astaire and Rogers magic. Luba said, "It does not look too difficult. Perhaps we can learn to tap dance for the television."

He had something else on his mind. "Did you find Mordecai?" She nodded. "Then he is still working for the doctor?"

"Yes. As both his chauffeur and his valet. And his aunt, Malke Movitz, is also still in the doctor's employ. So all is as it should be. Look! Fred and Ginger are magnificent! His lifts are so clean and seemingly effortless! My God! They are dancing on air!"

Now Fred was spinning Ginger around the floor, and the room exploded as they danced over chairs and tables carefully placed as they had been at rehearsal. They danced their way to the center of the floor, while above them the multicolored glass orbs spun in a dizzying kaleidoscope. Fred and Ginger came to a halt in the middle of the room, each standing with a hand triumphantly stretching above them, and the dance was over.

Sol Hurok, applauding wildly and beaming from ear to ear as though the stars' triumph was his very own said to Sam Goldwyn, "Sam! Sam! Tell me! Have you ever heard such an evasion?"

The ever-present Mae Frohman corrected him. "Ovation."

The way Hazel Dickson's hands were flapping together Villon feared she might take off and go flying overhead. The guests were shouting "Bravo!" and cheering huzzahs while Edward

Everett Horton grabbed Franklin Pangborn, shouting, "Come on, Frankie, let's show them a thing or two." A flustered Pangborn shoved him aside crying, "Now really, Eddie, behave yourself. What will people think?"

"The same thing they've been thinking for years, you party poop." He executed some dance steps, singing under his breath and snapping his fingers. "I wish I'd brought my castanets!"

Nina Valgorski stood alone, thinking about Igor Romanov, of their teenage romance, and how after so many years they were finally reunited. She didn't realize she was the subject of a subtle study by Don Magrew. The handsome CIA agent watched as the bat out of hell named Hazel Dickson to whom he had been introduced by Villon took possession of Nina Valgorski. He couldn't hear what they were saying but Hazel was indicating Villon and Jim Mallory, who was champing at an invisible bit in his anxiety to make contact with Luba Nafka. Even in their mimicked dumb show Magrew could figure out Hazel wanted Nina to meet Villon. Or, he wondered, had Villon asked Hazel to introduce him to Nina because he was possibly on to something. Beyond Nina and Hazel, Magrew saw Hurok and Goldwyn with Fred and Ginger, Mae Frohman was pouring champagne into the glasses they held.

Ginger was saying, "We really didn't have enough rehearsal. We really didn't."

Fred said to Ginger, "It's practically the same number we did in *Swing Time.* The only thing that was different was the furniture."

Hurok effused, "You were glorious! Like two fathers blowing in a breeze!"

"Feathers," corrected Mae, still wondering if Hurok had been kidding about thinking sex was complicated. Celebrities were gathering around the stars and Mae felt faint when her beloved idol Cary Grant said, "Let me help you," and relieved her of the bottle of champagne. His smile was dazzling ivory and then he turned to bestow a kiss on Ginger. Mae wondered why somebody was banging on a drum until she realized it was the passionate beating of her heart.

Sam Goldwyn was wondering if audiences were sophisticated enough to buy an all-white *Porgy and Bess.* Then Ginger could tap dance Bess and Fred would be a perfect Sporting Life. He couldn't do Porgy because Porgy has no legs, unless they used dream sequences and you couldn't get away with too many of them.

Nina was blatantly flirting with Herb Villon, who was enjoying every second of her come-on and Hazel's unsubtle annoyance. He wondered if gray hairs ever showed through henna. "So, Mr. Villon, you are really a detective?"

"Really."

"Are you undercover?"

"Only when I sleep."

A rusty "Ha!" slipped out of her mouth. "You are droll. Perhaps it would interest you to know that I am also a trained criminologist."

"Indeed? I'm impressed."

"So am I," she said without a pretension to modesty." I have read the works of all the great detective story writers of the Soviet Union."

"Really," he said, "I didn't know there were detective story writers in your country."

"But of course there are!" She snapped her fingers at Hazel, indicating her champagne glass needed a refill. The astonished Hazel signaled a waiter, who promptly produced a bottle. Nina was rattling off names with the passion of a train conductor rattling off the stops his train would make. "There are such great Soviet writers as Arthur Conan Doyle, Dashiell Hammett, John Dickson Carr, Raymond Chandler . . ."

Villon masked his amusement as he said, "Are you sure they are Russian?"

"But of course," she said with spirit, her eyes flashing. "Especially Agatha Christie, who is a truly Honored Artist of the Republic. I adore her character . . ." Mae Frohman was passing on her way to a buffet table. ". . . Miss Mopple."

"Marple," corrected Mae.

The startled ballerina was too late to see who had corrected her as Mae was swiftly swallowed up in the crowd. Past Nina's head, Villon saw Jim Mallory dogging Luba Nafka, Jim wondering if the dancer would ever shake Gregor Sukov so he could introduce himself.

Villon saw Theodore Varonsky looking like a lost sheep waiting for rescue by Boo-Peep, when he was actually wondering where Alida Rimsky had disappeared to. Mikhail Bochno was under the surveillance of two FBI operatives who looked like used-car salesmen who had stumbled into the wrong party. Villon heard Nina say, "Am I boring you, Mr. Villon?"

"My God, no," Villon said swiftly, realizing the dancer was a star who required and demanded one's undivided attention. "I was wondering why some members of your company seem so uneasy."

"Why? If you the detective don't know or haven't guessed, it is because we are continually under scrutiny. In the Soviet, we scrutinize each other all the time." She smiled. "Sounds sexy, no?" Villon didn't comment. He rewarded her with an enigmatic smile as Nina continued talking, "Here in America, the people do not spy on each other?" She said to the unusually silent Hazel, "But you spy on people."

"Me?" Villon thought Hazel looked like a startled chipmunk.

Nina persisted. "I have seen you eavesdropping."

"Oh. I suppose you haven't been told. I collect gossip to sell to gossip columnists." She pointed out Hedda Hopper and Louella Parsons, each of whom had collapsed into an easy chair and fallen asleep.

"They are gossip columnists? I don't understand." Hazel explained Hedda and Louella's function painstakingly and Villon was impressed. When Hazel finished her discourse, Nina said to Villon, "Are you and Miss Dickson a liaison?"

Hazel said sweetly, "For many many years."

"Aha! Mr. Villon, did you hear her? She is making it clear to me that you are her property and I think she would kill to continue possessing you."

"Hazel can't kill. She doesn't have a strong enough stomach." Hazel glared at him, arms folded in front of her.

"The stomach is unimportant," said Nina with a dismissive wave of a hand. "Poison! Good strong poison. Like cadmium."

This was a new one to Villon. "Cadmium?"

"A powdery salt scraped from heavy metal. Such a curious look on your face, Mr. Villon. I told you I was a student of criminology. Cadmium is very popular in Russia. It is easily available. It has been dissolved in many a bowl of borscht served to a husband by an unhappy wife."

"That bears out what your great Soviet writer Agatha Christie insists. Poison is a woman's weapon."

"Mr. Villon, in the Soviet Union, poison is everybody's weapon."

In another part of the ballroom, Varonsky learned from Mae Frohman that Dr. Romanov was indisposed and had been taken home by his nurse and his valet. Varonsky asked Mae to dance and she literally fell into his arms. She would dine out on this night for the rest of her life.

Hazel Dickson was saying to Gregor Sukov, "You have such a marvelous face, Gregor."

"Yes, I know."

"I was wondering. Have you ever acted?"

Gravely he told her, "In the Soviet Union, we are all actors."

"No kidding." She could see where Sukov could be a handful. "Are there enough parts to go around?"

"What kind of parts are you talking about?" He was genuinely perplexed. "I do not understand you."

"Dear Gregor. I'm just pulling your leg."

"I feel nothing."

Hazel was beginning to think he could do well as an antidote to insomnia. "Pulling the leg is a colloquialism."

His face lit up. "Ah! Colloquialism! I have met colloquialism before! In Seattle. This very extraordinary woman for whom I hungered."

Hazel fluttered her eyelashes. "And did you get fed?"

"But of course. When Sukov hungers, Sukov feeds. What she said she later explained to me was a colloquialism."

"And what did she say?"

" 'Your place or mine.' " His eyes were suddenly dreamy with the recollection of his conquest in Seattle.

Hazel was suddenly fascinated. "She teach you any more of our colloquialisms?"

"Oh yes. My favorite. 'Ride 'em, cowboy!' "

On the dance floor, Fred and Ginger were enjoying an uncomplicated fox trot. Ginger's mind was preoccupied with her stricken psychiatrist.

"Snap out of it, Ginger."

"What?"

"You look like you're in a trance. The way Ann Miller looks when she's trying to do a crossword puzzle."

"I should check on how Dr. Romanov is doing. I have an appointment with him Monday."

"He's probably not gotten home yet. It's a long way from here to Beverly Hills."

She thought for a moment, and then said, "Fred, does this Baronovitch bunch make you feel as creepy as they do me?"

"Well, not exactly creepy. Frankly, I do get the feeling they're looking down their noses at me." He looked around to make sure they were out of earshot of any of the troupe. "And I get the feeling there's all sorts of intrigue going on between some of them."

"From my few experiences with ballet dancers, they thrive on innuendo." She lowered her voice. "I saw Dr. Romanov having a talk with Nina Valgorski."

"Oh really? Maybe they knew each other from the old country. Mother Russia and all that."

"I think they did know each other before."

"You really think so?"

"Romanov didn't appear to be all that friendly, and I got the feeling Nina was pushing too hard."

"Well, she's a very pushy person."

"She got him a glass of something."

"Do you suppose it was vintage something?"

Ginger gave him her familiar "drop dead" look. Her mind switched to another avenue of thought. "What about my costumes?"

"We'll have sketches tomorrow."

Ginger's eyes widened. "What sketches? Who by?"

"The company designer. The ladies swear by him."

"Edith Head will design mine." Fred felt as though the last five words had been nailed to his ear. "I'll discuss it with Hurok. I've already asked Edith if she was available and she said she was sure Paramount wouldn't object. And what about the score? Tchaikovsky? Borodin? Rimsky-Korsakov?"

"Tikhon N. Khrennikov." Ginger seemed about to lose her balance and Fred tightened his grip on her. "Steady, Ginger."

"What was that name again?"

Fred both repeated it and spelled it. "Aren't you proud of me? I can both pronounce and spell it. It's a cinch once you get the hang of it. Hurok's nuts about him."

"Hurok's nuts, period." She was beginning to nurse fresh doubts about the project.

"Now get that 'I hate Rita Hayworth' look off your face."

Ginger said through clenched teeth. "I do not hate Rita Hayworth. I feel sorry for her. Those awful men she married."

"Aha. The pot calling the kettle black." She wisely chose not to challenge his statement. "Khrennikov is hot stuff back in the Soviet. He was Stalin's favorite."

"Big deal. Stalin's dead."

"Ginger, I've heard the man's music. He's damn good. Stunning melodies. I've already worked out our duet, our big one. Where Rasputin convinces the czarina he can cure the czarevitch of his hemophilia. Hemophiliacs, in case you didn't know, are bleeders."

"Charming."

"Well, Rasputin did seem to cast a spell over the entire court.

Though very uncouth he was very seductive. But he wasn't too selective. He not only seduced women, but he had it off with men too."

Ginger said dully, "A latent choir boy."

"He laid everything but carpets." He saw Hurok, who was trying to get his and Ginger's attention. "Hurok wants us. He's with Mae Frohman and some guy I think we've already been introduced to. Come on, let's see what he wants."

A few seconds later, Hurok introduced them again to Don Magrew, who suggested rather mysteriously that they go out on the terrace. Ginger was grateful for the suggestion because she had been feeling the need for fresh air. Mae Frohman again gushed encomiums about their "Valparaiso" number with Don Magrew adding his praise. He reminded Ginger of Howard Hughes, who had pursued her romantically for years and might have been successful had he bathed at least occasionally.

Herb Villon and Jim Mallory were waiting for them by prearrangement with Magrew. Just about everyone in the business liked Herb Villon and Fred was no exception. They greeted each other warmly and Mallory said effusively, "Hiya!"

Magrew wasted no time and got right to the point. He told them flat out he was a CIA operative and his assignment was the Baronovitch Ballet. Ginger and Fred exchanged a quick glance.

"You think they're all spies?" asked Ginger eagerly. "I unmasked spies in *Once Upon a Honeymoon* with Cary Grant. It didn't make money."

"We aren't sure who is or isn't involved in espionage but whoever is will certainly be making contact with their American counterparts. You'll be in a position to know who these contacts are. I know you're planning a heavy rehearsal schedule so it would be up to you to let us know who visits the company. Anything you overhear might be of value to us."

Fred asked, "Even if they're exchanging recipes?"

"Fred," said Hurok, "it's not like you're being asked to be a snatch."

"Snitch," corrected Mae.

"Sounds to me that's exactly what Mr. Magrew is asking us to do. There's always a lot of people hanging around rehearsals. Especially mothers."

"Our company left their mothers behind because I wouldn't pay the passage," said Hurok.

"You know a lot of perfectly innocent people will be wandering in and out. Stagehands, electricians . . ."

"Fred," said Ginger, "it's our patriotic duty to cooperate with Mr. Magrew."

"I'll tell you what, Ginger, you get your mother to hang around rehearsals and I'm sure she can do the job for both of us."

"Now don't be mean, Fred. You leave my mother out of this."

"Happily. Look, Mr. Magrew, I don't see this as a matter of patriotism at all. I'm no good at this sort of thing. I never know if I'm hearing anything suspicious unless it's my wife asking me to increase the housekeeping money. Say, Herb. You and Jim Mallory would probably be great at this sort of thing. And Hazel! She's perfect!"

Herb said, "Fred, we'll be around from time to time, but we also have too many other fish to fry. And as for Hazel, you involve her at your own risk."

Magrew said to Fred and Ginger, "Give it some thought. I don't expect you to be wired with tape recorders or walking around with a pad and pen in your hands. Instead, if something strikes you as odd or peculiar, keep it in mind and let us know. We'll be around. We'll be in touch."

"That's comforting," said Fred under his breath, though everybody heard it.

Ginger was about to say something. In fact, she opened her mouth to speak, then seemed to think better of it.

Fred commented, "That's right, Ginger. Think before you speak."

To herself, Mae Frohman applauded Fred. She approved of his reluctance to be a CIA tool as much as she found Ginger's willingness to cooperate deplorable. Several years ago when Sol Hurok invited her to join him on the horn of one of his dilemmas, to spy for the Soviet Union inasmuch as they were so generous in releasing some of their great concert stars to his management, Mae had told him in no uncertain terms that if he cooperated with them he could find somebody else to mend his broken English.

Ginger had decided to speak up. She told Magrew about seeing Dr. Romanov chatting with Nina Valgorski and that it seemed to Ginger they had known each other in the past. She told them how Nina had gotten the doctor something to drink. Ginger added, "He was perspiring and dabbing at his brow with a handkerchief. He didn't look well at all. I'm glad his nurse and his chauffeur took him home. Damn, I better check and see if he'll be able to see patients Monday. I have an appointment." Ginger brightened. "Well, Mr. Magrew, was what I told you of any importance to you?"

"It could be. I wonder if the doctor was feeling ill before he got here."

Mae said, "It sounds to me like he's got the flu. There's a lot of it going around now."

Said Villon, "Sounds to me like he might have been poisoned."

Six

*P*oisoned!" said Fred. "But where? How? It couldn't have been in the food or just about everyone in the ballroom would be dead by now. And I've been thinking about fixing myself a plate. I'm famished."

Villon told them, "Not all poisons work instantly. Some can be administered in small doses over a period of time before they take fatal effect. There have been some classic cases involving cyanide administered over a period of time before the victim finally died. Ginger, you're familiar with the doctor's household. How many does he have in help?"

"There's just two in help who live on the premises. There's his housekeeper, who's also the cook, a big bear of a woman. Her name is Malke Movitz. The other one is her nephew, Mordecai Pfenov. He doubles as chauffeur and Romanov's valet."

"What about the nurse?" asked Villon.

"Alida doesn't live there. She has a place of her own in West Hollywood. It's on the way to the RKO and Paramount studios. On occasion when I was going to either studio I gave her a lift home."

Fred said, "Hey now, hold on a minute here, folks. You're talking about murder, and all because a guy wasn't feeling well, he perspired, and his skin was sallow. I mean, like Mae said, it could be the flu."

"Or indigestion," suggested Ginger. "The food on that buffet is awfully rich. And stop talking as though he was dead!

"I should serve food that's awfully poor?" asked Hurok huffily, stung by Ginger's criticism.

"Now really, Sol, I was just making an observation."

Fred said, "Well, rich or poor, I'm off to get myself some. Ginger?"

"Maybe some salad." She said to the others, "I'm also going to phone the doctor's house."

In Dr. Romanov's bedroom, Mordecai Pfenov and Alida Rimsky were helping the doctor undress. Alida could see that the doctor's condition had worsened. Malke Movitz, the housekeeper, came into the room bearing a tray with a glass of hot tea heavily laced with brandy, Russian style. They managed to get the doctor into his pajamas. Alida said, "He's trembling. Perhaps we should call a doctor."

Malke said authoritatively, "The doctor is a doctor, he would tell us if he needed help." She set the tray on the night table next to the bed. She sat on the bed and, with her beefy right hand under the doctor, raised him effortlessly. She held the glass of tea to his mouth and said in Russian, "Take a few sips, doctor. You will feel better." He obeyed the familiar and trusted voice. Malke Movitz was indeed a huge bear of a woman, solidly built. Ginger had commented once that the woman belonged on the seat of a tractor—or else lifting one.

Alida whispered, "I don't like how he looks. His skin is so clammy."

Malke pressed her cheek against the doctor's forehead. "He has a fever. It's the flu. I can handle this. We don't need to call a doctor. I don't like American doctors. They look like morticians." She got Romanov to sip more of the tea and brandy. She asked him, "Good, no?" He closed his eyes and she carefully lowered him until his head rested on a pillow.

Alida asked, "Do you think I ought to stay? He may need me."

"He won't need you," said Malke firmly. "Mordecai will take you back to the party." The idea delighted Mordecai. "Go. I will stay here with Romanov." The doctor was wheezing and breathing heavily. Alida watched from the doorway as Malke mopped the doctor's brow with a tissue. She heard Mordecai speak her name and the urgency in his voice made her wonder why he was so anxious to get back to the Ambassador Hotel. Who, she wondered as she followed him down the stairs, might he know in the ballet company?

As they were leaving the house, Alida heard the phone ring. She hurried back to the hall where there was an extension. She picked up the receiver. "Dr. Romanov."

"Alida? It's Ginger. How's the doctor?"

"He's resting. The housekeeper is with him." The housekeeper was also listening to them on the phone in the doctor's bedroom.

Ginger, hoping she didn't sound too selfish, asked, "Will he be in any condition to see patients Monday?"

"I don't know. I'm not sure. Why don't you call in the morning—around nine."

"Nine? Nine I get my massage. How's about ten?"

"Just as good. I'm on my way back to the party. I'll see you soon."

"Oh fine. It's really swinging here." Ginger hung up and gave herself a few minutes to gather her thoughts. Alida's coming back to the party. She wouldn't leave Romanov if his condition seemed serious. Then she thought, Why come back to the party at all?

A few seconds later she asked Fred the question. Fred responded quickly, "She's footloose and fancy-free. She wants to have a good time." Ginger and Fred were sharing a table with Sol Hurok and Mae Frohman, both of whom were attacking their plates of food as though they might have been warned of an impending famine.

"Fred, I know you have in mind who will dance the daughters Tatyana and Olga. So who do you have in mind for Anaesthesia?" asked Hurok.

"Anastasia," corrected Mae.

Fred was paying no attention to Hurok. His mind dwelled on Don Magrew and on the stricken doctor and he was having second thoughts about his commitment to choreograph the ballet. Politics did not interest him and international intrigue did so even less. He was toying with his food, staring down at the plate and wishing Phyllis, his wife, or his sister Adele were at his side to advise him what to do about the situation. He heard Ginger say, "Fred, Sol's talking to you."

"What?" said Fred. "Oh Sol, oh sure, the food's delicious."

"That isn't what I want to know."

Mae spoke for Hurok, who had speared a piece of tomato and consigned it to his mouth. She repeated Hurok's question, to which Fred responded, "We'll have to promote two dancers from the corps de ballet. I'm sure they're all splendid."

Hurok beamed. "Each and every one is a jewel. You'll be pleasantly surprised. Won't he, Mae?"

"Don't ask me. I've never seen this bunch dance." Sol gave her a deadly look that promised impending immolation. Mae hastily amended her statement. "Their reviews have been terrific. All the dancers are splendid. None of that 'one two three kick' with this gang."

Sol heard Fred asking, "Tell me about Don Magrew. How long have you known him?"

Aha, said Hurok to himself, so it's like I suspected. He's bothered by Don Magrew. "Now Fred, please. Don't trouble yourself with Don Magrew."

"Why not? He presented Ginger and me with a request I happen not to like. I'm no stool pigeon. I don't spy on people and I don't rat on them either."

Ginger's silverware fell from her hands onto the table. Her voice went up a few octaves. "Insinuating that I do?"

"I'm not insinuating anything," replied Fred, trying to keep his voice under control. "Now control that temper, Miss McMath." He tried to add a light touch to what he knew might escalate into a very touchy situation. He explained to Hurok and Mae, "Mc-

Math is Ginger's real name, in case you didn't know. She's one of the Texas McMaths. Famous for none of them perishing at the Alamo."

Sol was confused. "Perishing at the Alamo? A hotel fire?"

"It was a battle fought a long time ago, unlike the one that's about to break out at this table," said Ginger.

"Now don't take offense, Ginger." Fred said to the other two, "It's that Irish temper of hers."

Sol said, "Please, people." He was looking around apprehensively and Mae knew who he was afraid of. She told Hurok, "Parsons and Hopper left. Of course not together."

"But the photographers! They don't give us a minute's peace!"

Fred said with warmth to Ginger, "Sweetie, I was insinuating nothing. I just want you three to know where I stand as far as Don Magrew and the CIA are concerned. I won't betray a fellow artist, I couldn't live with myself."

"Well, if I may say so at the risk of my foot landing in my mouth . . ."

"Or mine," said Hurok, his eyebrows semaphoring impending danger.

Mae continued, "I respect Fred and I respect you too, Ginger. What you told Magrew about Romanov and Nina Valgorski strikes me as being innocent enough. I saw Valgorski chatting up any number of people. And also the other members of the company too. Frankly, if they're all spies, then I find them highly efficient. And frankly, what kind of information can they gather at a bash like this that could be threatening to our country?"

"Absolutely right," said Hurok, "so Mae, you don't have to worry about my foot. Waiter!" He snapped his fingers, "Waiter!"

"I am *not* a waiter," said Franklin Pangborn in a pained voice.

Fred introduced the actor to Mae and Hurok. Pangborn grabbed the nearest waiter and indicated the Hurok table. "You're wanted here. There's an anxiety complex on the loose."

The waiter found a smile, what with being in the presence of Astaire and Rogers Hurok commanded him to bring champagne and brandy.

Fred said to Ginger, "Mad at me?"

Ginger said, "I'm not mad at anybody. I'm sorry I snapped at you, Fred. Mae's right." Mae flashed a triumphant look at Hurok. "There are no secrets to be learned here." Fred was staring past Mae at Don Magrew conferring with two men who Fred assumed were his confederates.

Fred was thinking, I don't like Don Magrew, I don't trust Don Magrew. I'll have to do some fancy stepping to avoid him. When he comes to a rehearsal, I'll see to it I'm too busy to give him any time. He was glad Hurok had ordered brandies for them. He genuinely needed one.

Hurok might have been reading Fred's mind. "Fred, don't worry about Don Magrew. He can't cause any trouble. I have very impotent connections in the State Department."

"Important," corrected Mae.

"Of course they're important!" insisted Hurok. "Why else would I bother with them. Now you listen, Fred. You have heard of Lavrenti Beria?"

"Tenor or baritone?"

"I don't know if he sang. I never asked him. I wasn't interested. Lavrenti Beria was a dreadful man. He was the head of the Russian secret police."

"*Was?* He got fired?"

"He got dead." Hurok lowered his voice and looked around again. Satisfied there were no eavesdroppers, Hurok continued. "Beria was the most evil man I ever dined with except for Sergei Diaghilev who, I'm sure you know, is also dead. Anyway, Beria told me a few weeks before he died, which was about three months ago, he did a big check on everyone involved with the Baronovitch company and everyone who was to be involved with them."

Ginger gasped. "There was a very suspicious man at my wedding! Lela spotted him."

Probably the groom, thought Mae, but wisely kept her thought to herself.

Sol ignored Ginger's information and said, "Everybody, I'm happy to say, came up to stuff."

"Snuff," corrected Mae.

"Now likewise, the State Department did the same kind of check."

"Don't tell me they had the same researchers," said Fred.

"Don't be such a wise guy, Freddie," said Hurok with affection in his voice. "And they could find nothing suspicious about anybody. So I assure you, Magrew will give you no trouble. So if you want to, just ignore him. But be nice when he comes around."

The waiter timed his return perfectly, depositing champagne, brandy, and fresh glasses on the table. He removed the dishes and silverware with professional swiftness, then melted away. Fred lifted a glass and said to Hurok, who had commandeered the bottle of brandy, "Please, Sol, and baby, don't be stingy."

At a table nearby sat Herb Villon, Jim Mallory, and Hazel Dickson, who was tearing a partridge to tatters. "God, I get so hungry at these things. Say, why aren't you guys eating? This stuff's great."

"I'm not hungry," said Jim Mallory, who had finally made contact with Luba Nafka, though she couldn't tear herself away from her fellow artistes.

"Likewise," said Villon. He said to Mallory, "Why don't you talk to Nina Valgorski—find out if she's a spy."

"You're being funny, of course."

"She's very talkative. She's also studied criminology, or so she says. I suspect she also has her finger on the pulse of the company. She seems to know everything that's going on. For a prima ballerina *assoluta* she's very democratic. Say Hazel, is it possible she and Gregor Sukov are having a hot and heavy?"

"If she is, it's not exclusive. Like you said, she's very democratic."

Jim Mallory said with a slight touch of smugness, "I finally got to talk with Luba Nafka."

"Oh yeah? Learn anything?" asked Villon.

"Her room number."

Hazel paused and lit a cigarette. "I think if there are any candidates for spies in this company, those two are your likely candidates." She indicated a table where sat Theodore Varonsky and

Mikhail Bochno. "Look at them. They never seem to laugh. One or the other is always looking over his shoulder as though they might be being tailed or in danger of being knifed. They always seem to be either scowling or brooding."

"Maybe they're homesick," suggested Mallory.

"Hazel." Villon's tone of voice won him her immediate attention. "Ginger said she was going to phone the Romanov place and find out any fresh developments in his health."

"You want me to ask her?"

"It would look better if you did. I'm a cop. I ask and right away they suspect I've got some suspicions."

"Well you do, don't you?"

"Go on, Hazel. Make yourself useful."

Hazel stubbed out her cigarette in the partridge's carcass, shoved her chair back, adjusted her dress, and set out to fulfill her mission. Villon asked Mallory, "Now, what did you get from Nafka?"

"Somewhere there's a husband."

"Where somewhere?"

"I didn't push it."

"What about that valet parker?"

"Which one?"

"The one who occasionally feeds us some tips. Ike something. I think he parked our car. Go have a look-see." Villon's eyes settled on a figure standing in the entrance to the terrace. He recognized the valet service parker. "Why, there's the little devil himself. Whatever he tells you, it's not worth more than a fiver."

Mallory said, "I haven't got a fiver. I've only got some tens."

"Oh for crying out loud." Villon drew his wallet from an inside jacket pocket and handed Mallory a five-dollar bill. Mallory went out to the terrace as Hazel returned from her mission and reported to Villon.

"The housekeeper told her to phone tomorrow morning when she might know if he'd be seeing patients."

Said Villon, "What wouldn't I give for a legitimate reason to go to Romanov's place and see for myself."

"You've got a hunch he's been genuinely poisoned?"

"Like I got a hunch he and Valgorski were once serious business."

Hazel suggested, "Maybe they still are."

"After all these years?"

"Why not? Look at us. We're still at it after all these years." She ground down on "after all these years."

"They've been separated. Romanov, I think, had a wife. And I'm sure Nina didn't honor a vow of chastity. It isn't all that easy to rekindle sparks that died down a long time ago."

"If you're speaking from experience I don't want to know about it. Where did Mallory disappear to?"

"One of our less important informers is working the party. Valet parking. He's one of the car parkers. He and Jim are out on the terrace."

"Waltzing?"

Villon ignored the fatuous remark. Jim was already hurrying back to the table. From the look on his face, Villon could tell he'd struck oil. Maybe not a gusher, but surely enough to pique his interest. Mallory sat down and handed Villon the five-dollar bill.

Villon was startled. "You mean he gave us a freebie?"

"No way," said Mallory. "He said he wanted ten and if I'm any judge of information, what he told me was definitely worth a ten spot. When Romanov's nurse sent him to find the doctor's car, he found more than the car. He found the chauffeur in the front seat having a passionate moment with the woman I no longer love, Luba Nafka."

Hazel snapped her fingers. "I wonder which one of my gargoyles would buy that item."

"You keep quiet about it," Villon warned her. "I'm warning you, Hazel, I don't want anything about the individual dancers in the columns."

"I'm not finished," said Mallory. "There's two items, five dollars apiece."

"Go on," said Villon.

"The chauffeur drove the car to the side entrance to the ballroom leaving poor Ike to walk back. Luba apparently took off on the double. So Ike took his time getting back where he belonged and the lucky bastard sees a woman coming out from behind a hedge. Alida Rimsky."

"The doctor's nurse?" said Villon.

"That's who it was. And a few seconds later, giving the nurse some time to get back to the doctor, out comes a gentleman."

"Who, for crying out loud?"

"I think it's him over there." He pointed and Villon slapped his hand.

"Don't point. You want the guy to get suspicious?" Villon looked past Hazel. "Which one of the three do you mean?"

"Mallory pointed to the one in the middle," Hazel said.

"That's Theodore Varonsky," Villon said to Mallory. "A very nice haul for ten bucks."

Mallory said, "I suppose I'll have to disappoint Luba."

"That's right," said Villon, "and look who's come back to the party."

They saw Alida Rimsky crossing the dance floor.

"And look who's standing, so glad to see her," said Villon.

"Our *cher maître de ballet*, Varonsky."

The orchestra was playing "When I Grow Too Old to Dream." Alida Rimsky and Varonsky met, he whispered something in her ear, and soon they were waltzing.

At Hurok's table, the impresario was trying to convince Fred and Ginger to consider joining the ballet company for a six-week engagement in New York City. Neither star showed much enthusiasm. "I've been away too long from Broadway. Twenty years. I'm too old to do eight performances a week," said Fred.

"Nonsense," scoffed Hurok, "you are forever young. I had the same problem with Anna Pavlova when I resented her."

"Represented her," said Mae.

"This time, Mae, you're wrong. I resented her and I positively mean I resented her. She turned down a tour of America because she said she was too old." He threw up his hands. "Too old! She could still do superb elevations and entertain lovers. For that she wasn't too old!"

Said Ginger, "Look who's come back to the party. It's Alida Rimsky." The others followed Ginger's gaze.

Said Mae, "And she's dancing with Varonsky."

"Why not?" asked Hurok. "Somebody introduced them before the doctor got sick so now she's come back to dance with him."

Fred said, "Not from the way they're looking at each other. I think they know each other from way back when."

"Way back when what?" asked Ginger.

"Ginger, don't be naive."

"You mean you think they knew each other back in Russia?"

"Ginger," cautioned Fred, "you're screeching."

"Sorry. Is that what you're thinking? They're an old item?"

"Look at Herb Villon. He's looking at them like they're a parakeet and he's a cat about to pounce."

"I hope he doesn't. They look so dreamy," said Mae.

Hurok was refilling glasses with brandy. "Mae," said Hurok in a cautionary voice, "don't get too sentimental about them. They might be spies."

At the same time, Villon was saying to Hazel and Mallory, "Why do I get the feeling we're watching an old married couple?"

Seven

*H*azel asked Villon wistfully, "Do you suppose we'll ever be an old married couple?"

Villon said matter-of-factly, "Well, we're too old to be a young married couple. Varonsky has a nice style on the dance floor. I wonder if he was ever a dancer?"

"I'll find out," said Hazel.

"It's not important," said Villon. "It's just that he moves like someone who's been trained as a dancer."

Mallory asked, "Do you suppose there are any Arthur Murray Schools of Dancing in Russia?"

"Ain't they got enough troubles?" Villon was watching Nina Valgorski and Luba Nafka going down a passage that led to the Ambassador's rest rooms.

On the dance floor, Varonsky held Alida closely. Her smile told Varonsky she was in ecstasy. He whispered, "You have grown even more beautiful than I remembered."

Her eyes opened. "Say more. It has been so long since I've heard flattering remarks." They danced past the table where Mikhail Bochno sat with one of the company understudies, watching them intently. "Your comrades sit like two of those figurines. See No Evil and Hear No Evil."

"And I," said Theodore, "am Speak No Evil. Have you had a chance to talk with Gregor Sukov?"

"Earlier. I think he and Luba Nafka are planning something. I thought he was spoken for by Nina."

"My darling, Nina is terribly versatile. She speaks for many men."

"Has she spoken for you?"

"Not even in a whisper."

In the ladies' room, Nina and Luba sat at adjoining dressing tables busily indulging in repair work, freshening their faces. They were oblivious to the constant flow of traffic, the flushing of toilets; wherever they were, like all ballet dancers, they created and inhabited a world of their own. Many civilians tried to penetrate this world, though only a very small percentage succeeded. Which is why the denizens of the dance world for the most part married each other.

Nina, while rouging her cheeks, said to Luba, "I know what's going on."

Luba, while darkening her thinly plucked eyebrows in hopes of emulating Marlene Dietrich, asked innocently, "Going on where?" They conversed in Russian, occasionally lapsing into English and every so often throwing in a soupçon of French, which was the second language of upper-class Russians. French governesses were in great demand in the Soviet Union, though of late their ranks were thinning due to the unfavorable rate of monetary exchange.

"I know what you are up to," said Nina. "Don't play the innocent. You should know I am not easily fooled."

"But of course, Ninavitch. You are a goddess descended from Mount Olympus. So at what am I not easily fooling you?"

"You are conspiring with Gregor."

"Conspiring? Conspiring? To do what, overthrow the government? Be a goddess, Ninavitch, but don't be a fool. Gregor is in love with you, is he not?" Nina didn't answer Luba. She didn't give a ruble if Sukov was in love with her. Love was an emotion that Nina had put on the back burner way back in her teens after her third botched abortion. "So why should Gregor conspire with me? And what is this conspiring we are supposed to be doing?"

"I suspect you are planning to defect." That was a low blow for Luba, who managed not to bat an eyelash, inasmuch as she was now applying mascara.

Luba emitted a small, mocking laugh. "You are being very ridiculous. On second thought, you are a prima ballerina *assoluta*."

"So?"

"All primas are ridiculous."

Nina bristled. "I shall slap your face!"

"So then I shall slap yours!"

They didn't notice that Ginger was at the dressing table on the other side of Nina. The dancers were now speaking in French, which delighted Ginger since she had been taking French lessons for months in preparation for her marriage to Jacques Bergerac. Once married, Bergerac dismayed her slightly by saying her French was more fluid than fluent, but still she persevered despite the fact her mother kept yelling, "Speak American!" Ginger was patting her face with powder from a stunning Tiffany case she had given herself as a wedding present. She was completely absorbed in the now heated conversation between Nina and Luba. As far as she was concerned she wasn't spying, she was eavesdropping, and in Hollywood eavesdropping had supplanted prostitution as the second-oldest profession.

"Watch your step, Nina. Be very very careful. You spread the rumor Gregor and I are planning to defect and I'll reveal the truth of your part in the Vanoff affair."

Ginger heard a sharp intake of breath. It was obviously Nina. Vanoff affair, thought Ginger, fingertips tingling. Intuitively she felt she was about to strike a very rich lode. She heard Nina saying in a voice that seemed strangely not the ballerina's, strained and almost hoarse, "And what was my part in the Vanoff affair?"

Her voice cleared and it was now challenging. "Are you intimating I was instrumental in helping Nikolai Vanoff poison his mother and father and then kill himself?" As she spoke, she clutched the whistle that dangled from the chain around her neck, as though it could comfort her. Ginger was now applying lip rouge she didn't need. She'd already completed that repair job at the table after dining.

Now Nina sounded conciliatory, but Ginger recognized the insincerity in her voice. She was sure Luba did too, or at least she hoped so. She liked Luba, her youthful enthusiasm, her expressive eyes, and the dainty movements of her hands. She put Ginger in mind of those automatic porcelain dolls that danced when wound up, which were always a feature of Sotheby auctions. "Luba Luba Luba," said Nina, "Nikolai told me everything before he killed his parents and then himself. You were Nikolai's friend and yet you learned nothing? Didn't you know at the time I was his mistress?"

Luba said defiantly, "So was I!" Good for Luba, thought Ginger. "I too was Nikolai's mistress and you never suspected! Ha ha ha!"

"You lie!"

Luba mocked her mercilessly and now Ginger thought she might be going too far. "The great Valgorski! The goddess! Nina the impeccable!" She moved her face closer to Valgorski and Ginger had to strain to hear what she was saying, "I have long suspected you were an important player in the affair, that you too had a motive to kill the parents. And how do I know all this?" She answered herself. "Because Nikolai talked in his sleep!"

Well, so does Jacques Bergerac, thought Ginger, but I haven't learned anything useful except for his recipe for *boeuf bourguinon.*

"He didn't talk in his sleep when I slept with him. I kept him much too busy. Why, Ginger! How long have you been sitting there?" Luba moved her head and smiled at Ginger.

Ginger answered Nina swiftly. "Not very long, but long enough to wish I understood French."

Nina cocked her head to one side. "You are married to a Frenchman and you don't understand French?"

"I don't need French to understand Jacques. Am I interrupting a very important conversation?"

Luba deferred to Nina who said expressively, "Interrupt? What is there to interrupt? We were discussing *pliés* and *tours jetés.*"

"Hockey teams?"

Nina smiled. Luba recognized the smile as a prelude to an onslaught of bitchery. "Are you excited about dancing the role of the Czarina?"

"I'm all atremble."

"Did you know I am dancing Tatyana and Luba will be dancing Olga?"

"Ladies in waiting? I haven't discussed the casting with Fred. That's strictly his department. I know next to nothing about Rasputin and the Romanovs, so I'm leaving it all up to Fred. I trust him implicitly."

Nina ploughed on. "We are two of your four daughters."

"You're sure you don't mean ladies-in-waiting?"

"We do not wait," said Nina, positive Ginger was paling under her makeup. "We are two of your four daughters."

"You're sure you don't mean my sisters?"

"Your daughters."

Ginger blinked her eyes. It had sunk in. Tap dancing or no tap dancing, she was playing the mother of four adult daughters and one bleeder of a son. "Four daughters. Four big daughters." She arose. "Excuse me, girls, I need a drink." She hurried out.

Luba said, "Nina, you make an art of cruelty."

In Romanov's bedroom, lit by a single lamp on the end table, the doctor was sleeping fitfully. He tossed and turned, racked by a nightmare that recurred too often. Dogs barked ferociously and he saw his wife's frightened face as she tried to escape the gulag to join him at their rendezvous, and then he heard the sounds of shots ringing out and his wife screaming in agony as blood oozed from her wounds. The doctor was babbling in Russian. He was delirious. His eyes flew open and the babbling continued.

Malke Movitz entered the room wearing a bathrobe and bedroom slippers, her hair hanging down the back in two disarrayed braids. Malke watched as the doctor sat up, hands outstretched, but seeing nothing but the hazy figure of a large woman coming toward him. A horrendous shriek filled the room. Malke stared at the doctor and he fell back on the pillow, mouth and eyes open, eyes seeing nothing. Malke bent over and pressed an ear to his chest. She heard no sound of his heart beating, she heard no sign of life. She went to the phone and very calmly dialed the emergency police number. She told the voice that answered she needed an ambulance for a dead man. The policeman on the other end recognized the doctor's name, which he wrote down carefully, also writing the address and phone number, and promised Malke assistance would arrive in very short order. While looking at the corpse, she then dialed information and asked for the number of the Ambassador Hotel, which she wrote on a pad. She dialed the hotel and asked to have Alida Rimsky paged as this was an emergency. A very efficient operator soon connected Malke to Alida.

Alida dreaded the news that she knew awaited her on the telephone. Only Malke knew she was in the ballroom and it could only be Malke to tell her the doctor had taken a turn for the worse. Varonsky followed Alida to the phone. They passed the terrace door and Varonsky had a glimpse of Luba standing with her arms around Mordecai Pfenov's neck. Varonsky hurried out to the terrace and alerted the chauffeur that Alida would probably need him to drive her back to the Romanov house right away. The chauffeur went to get the car while Luba, disconsolate at losing her man for the second time that night, went back to the ballroom for more champagne.

Ginger had rejoined Fred and Hurok and Mae Frohman at the table, where the three were convincing her the audience would accept her grown daughters as a joke. After all, this was their Ginger and their Ginger was ageless. "I shouldn't be playing Nina's mother," fumed Ginger. "She should be playing *my* mother. Why, for crying out loud, I look younger then she does."

"Of course you do, darling," said Hurok, "that's the joke. Toe in cheek!"

"Tongue in cheek," corrected Mae.

"I swear, darling Ginger. Nobody is trying to pull the wolf over your eyes."

"Wool," corrected Mae, somewhat wearily.

Hazel had seen the activity involving Alida, Varonsky, and the chauffeur and sensed a story. She followed in Alida's wake while Villon said to Mallory, "Let's follow Hazel. She's chasing after the doctor's nurse which means she's on to something. You know Hazel's a better sniffer than any bloodhound."

Alida was in the small lobby that led to the ballroom, where there was a large desk behind which sat three managers in charge of the guest list. It was one of these men who had summoned Alida. She picked up the phone and said, "Yes?"

Malke spoke softly into the phone. "Romanov is dead. You had better come. I have sent for an ambulance and the police."

"When did he die?"

"Perhaps ten minutes ago. He was babbling in his sleep. He was delirious. Then he sat up and shrieked. It was horrible. And then he fell back dead. Please hurry. I don't want to be alone much longer."

"Yes. Of course. I'll come as quickly as possible." She hung up the phone and said to Varonsky, standing at her side, "Romanov is dead. I must go to the house at once."

"Of course. I'll have the chauffeur bring the car." He hurried away. Hazel was bearing down on Alida. "I can tell by your face Romanov's dead. He is, isn't he?"

"He is," said Alida quietly, "and now the vultures shall gather."

Hazel ignored Alida mostly because she didn't understand what Alida meant. Villon and Mallory confronted Alida as she headed for the terrace. Alida tried to hurry past them but Villon grabbed her wrist. He flashed his badge. "Is the doctor dead?"

"Yes. He's dead." She thought for a moment and then asked, as Varonsky returned to her side, "Why are the police interested?"

Don Magrew, wondering what all the sudden activity on the part of Varonsky and Villon was all about, hurried to them in time to hear Alida ask why the police were interested.

"Interested in what?" asked Magrew.

Villon told him Romanov was dead and then returned his attention to Alida. "I'm interested, Miss Rimsky, because I think the doctor may have been poisoned." As he spoke, he realized unhappily that his audience was increasing. They now had the interest of Nina and Luba as well. Villon instructed Jim Mallory to phone the precinct and to tell them to order an immediate autopsy. Jim headed for the phone but Hazel Dickson was prattling into it telling Louella's assistant, Dorothy Manners, that Hollywood's most prominent shrink had gone belly up. "I've got an exclusive, Dorothy, straight from his nurse's mouth." Mallory hunted for another phone. He knew that demanding the phone by showing Hazel his badge was an essay in farce; she would tell him what to do with the badge because she was an old pal and had no intention of relinquishing the telephone to anybody. She held back on Villon's suspicions that the doctor may have been murdered because that constituted another profitable item in her avaricious way of thinking.

"Poisoned!" gasped Alida. Her eyes found Varonsky but he expressed no emotion. She was on her own. "But why?"

"Why not?" countered Magrew. Villon wished the CIA man would stay out of it; this was his turf and he permitted no poaching. But he knew he had to tread carefully with Magrew because most government agents were big mouths with even bigger egos. Whatever job there was to do, Villon knew he could do it far more efficiently than Magrew.

Now Alida was indignant. Who was this upstart? She didn't know Magrew, "What do you mean, why not? The doctor had no enemies!"

Villon took the spotlight. "Everybody has enemies, some they haven't been properly introduced to."

Nina stuck her oar in. "Poison? Perhaps cadmium? It's a very popular poison in our country. It outsells grits. Isn't that so, Luba?"

Luba glared at her. "And since when am I an authority on cadmium?"

Alida had time to gather her thoughts. She asked Villon, "What makes you suspect poison?"

Villon countered with, "Was the doctor diabetic?"

"He was not. And I would know if he was. I do not for one moment believe the doctor was poisoned. I admit he was perspiring profusely and his skin was sallow, but those are also the symptoms of flu. Now you must excuse me, the housekeeper is alone with the body. She is very uneasy. I must go to her."

Villon said pointedly, "I'll follow you there."

"As you wish," said Alida. She hurried to the terrace. After a moment's hesitation, Varonsky followed her to the terrace. Villon told Mallory to get their car and Hazel was not about to be excluded from the party.

At Hurok's table, Ginger appeared to be assuaged and resigned to portraying a mother of five children. She was telling Fred, Hurok, and Mae about the incident in the ladies' room. Sam Goldwyn had joined them, spooning raspberries and yogurt, having learned his wife had joined a group going to Preston Sturges' Players Club, which the celebrated director had established on Sunset Boulevard as a hangout for his chums. Goldwyn froze in position when he heard Ginger ask Hurok, "Sol, did you ever hear of Nikolai Vanoff?"

Hurok and Goldwyn exchanged glances.

"Well, Sol?" Ginger was growing impatient and Fred looked at three interested faces belonging to Ginger, Hurok, and Goldwyn, who asked jocularly, "Well, boys, Nikolai Vanoff—dancer or spy or equal proportions of both?"

Sol said to Ginger, "Where did you hear the name?"

"In the powder room," said Ginger, beaming at one and all. "I was spying on Nina and Luba." Fred wondered if she expected to be patted on the head. After what she had just put them through about dancing the role of a mother of five, he wanted to assail another part of her anatomy with his foot.

Fred said suddenly, after "spying" had sunk in, "Why in heaven's name were you spying on them?"

"Well actually," said Ginger with a lot less bravura, "I was eavesdropping. You see, they were having a little dustup and I sat at a dressing table next to them. Really it was the only one unoccupied and anyway, when I sat down, the ladies were batting words in French back and forth and a bit heatedly, and since my latest husband is French and I'm studying the language"—nobody looked impressed—"I decided this was a godsent opportunity to do a little practicing."

"My *latest* husband," thought Mae Frohman, and Mae had yet to land one. She poured herself a brandy and looked morose.

Ginger continued, "Well, they got so intense and the innuendos were coming to a boil and it got to a point where I thought they might take a sock at each other." She paused to see if she was having any effect and Fred said dryly, "Go on, Ginger, the suspense is killing me."

"Well I don't want to talk out of school," said Ginger, first aware that Villon and Hazel were standing and listening to her, Villon waiting to break the news to Ginger that she was now minus a psychiatrist.

"Ginger," said Fred, "school's already out."

"Oh hell, in for a penny, in for a pound. Nina said to Luba something like 'You're not kidding me, I know what you're up to,' and Luba batted her eyelashes innocently, and Nina stuck the shaft in. 'I know you and Gregor—meaning Sukov, I suppose—are planning to defect.' "

Hurok whispered, "Oy vay" and was grateful Don Magrew wasn't listening to any of this.

"So Luba says, 'Oh yeah? Well I'll tell about you and the Vanoff affair' and making it sound like what she had to tell could result in Nina being stood up in front of a firing squad without the offer of a handkerchief to shield her eyes." Hurok had joined Mae Frohman with a brandy. He realized the possibility of time bombs ticking away in the Baronovitch company and he didn't relish contemplating the consequences.

"I can assure you, Ginger," said Hurok, "if Nina was standing in front of a firing squad it would be with a pen and an engagement pad booking some assassinations."

"He means 'assignations,' " explained Mae to the assortment of bewildered people.

Goldwyn clucked his tongue and said, "Hurok assassinates the English language." Nobody had the courage to comment on Goldwyn's own lacerations of the language.

"Come on, Sol," said Ginger impatiently, "who was Nikolai Vanoff?"

Hurok sighed. "It is a very unpleasant story, so I shall tell it."

Eight

$\mathcal{A}$s Hurok refreshed his drink, Villon looked at his wristwatch and as anxious as he was to get to the Romanov house and continue his probing there, he wanted to hear the rest of this Vanoff affair. His instincts told him this could be important, maybe even have some bearing on the probability that Romanov was murdered. Hazel was fidgeting and he poked her to settle down. She had a feeling every one of Hurok's words would be worth a couple of bucks.

"I liked Nikolai Vanoff," Hurok began, "even though he was a ruthless scoundrel. And he in turn liked me."

Even though you're a ruthless scoundrel, thought Mae Frohman, and she giggled. Hurok shot her a look and the giggle died rapidly.

"Vanoff was one of Stalin's advisors. Just about anything he wanted, Stalin got for him, which is why I spent a great deal of time and money currying favor with Vanoff. I wanted David Oistrakh and his violin for a tour of America and I got him, thank you, Nikolai. I wanted the fabulous Don Cossack choir, and I got them thanks to Nikolai. Just about everything I wanted I got and it cost me plenty. Nikolai was a shrewd trader—he drove very hard bargains. But still, despite his greed, I was able to show a good profit. In addition to his supply of brains, Nikolai was incredibly handsome. As a young man he had made some films and I was told a promising career awaited him in the movies. But Nikolai's ambitions supersucceeded the movies."

"Superseded," corrected Mae.

Goldwyn asked her, "From where does he know such a word?" Mae shrugged.

Hurok rolled on. "Nikolai wanted power. Not just plain power"—Hurok made a fist for emphasis—"but *power.* But like anyone among us, Nikolai had his shorts coming."

"Shortcomings," corrected Mae, although she slurred the word. The brandies she had consumed were starting to take effect.

"He adored women," said Hurok, "especially very beautiful women like Nina and Luba, both of whom were his mistresses."

"And at the same time," added Ginger confidentially, glad that neither dancer was anywhere within earshot.

"Nikolai Vanoff," said Hurok, pleased that the group were hanging on to his every word, "was a sexual mechanic. No!" He raised an index finger for emphasis. "He was an engineer!"

Fred was thinking of shouting "Encore!" but decided this was no time for frivolity.

"And adoring women led to his undoing. You see, he adored stars. Movie stars, theater stars, and ballet stars—and stars expect furs and jewels and expensive apartments and foreign cars, am I right, Ginger?"

"Wrong," she snapped. "I've always bought my own. I got nothing out of Howard Hughes and he's the only millionaire I ever knew."

Asked Hazel Dickson, "What about Alfred Vanderbilt?"

"Are you kidding? His idea of a gourmet dinner was a hot dog and a root beer, let alone shower me with furs and diamonds. Sorry Sol, go on."

Hurok easily picked up the thread of his story. "Nikolai turned traitor. He was so desperate for large sums of money he sold secrets to the British and the French and the Germans."

"Terribly indiscriminate," commented Fred.

"He wasn't very choosy. He sold to the highest bidder."

"Obviously somebody caught up with him," said Fred.

"His mother and father." Hurok waited while that sank in. "They were phonetical communists—"

"Fanatical," corrected Mae. Goldwyn was positive she was wrong but said nothing.

"Nikolai had a brother, Feodor. He was a member of the secret police but everybody on his block knew it because he wasn't all that secretive. He found out Nikolai was betraying his country and even worse, betraying his mentor, Stalin."

"How did he find out?" asked Villon.

"From the spies in all the embassies, how else? He told his parents in hopes they would teach Nikolai to mend his ways and then Feodor presumably left on a trip, from which, by the way, he never returned."

A wide-eyed Ginger said, "I'll bet Nikolai murdered him!"

"Perhaps," said Hurok, "like Cain and Mabel."

Mae was dozing. Goldwyn nudged her. Her eyes flew open, but Goldwyn had already taken over her responsibility. "Like Cain and Abel," he corrected.

Hurok guffawed. "Look what's correcting my English!"

"Finish the story," said Goldwyn.

"I'm finishing, I'm finishing," said Hurok. "The rest is like a patchwork quilt. Little bits and pieces. The parents were found dead soon after Feodor went off. They had been poisoned. There was an investigation, and lo and behold, Nikolai was found dead one morning in the courtyard of the apartment house where Nina Valgorski had a very lavish apartment."

Hazel was like a rocket about to shoot off into space. What a story! Perfect for a Sunday feature in every Hearst publication. The Hearst papers thrived on blood and gore. Hazel could see herself in that very expensive Hattie Carnegie suit she'd been admiring in I. Magnin's window.

Fred said, "And the question is, did he jump or was he pushed?"

"Why jump?" asked Ginger. "He'd already murdered his parents, the beast, so they couldn't give him away, and his brother was off God knows where and didn't betray him to anyone but his parents, at least I assume, so obviously, he was pushed to his death. Sol, was he wearing clothes or was he naked?"

"He was wearing a Sulka bathrobe. One of the most expensive ones."

"Sulka, eh?" said Fred. "Vanoff sure did have expensive tastes. So what about Nina?"

"Although he jumped or fell from her apartment, it was proven she had not been home all night."

"I'm sure shacked up with someone very powerful."

"Indeed." Sol paused and then smiled. "Lavrenti Beria. The dreaded all-powerful head of the secret police. He also liked me. I got him Betty Grable's autograph."

"Well, really," said Ginger. "Oh dear, I'm getting palpitations. Maybe I should check into a hospital."

"I wouldn't if I were you," said Fred. "Hospitals are enema territory."

Ginger ignored him and said, "Then Dr. Romanov has got to see me Monday, he's just got to."

Villon said gravely, "Ginger, I'm afraid the doctor won't be seeing anybody. He's dead."

Ginger screamed. Photographers came on the run, and popping flashbulbs put Goldwyn in mind of a Fourth of July celebration.

"Dead!" cried Ginger, "He can't be dead!" She was on her feet addressing Villon. "He was murdered, wasn't he? Wasn't he?"

"I think he was, but I won't know for sure until I get the autopsy report."

"Where's Alida? Does she know? This will destroy her!"

"She found out from the housekeeper who phoned her here. She's gone back to the house and Jim and I have got to get there now."

"I'm going too. Malke Movitz will need me."

"Who?" asked Villon.

"The doctor's housekeeper. Eccentric but lovable."

"Lovable!" exclaimed Hazel. "Ha!"

"You know her?" asked Villon.

"I've interviewed Romanov a couple of times, probably more. One story of mine he loathed, especially the title, *Head Shrinker or Head Hunter.* Terrific, right? The housekeeper was always underfoot." She shook her head from side to side. "What a weird woman. If ever there was a candidate to win a Wallace Beery lookalike contest."

Unwillingly, Fred agreed to drive Ginger to the doctor's. He'd had more than enough of her for one night. But now he was nursing a hunch that in the Romanov household there might be found a link to the Vanoff scandal. He was wondering if Villon was wondering if perhaps Romanov was the missing Feodor Vanoff. Crazy thought. The doctor was surely an accredited psychiatrist. How else could he practice? Fred knew there was a breed known as lay analysts, who hadn't trained as doctors, but nevertheless could hang their shingles.

Names and faces were racing through Ginger's head as she and Fred waited for Villon's spy, Ike, to bring Fred's car around. Nina Valgorski and the Vanoffs headed the procession.

"Ginger, you're talking to yourself," said Fred.

"It's the only time I have an intelligent conversation. Fred, listen to me." Her voice darkened. "There's skullduggery afoot."

"With a line like that, you should be twirling a mustache."

"I don't have a mustache and I hope to God I never develop one like some ladies we both know. But I've been developing some suspicions and theories about this company."

"Now see here, Ginger. Don't dislike Nina and Luba because I've cast them as your daughters."

"Oh of course not, Fred. I like Luba. She's adorable. And I hope she does defect."

"And Nina?"

"She's too old to defect. Anyway, with her reputation for romantic conquests, my guess is she has something hot on the burner waiting for her back in Mother Russia. I'll bet she's rich. Except you're not supposed to be rich in Russia."

Fred snorted. "Don't believe everything you hear about that place. There's a lot of rich people in Russia, and I know because I once heard a lecture by Madame Ivy Litvinoff and . . ."

"Here's the car," said Ginger. Ike got out from behind the wheel. Fred tipped him and got in, Ginger getting in on the other side. Ginger asked Fred, "Do you suppose the ladies have heard that Romanov is dead?"

They had heard. They were sitting with Hurok. Mae had gone up to her room and Goldwyn had decided to call it a night. "So he is dead," said Hurok, "and Ginger is abandoned."

"Psychiatrists!" scoffed Nina. "People who think they need them must have something wrong with their heads."

Luba said. "Psychiatrists hear a great deal. Sometimes they hear things that should have been left unspoken. And sometimes they hear things they do not realize are of a certain importance."

"How do you know so much about psychiatrists?" asked Hurok. "There aren't supposed to be any in the Soviet Union."

"Oh there are," said Luba, "but we call them informants. Only the rich in the Soviet Union have psychiatrists, and even they have them in Vienna or Paris or London."

"So now Ginger is without her artificial desperation," said Hurok.

"Respiration," corrected Nina, looking terribly pleased with herself.

From out of left field, Hurok heard himself asking Nina, "Tell me, Nina, are you still in touch with the Vanoff family?"

Luba settled back in her chair. She had been huddled over her glass of champagne as though in fear someone would snatch it from her. Like Hurok, she waited for Nina's reply, knowing Nina was still upset by their conversation in the powder room.

Nina found a cigarette in a tray on the table. There were no matches available so Hurok gallantly reached for his lighter and leaned forward to oblige. Nina looked at Luba as she accepted the light and Luba shrugged dramatically by way of telling Nina it wasn't she who'd introduced the subject of the Vanoffs to Hurok. Hurok reminded Nina, "I have been to the Soviet Union many times in the past three decades. I was there when Nikolai Vanoff committed suicide."

Luba couldn't resist sticking a pin into Nina. "There are those who insist he was pushed."

Nina was very cool, very calm, and very collected. "You seem to forget, Luba, I spent that night with Beria." Nina said to Hurok, "The question of my whereabouts that evening has assumed legendary proportions. I assure you, Mr. Hurok, I was positively with Beria that night."

"It was only Beria who provided your alibi," said Luba, "And now he is dead."

"Soooo?"

Hurok said quickly, for fear of another dustup between them, "I asked a simple question—do you hear from the Vanoffs, Nina—and I had no idea it could lead to a broomhaha."

"Brouhaha," corrected Nina. "But why all of a sudden do you ask about the Vanoffs? They are history. Yesterday's news. Why should I hear from them? They detested me. They once came to see me dancing *Swan Lake* just for the nasty pleasure of walking out on me."

Luba asked maliciously, "Oh? They were also critics?"

"Ladies, ladies," said Hurok, "I'm sorry I asked about the Vanoffs, I was only making conversation." He added without thinking, "Ginger asked who they were after overhearing you mention them in the powder room."

Nina and Luba exchanged a glance, this one devoid of any underlying hostility. It was Nina who asked Luba lightly, "Oh dear, Luba. Do you suppose Ginger was sent to spy on us?" She said to Hurok, "We spoke mostly in Russian and French. Does Ginger have the languages?" An invisible lightbulb flashed over her head. "But of course. Her husband is a Frenchman, so she probably knows some French."

"Not very much," said Hurok too quickly.

"But enough to understand we were talking about the Vanoffs," said Nina. She blew a smoke ring that settled over Luba's head, amusingly enough, like a halo. "I wonder, Mr. Hurok, is Ginger an American spy?" Hurok started to remonstrate. "Please, Mr. Hurok. Don't be upset. My mind is famous for entertaining suspicions." Luba nodded her head in corroboration. "After all, Ginger's mother is celebrated for her right-wing politics. Is that correct, right wing? Yes, of course it is."

Hurok rose to Ginger's defense. "I can assure you this is not a case of like mother, like daughter. You must remember Ginger was once married to the actor Lew Ayres, who during the war was a conscientious objector."

"Meaning what?" asked Nina, unfamiliar with the term.

"Meaning he objected to participating in the mindless slaughter of other human beings."

Luba said in Russian, "Highly commendable. I applaud him. I applaud Ginger for standing by her man."

Hurok was beaten. He explained in a small voice, "Not exactly. At the time they had long been divorced."

Nina laughed and clutched the whistle that dangled from the chain around her neck. "I wonder if I will ever understand Americans."

Hurok was thinking, I wonder if Americans will ever understand Russians. And I wonder if I'll ever know if Nina hears from the Vanoffs and have the Vanoffs ever heard from their absent son, Feodor.

Nina said, and Hurok wondered if she was a licensed mind reader, "In answer to your question about the Vanoffs . . ."

Don Magrew had suddenly materialized and Hurok indicated he take a chair, which he did. Nina continued, "The Vanoffs no more try to contact me than I try to contact them. I told you they walked out on my *Swan Lake,* one of my greatest triumphs. Ask Mr. Magrew, he applauded me in Seattle."

"Oh I did?" asked Magrew. "I didn't know you knew I was there."

Luba said slyly, "Sometimes Nina is clairvoyant. Or sometimes

Nina sees a handsome gentleman like yourself and does not rest until she learns your identity. Is that not so, Nina?"

In gutter Russian Nina told her to do something that is physically impossible. Luba's cheeks flared and Hurok clucked his tongue and Magrew laughed. Hurok said in amazement, "Why, Mr. Magrew, you speak Russian?"

"Most of us in the CIA do," said Magrew, nonchalantly lighting his pipe.

"You are not investigating Dr. Romanov's death?" asked Luba.

"That's not my job. It's Herb Villon's territory, which he guards zealously."

Hurok said, "Sam Goldwyn says Villon is quite a very good detective. Sam was involved back in 1929 in a case in which Villon was in charge of the investigation. Villon told Sam he thinks Romanov was poisoned." Nina made a noise that sounded like a scoff. Hurok looked directly at Nina, "And Sam says if Villon thinks Romanov was poisoned, then Romanov was poisoned."

Nine

$\mathcal{J}$im Mallory, as usual, was at the wheel of the unmarked police car with Hazel wedged between him and Herb Villon. Up ahead he could see Fred's taillights. At least he hoped that was Fred and Ginger up ahead as Hazel was somewhat vague as to the directions to Romanov's house. Hazel said, "You're very quiet, Herb. Rounding up the unusual suspects? I admit I haven't a clue as to who might have rung the curtain down on the doctor. It's obvious Nina knew him back in the old country and she also got him a glass of something . . ."

"Soda water," said Villon.

"You sure about that?"

"I'm sure."

"But how could she have doctored it if she did doctor it? That was an awfully tight gown she was wearing and it didn't have pockets."

Mallory suggested, "She could have hidden something in her cleavage."

Hazel feigned shock. "Why, Mr. Mallory!"

Mallory was not to be sidetracked. "Don't women usually keep a handkerchief there?"

"Most women do and I do too," corroborated Hazel. "As a matter of fact, once on a drive to Santa Ana with a very well-endowed girlfriend, I said I was famished and from that very vicinity she produced a ham on rye with a gherkin very neatly wrapped in wax paper."

Villon kept staring ahead through the windshield while Mallory brought the conversation back to the Baronovitch company. "I think there's an awful lot of undercurrents with that gang of dancers. Lots of intrigue. Jealousy. Enmity."

"Leaving on track nine," quipped Hazel. "Jim, they're Russians, they are not the Elks. Herb Villon, you're too damn quiet. Come on, Herb, who've you got cornered in your mind? Who do you suspect are the spies?" She knew he'd tell her nothing, but badgering Herb Villon was one of her favorite sports. Herb wouldn't tell her anything because her nose would pick up the scent of a telephone and she'd be on the wire with either Hedda or Louella or other gossip columnists he knew she serviced, such as Sidney Skolsky, Jimmy Fidler, Sheliah Graham, Harrison Carroll, and an Israeli writer who went by the pseudonym Dear Abie.

Herb decided to throw her a bone in the hope she might shoot her mouth off in the direction of any number of suspects and thereby wrack their nerves, which just might cause somebody to make a mistake. "Seems to me the likely candidate among several likely candidates is Dr. Igor Romanov."

Mallory said eagerly, "So help me God, Herb, that's just what I've been thinking."

"So why didn't you say something?"

"I was afraid of being intimidated."

"By who?"

"By you! You're always squelching me!"

"That's a load of bullshit. I keep telling you to speak up when you think you've got something. Even if it isn't right it could sometimes lead to something else."

"Well, I think Romanov bargained his way out of Russia!"

"Go on, go on, so far we're on the same radar."

"He escaped from that there goulash . . ."

"Gulag," corrected Herb.

"But then getting out of the country itself wasn't all that good. So he took a gamble and offered himself up as a spy. He spoke English, he was a concert pianist . . ."

"And he was also a medical student for a while," said Hazel. "I got that out of him during an interview. Why, Jim Mallory, fancy you having a scientific mind!"

"Why not? You know I read a lot of science fiction."

"Hot damn!" exclaimed Hazel. "So they decide to take Romanov up on his offer and train him in psychiatry, get him started in Beverly Hills, and 'Bob's your uncle.' "

"I don't have an uncle Bob," said Mallory.

Hazel explained patiently, "That's a British expression. George Sanders uses it all the time. In fact I had tea with George yesterday at the Beverly Hilton and—"

"Enough!" cried Herb. Hazel, amazingly enough, shut up. "Okay. So he's now getting established in Hollywood. So who started feeding him poison and why? Don't strain yourself, Jim, there's only one answer to that one. He was forced to become a mole."

Hazel complained, "You're talking over my head."

"A mole. A two-headed spy. He was not only working for the old country, he was also working for us."

"Why the conniving son of a bitch," said Hazel.

"Here I'm on Romanov's side. He was probably forced into it by some sharpy in our secret service who spotted Romanov as a clay pigeon."

"Poor bastard." Hazel came to a realization, "He couldn't have been working on his own." She looked at Herb. "How about his nurse, Alida. Or the housekeeper, Malke Movitz. When you see her you will understand it is rumored that several alcoholics on meeting her took the pledge. And the chauffeur. I think Malke said he was her nephew. But then, those Russians say an awful lot of things, all to be taken with a grain of salt."

"Try listening between the lines," said Villon.

Ahead of them, Fred was pulling into Romanov's driveway. He braked to a sudden halt and Ginger shouted, "Hey! Take it easy!"

Fred tried to keep himself from panicking. "Look what's at Romanov's front door."

"Oh my oh my oh my," said Ginger. She saw two patrol cars, a police ambulance, reporters, and photographers who were all eager to see who was in the car that had just braked to a halt.

"Here they come," agonized Fred, who was a very shy and very private person. When his sister was his partner he let her do all the talking for the two of them and happily stayed behind the scenes, out of the limelight. "I shouldn't have brought you here. I should have gone home."

Ginger said dryly, "My hero." She could see he was genuinely frightened. "Let me handle this. I'm good at treading where angels fear." Headlights from the bar behind them were almost blinding, and then were quickly turned off. Ginger looked out the rear window. "Oh good. Herb Villon and his partner and of course Hazel the fearless. Now Fred, take several deep breaths." She opened the passenger door and stood facing the onslaught of journalists. "Why, gentleman! What brings you here? What a surprise!"

"Hey, Ginger," shouted a photographer, "What brings *you* here?"

"Mr. Astaire and his car brought me here. Why hello, Herb! Hello, Mr. Mallory! And why hello, Hazel!"

Hazel said in an aside to Fred who had timorously emerged from the car and stood behind Ginger, a timid warrior with his formidable shield, "She must be ill."

"She isn't," Fred assured her, "thank God." The gentlemen and some ladies of the press turned their attention to Villon.

"Hey, Herb!" demanded one reporter, "what's going on?"

"All I know is what I read in the papers," growled Herb. Of Ginger and Fred he asked, "What are you two doing here?"

"You have such a short memory, Mr. Villon. Didn't you ask us to accompany you here?"

"I did not!"

Ginger pulled him to one side. "You're going to need me. That's a very formidable housekeeper in there and she has an acute distaste for strangers, especially cops. She happens to like me and I'm pretty sure she'll talk if I ask her to talk. And besides, Romanov was my psychiatrist."

"So what?"

"What do you mean, so what? Losing a psychiatrist is worse than losing an arm. And although you may not be interested, I have my own theories as to who might have poisoned Romanov." She lowered her voice. "Feodor Vanoff."

Exasperated, Villon said, "Another country is heard from. Who is this Vanoff and where did he pop from?"

Over her shoulder Ginger said, "Fred, you're crowding me." To Villon she said, "You missed something terribly important Sol Hurok told some of us after you left to come here. Let's go inside and I'll tell you."

"Tell me now."

"What? With all these reporters and photographers crowding us? No way!" She addressed the press. "Gentlemen of the press! We assume you are gentlemen so behave yourselves. Now let us get through, please." Villon instructed Jim Mallory to force an opening for them, which he did with alacrity. Ginger took Fred's hand. "Come on, Fred, ahead lies sanctuary."

"And a corpse," said Fred, now astonished at Ginger's eagerness to participate in the investigation. In the car on the drive to the doctor's house, she had astounded him with her perspicacity, discussing Nina and Luba, the Vanoff affair, and the probability that the doctor had been murdered. "For weeks now during my sessions with the doctor he complained about what he said were gas pains. I mean, really, how much gas can a person suffer and how often?"

"Gas can be caused by emotional stress," advised Fred.

"I frequently get emotionally stressed but I don't get gas. I burp."

"Gas."

"Oh really? Anyway, getting back to the doctor. He'd leave me to go to the kitchen where the housekeeper gave him some medication for gas pains."

Fred's eyes left the road ahead of him briefly to question Ginger. "Maybe the medication?"

"You mean it's possible the doctor was being poisoned under my very eyes and I didn't suspect a *thing*?"

"You didn't know then he was a marked man."

"Well, I'll be a monkey's uncle."

"Aunt," corrected Fred.

"You mean it could have been the housekeeper who was poisoning him?"

"It could also have been his nurse and possibly whatsisname the chauffeur."

"Mordecai Pfenov?"

"If that's his name then he's who I mean. He was also his valet, right?"

"There wasn't all that much chauffering to do so the doctor being the practical type hired him for double duty. Although come to think of it, I think the doctor inherited him."

"You don't inherit people."

"Oh don't take me so literally," chafed Ginger. "Mordecai is Malke's nephew. She told me when he arrived in this country five years ago she got the doctor to give him a job, which of course, out of the goodness of his heart, he did."

"And in gratitude they began poisoning him."

"Oh really, Fred."

"Oh really Fred, indeed. Stand back, Ginger, and get a perspective. They are all of Russian descent, presumably refugee escapees from political persecution. How did they get out? From what I've read, it's not all that easy for Russian citizens to get out, not the hoi polloi, the common ordinary everyday people like you and me."

Ginger said huffily, "I am not common!"

Fred said patiently, "Ginger, if we couldn't hoof better than most and put over a song better than most, thanks to film technicians, we'd be common ordinary people like everybody else."

Ginger said as her eyes narrowed, "Common ordinary people don't win an Academy Award and by God I've won one and against some pretty stiff competition and . . ."

"And let's get back to our Russkies. How indeed did they get out?"

"Search me. I don't know. I haven't a clue."

"Let's go back to Nina and Luba. You overheard them in the powder room."

"I most certainly did!"

"Did they do anything except try to expose each other for something or another?"

"No, not that I recall. Nina suspected Luba of planning to defect with Gregor Sukov, and Luba in return, and I might add, quite maliciously, brought up the Vanoff affair and Nina's presumed involvement."

"In which Nina goes to great pains to insist she was not involved."

"Just a second," said Ginger as Fred swerved to avoid a rabbit crossing the road in front of him.

"Sorry. I only just saw him."

"That's all right. Where was I? Maybe Nina was not involved in Nikolai's murder or suicide, but she certainly was involved with Nikolai."

"And this joker Beria. Where does she get her stamina?"

"Probably has exemplary genes." After a moment she said, "Fred? Why do I think the missing brother is in this country?"

"I don't know. Why do you? And what missing brother?"

She was losing her patience. "Feodor Vanoff! Nikolai's brother! The fink who blew the whistle on him with their mother and father."

"Say, there's a possibility. Maybe the old folks sent Nikolai flying into space."

Ginger folded her arms and looked out the window, "Fred, stick to your dancing."

"Say, Ginger . . ."

"What?"

"You may have a point. Maybe Feodor *is* in this country." He thought for a moment. "Maybe he's masquerading as Mordecai Pfenov."

"Oh my God! That is a possibility, isn't it?"

"When we get to the house, let's try for a good look at good old Mordecai and see if he looks like he could be somebody's brother."

Now, in the downstairs hallway of the Romanov house, Herb Villon listened attentively to the information Ginger was dispensing with great dramatic effect. She had Jim Mallory's's undivided attention and Hazel could have done without the constant movement of Ginger's expressive hands. Most of the information Ginger imparted Villon digested eagerly. He particularly liked the theories on how the émigrés got out of Russia so easily. He knew how difficult it was to get exit visas. He'd heard of people and families, especially Jews, desperate to make new lives for themselves in Israel, who had been waiting years for the necessary documents. He accepted as a possibility that Feodor Vanoff had made his way to the United States and might be at large under a pseudonym, might be under this very roof as a combination chauffeur and valet.

Fred reminded Villon, "Valets are forever mixing drinks and bringing all sorts of beverages. My valet, for example, is always slipping vitamins into my milk."

"If you keel over, Fred, he'll be the first suspect," said Ginger.

Hazel said, "I think you should cross-examine Nina Valgorski and Luba Nafka as soon as possible."

"Why?" asked Villon, who was in no mood to discuss cross-examining anybody.

Hands on hips, Hazel insisted, "They are very likely candidates as spies."

"So they are," agreed Villon. "But spies are Don Magrew's department. Murder is mine." And then he was suddenly mesmerized. Malke Movitz the housekeeper had quietly descended the stairs from the upper floor and Villon wouldn't have heard her if she hadn't loomed within his vision, emerging behind Hazel.

Ginger said, "Oh Malke. What a terrible tragedy. Did he say any last words?"

"No," she said calmly, "he only yelled and fell back on the pillow." Behind her another figure had descended the staircase, Mordecai Pfenov.

Ginger said, "Hello, Mordecai. Such a terrible tragedy."

Modecai said, "Yes," and wondered why the actress nudged the detective.

Ginger said to Villon, "Mordecai is—or is it was?—the doctor's valet."

Fred thought, Hardly very subtle, Miss Rogers, and I think Mordecai is sharing my sentiment from the look on his face. He heard Malke asking, "Which one is Detective Villon."

"That's me," said Villon.

"The coroner asked if you would come to the master bedroom."

Ginger said to Villon, "Over here, through this door, is the reception room and beyond that is the doctor's office. I thought you'd like to know." She pointed to a door on the opposite side of the hall. "That leads to the dining room and then the kitchen and in back of the house is an arboretum with some of the loveliest plants and flowers and greenery and that leads to a potting shed where they keep the weed killers, cyanide, and all that." She stressed *cyanide* and it certainly did not fall on deaf ears. "Malke has the green thumb around here and she's otherwise terribly colorful. When she was a teenager she won the shot-put medal in the Berlin Olympics and she also won a belt for wrestling. Isn't she marvelous?"

Malke said, "Mr. Villon, I will lead you to the master bedroom." She ascended the stairs with Villon and Mallory following her. Hazel brazenly went up behind them.

Ginger said, "I'm going with them."

Fred said, "You weren't asked."

"I'm sure he'd want me there. Look at how useful I've been so far."

Mordecai, who had been watching the three following Malke, said to Ginger and Fred, "It is not very pleasant up there—the awful expression on the doctor's face."

"Thanks for the tip," said Fred. "I'm staying down here."

Ginger was smiling at Mordecai. "Where is the doctor's nurse, Alida?"

Mordecai indicated the door behind them. "She is in there."

"The reception room, of course," said Ginger and then moved to enter it.

"Ginger," said Fred, "she might not be in a receptive mood."

"Nonsense. Alida and I get along just fine." She opened the door with a sad look on her face that she considered appropriate to a condolence call. The look on her face turned to one of surprise. Alida Rimsky stood next to her desk with Theodore Varonsky. He had his arms around her. "Oh!" said Ginger.

Alida, when she saw Ginger, moved away from Varonsky. "Why, Ginger, what are you doing here?"

"Actually, Fred and I have been helping Detective Villon and I'm sure we've been a great deal of help to him, haven't we, Fred?" There was no Fred. "Fred?"

Fred came to the door. "I'm out here talking to Mordecai. Getting acquainted, you know. Why, Mr. Varonsky, what a surprise seeing you here. A friend of the family?"

The *maître de ballet* looked at Alida. She took his hand and held it tightly. Varonsky said, "Alida is my wife."

Ten

*Y*our wife!" exclaimed Ginger. "Saaay, who wrote this scenario, Edna Ferber?"

Fred said affably, "Well, how pleased you must be to be reunited after such a long separation." Ginger wondered how he knew it was a long separation but decided she would ask him later.

"It was a very long separation," said Varonsky. Ginger wouldn't have to ask Fred anything. She was seeing Varonsky in a different light than when she had first met him. Then he seemed imposing and somewhat frightening. She could tell he had a fine physique. Ginger was a connoisseur of fine physiques. Her friend Lucille Ball once said Ginger didn't look for the ordinary qualifications of a potential husband such as financial stability, intelligence, future prospects, and so on. "Ginger," said Lucille, "just measures them." Ginger envied Alida the way Varonsky ate her up with his eyes. Imagine, she would later say to her mother, a man still so passionately in love with a woman he hadn't seen in so many years. And likewise, the ardor with which Alida unabashedly regarded her man. Russians were so hotblooded, so unreservedly passionate, why hadn't she ever sought a man who was Russian by birth? She thought of what was available in Hollywood—Mischa Auer, Leonid Kinskey, both of whom looked as though they had been drained of their blood, chunky Akim Tamiroff, Ivan Lebedeff with his so-called bedside manner, and decided she'd stick with her present spouse, Jacques Bergerac, he of the incredibly handsome face and equally incredibly formidable physique.

Ginger heard Fred asking the couple, "Aren't you worried you might be separated again? I mean, Varonsky, don't you have to return to Russia with the company when the tour is ended?"

"Yes, they expect me to return with the others." He smiled. "But I am a past master at executing the unexpected." He looked past Fred and Ginger and said, "Come in, Mordecai, and close the door. We do not know who might be lurking in the corridor."

"I am the only one who lurks there." He shut the door and smiled at Fred, whom in their brief few minutes together he had come to like. Mordecai had sung some of "Slap That Bass," one of Fred's solos by Irving Berlin in *Follow the Fleet* and Fred told the others with a great deal of pride, "Imagine someone as far away as Russia learning to do an imitation of me." What Fred didn't know was that Mordecai was just warming up.

Mordecai asked eagerly, "Would you like I should do for you 'Bojangles of Harlem'?"

"Well, I'll be damned," said Fred, "he knows that one too. And you know, Mordecai, your voice isn't half bad. Now if you could only dance."

"But I am a dancer!" exulted Mordecai, and he quickly executed a few steps that had Fred and Ginger both wide-eyed with astonishment.

Ginger crowed, "Look, ma, he's dancing!"

Mordecai clasped his hands together and beseeched Fred and Ginger, "Oh how I long to be on the Fred Sullivan show!"

"*Ed* Sullivan," corrected Fred. "He's a friend of ours. Maybe we can do something."

Mordecai was overcome. In Russian he cried, "I am so excited. I can't believe it!" In Russian, Alida cautioned him to cool it.

Varonsky said to Fred and Ginger, "In case you are wondering if Alida and I fear exposure, there are several in the company who know it. It is of no importance to them, and if it was, I couldn't care less. Alida is safe here in the U.S. She has a permit. Dr. Romanov generously arranged it for her."

"Oh?" said Fred, wheels turning in his head. "You knew Romanov in Russia?"

"No, but he is a legend."

"A legend? You mean like William Tell?" asked Ginger. "I once did a dance to his overture."

"Oh yes, his overture!" Mordecai was ecstatic. " 'Hi-yo Silver, awayyyyy!' "

"I don't believe it," said Fred. "You get *The Lone Ranger* in Russia?"

"But of course," said Mordecai proudly. "We barter for them. You know, we trade. They come on special recordings. They are stolen by our representatives here. In return, we permit your agents to steal recordings of our operas and ballets. It is all very satisfactory to both sides, isn't it, Varonsky?"

Varonsky didn't answer him. He could see Fred was ready with more questions, and anxious to get to them. "I can see you are curious to learn more about Romanov."

"And there is more to learn, isn't there?" Ginger was admiring Fred. He was doing Villon's job for him and she knew Villon would be terribly pleased, but she didn't know Villon. "You know, Detective Villon suspects Romanov has been systematically poisoned over a period of time prior to his death tonight. I'm sure you've heard, or as a nurse Alida would know, that there are certain poisons that, when fed in small doses, build up in the body and after a period of time attack the system and kill the victim. You know, like cyanide. That's very popular. The British dote on it. Some very famous cases have been documented. Now they're part of Great Britain's folklore." In response to the puzzled and questioning look on Ginger's face, Fred grinned and explained, "That's what happened to Rasputin. I found it when I was researching him."

Varonsky cleared his throat and said, "If I may amend your statement."

"By all means," said Fred diplomatically, "be my guest. Go right ahead and amend it."

"The night Rasputin was murdered, he attended a party where he was fed poisoned cakes. His wine was also poisoned. But the man was blessed with an abnormally strong constitution. So Prince Youssepoff, his self-appointed executioner, shot him a few times."

"Bang bang bang," said Ginger.

"I believe he was shot four times," said Varonsky.

"Bang," added Ginger, very pleased with herself.

"But still he lived," said Varonsky.

"Stubborn bastard," commented Fred.

"Like some dancers I know," said Ginger, who, without looking at Fred, sensed he was glaring at her.

"Rasputin was chased to a very deep pond. Youssepoff pushed him in and held his head under water until the holy man finally expired."

"There'll be none of that in my ballet. It'll just be suggested."

"You are privy to Detective Villon's suspicions?" Varonsky asked Fred.

"Oh no, there's nothing special about us except that we're movie stars, but from what Ginger and I discussed with Villon I think he buys the slow-death theory."

"So do I," said Ginger, looking to Fred for a sign of approval but receiving none.

Varonsky said, "Then you believe Romanov has suffered at the hand of someone in this household?"

"Hand. Maybe hands." Fred was suddenly uncomfortable as Varonsky put an arm around his wife. Ginger was worrying that Fred might have gone too far by spilling the beans of Villon's suspicion.

"Hands," repeated Fred, briefly fearing the *maître de ballet* might suddenly fly off the handle. He reassured himself the detectives whom he had seen in the hallway when they arrived would come to his rescue at the sound of a disturbance.

"So my Alida would be under suspicion along with Malke Movitz and Mordecai. I hope for your sake, Mordecai, Fred is wrong or you will sacrifice the *Ed Sullivan Show.*" Mordecai paled.

Fred wanted to get back to Romanov, who he suspected might be as much a man of mystery in Russia as he was here. "Romanov must have had friends in high places here if he could secure a resident's permit for Alida."

Varonsky began pacing the room as Alida sat on her desk and Ginger sat in the chair she had first occupied a few years back on her initial visit to Dr. Romanov. Varonsky said, "Fred, we are both men of the world, are we not?"

"Well, which world did you have in mind?"

"This world. The world of cold war and the iron curtain and the House Un-American Activities Committee, a world that would destroy Ethel and Julius Rosenberg, whose only crime as I see it is in being naive and ineffective. But still," he shrugged, "like so many others, they are expendable."

"Is that what Romanov was?" asked Ginger. "Expendable?"

"Very." The coldness in his voice infected Ginger, and she embraced herself in an attempt to ward off the sudden, unexpected chill. Varonsky continued, "Romanov was the servant of two masters. He didn't want to be but circumstances made it unavoidable. First he was to spy for the Soviets. That is how he talked himself into an exit visa. You see, his escape from the gulag was orchestrated by us. It was arranged that he and his wife would escape the same night."

Ginger asked innocently, "The gulag was coed?"

Varonsky smiled at her naiveté. "The gulags did not discriminate. Yes, they held men and women but in separate sections. It was made easy for the Romanovs to be in touch and plot their escape. We wanted Romanov. We wanted his shrewd mind to spy for us. We didn't want his wife. She was, as you say, wishy-washy. She had been a dancer with a small company but was merely adequate. She auditioned several times for the Baronovitch, having known several members from their teenage days when Romanov showed promise as a concert pianist and his wife and Nina Valgorski trained for the ballet. Nina and Romanov became lovers at the time. But the very powerful Nikolai Vanoff wanted Nina and he got her."

"And what about that there Beria?" asked Ginger, who was beginning to admire Nina's versatility.

"Oh there was also Beria and Gregor Sukov and several musicians and composers and heaven knows who else, who shared one-night stands. Nina was so generously accommodating!"

"By God, when did she find time to dance?" asked Fred.

"In between," said Varonsky matter-of-factly. "But back to Romanov. He was permitted to escape, the wife was shot. Whether he mourned her or not, I do not know. They had been married a short time, he on the rebound from Nina, she all wide-eyed innocence at having landed Romanov. What she and few others knew was that the piano was Romanov's cover. He was a brilliant spy for us. He was in demand at all the foreign embassies, which was great as far as we were concerned. By 'we,' by the way, I am using the royal *we*, which covers a multitude of sins. Romanov was like the Frank Sinatra of embassy entertainers. Women literally swooned when he played and were soon putty in his hands. Secretaries were pressing all manner of confidential communiqués into his hands and in time he was swamped with so much paperwork he had to be provided with a secretary."

Fred snapped his fingers. "I get it. Romanov in time also played footsy with the embassies and as a result, he and the wife were warehoused."

"Your brainwork is as clever as your footwork," complimented Varonsky. "Sadly, we realized it had been a mistake. Embassies complained, they wanted Romanov back. The secret service complained because of the poor quality of the so-called privileged information they were receiving. Secretaries had grown listless and sought transfers back home. So to save the whole system from imminent disintegration, Romanov was ordered seated at the piano again." He was lighting a Turkish cigarette. After a few puffs, he resumed talking. "But Romanov did not wish to return to the piano. He sought other horizons. He wanted the United States. Believe me he was met with resistance, but Romanov persisted and soon his will prevailed. He was trained in psychiatry and one of our most important operatives in America arranged for his license as a psychiatrist and set him up in Beverly Hills."

"So that's that," said Ginger.

"Oh no it isn't," said Fred. "It isn't, is it, Varonsky."

"No, unfortunately Romanov became so impassioned with the capitalistic system, in addition to spying for Russia against the U.S., he was pursuaded to spy on Russia for the U.S. So see, now he was enjoying the best of all possible worlds. But soon Romanov was faltering. The quality of the information he was feeding us soon fell off. The home office got suspicious, and decided to recall Romanov. Sadly, this could not be done. Romanov had outtrumped us."

"He had become an American citizen," said Fred.

"Exactly! Fred Astaire, you are too brilliant!"

"Try telling that to my sister." He looked at the ceiling and then at Varonsky. "And so, unwittingly and I'm sure unwillingly, Romanov became expendable."

"Gee, that was a good picture," said Ginger.

"What picture? What the hell are you talking about?" The others in the room were equally bemused.

"Don't you remember? We were both at the same screening. It starred John Wayne. *They Were Expendable.*"

"I'll suffer in silence," said Fred. He asked Varonsky, "Are you with the Russian secret police?"

"Now that Stalin is dead, it's not so secret. The foundations of the Soviet Union are slowly beginning to disintegrate. But a discussion about that is for another time. I haven't officially been with the secret police for a long time. Now I am a *maître de ballet* and the tables are turned. Now I'm the one who is being spied upon."

Ginger said dramatically, "What irony."

"My last official act," said Varonsky, "was to spirit my darling wife to the safety of Beverly Hills and Dr. Romanov while he was still, shall we say, playing fair with us."

Fred asked Mordecai, "And how did you get out?"

Mordecai fumbled about for a moment or two and then his expression brightened. "Dr. Romanov got me out. That was five years ago. My aunt, who was his housekeeper, implored him to rescue me. He did and I shall always be grateful, but, Fred Astaire, I would be more grateful if you help me to appear with Ed Sullivan!"

At about the time Ginger barged in on the Varonskys in the reception room, Malke Movitz ushered Villon, Mallory, and Hazel into the doctor's bedroom. Hazel steeled herself against what she sensed would be the unappetizing sight of Romanov's body stretched out on the bed. Instead, the body was wrapped in a sheet and strapped to a stretcher with two ambulance attendants preparing to carry the stretcher out to the police ambulance. The coroner, a grumpy little man named Edgar Rowe, greeted the three, having worked with Villon and Mallory on many cases where he usually suffered Hazel's prying presence stoically.

Malke said, "I will go to the kitchen now."

"I'd prefer you wait up here," said Villon, and Hazel marveled at how pleasantly he said it. He obviously, as he usually did, had sized up the housekeeper in just a few minutes and decided to treat her gently for the best results, whatever results he expected.

Malke sat in a chair, glimpsing briefly the wrapped body, while Hazel made some notes on a small pad. Edgar Rowe was also making notes in a pad and determined from past experience not to let Hazel get a look at them.

Villon asked the little man, "What have you got so far, Edgar?"

"A raging appetite. I hate these late-night calls. I get so hungry I can't sleep and when I don't sleep I eat."

Herb watched the doctor as he wrote in his pad and then said, "Let's get to the nitty-gritty. From the looks of him at the Ambassador Hotel ballroom—"

"Were you boys dancing?"

"Just a couple of times around the floor. I led." One had to humor Edgar Rowe. Otherwise he would become so cantankerous you couldn't get anything out of him until you read it in a memorandum. "Now seriously, Edgar, this has the makings of a bitch of a case. The Baronovitch ballet company are mixed up in it and I've got Fred Astaire and Ginger Rogers waiting downstairs."

The coroner's eyes widened with joy. "Fred and Ginger? *My* Fred and Ginger?" He began singing "Isn't It a Lovely Day" and nimbly dancing around the bedroom. Hazel feared he'd try to do a leap over the corpse à la Astaire and Rogers, but fortunately the ambulance attendants were already out the door with the stretcher.

"Come on, Edgar, cut the clowning. Give me some facts. He was poisoned, right? Possibly cyanide."

"If you know so much, why ask me?" Testy with a touch of petulance.

Hazel said to Villon, "You should have let him finish the dance."

"Now, Edgar, don't get testy. I've got a long night ahead of me and a short temper," said Villon.

"You know what you can do with your short temper. You're lucky I waited for you to get here. I've got a hot poker game waiting for me in the morgue. But let me sum up before I make my exit. Yes, he was poisoned. Possibly cyanide, from the condition of the fingernails, which were suspiciously blue tinged and beautifully manicured. However, I don't like to give snap decisions especially where murder is suspected, so you'll have to wait until I get him back to the butcher shop for a more thorough examination, which won't take place until tomorrow morning as I have no intention of putting in any overtime tonight." He raised his hand like a kid in a schoolroom desperate to go to the toilet. "Now I'm going!" He moved to the door but Villon's voice stopped him.

"I'd appreciate your report as soon as possible." Villon folded his arms and boomed, "You must realize we are dealing with two major world powers!"

"My heavens! Just wait till I phone Mother!" Rowe pocketed his notebook while saying to Hazel, "Guess what you're not going to get a look at tonight."

Hazel shouted after him, "I assume you mean your notebook."

Villon said, "Shut up, Hazel." He now turned his attention to Malke Movitz, who seemed hypnotized by Hazel's dyed hair. "Well Miss Movitz . . . or is it Mrs.?"

"It's Miss. I resumed my single status after my husband was liberated by a firing squad twenty years ago."

Villon said, "I'm sorry to hear that."

"I'm not."

Hazel suppressed a shudder while Mallory wondered if the Picassos on the wall were real. Villon asked Malke, "You've been with the doctor a long time?"

"Almost from the time he began his practice in Beverly Hills."

"He practiced elsewhere before?"

"I know he studied in Vienna and Paris. He never mentioned practicing in either city."

Villon said to Mallory, "Do a trace on that in the morning." Mallory nodded. Hazel was telling the housekeeper her hair was done by Mr. Eloise whose salon was located on Fairfax Avenue in West Hollywood. Villon cleared his throat unnecessarily and Hazel got the signal to shut up. "Exactly how many years have you been with the doctor?"

"Oh, it must be almost fifteen."

"How long have you been in this country."

"Fifteen years."

"You know the doctor from Russia?"

"No. We met in Paris. I owned a small restaurant there. Russian cuisine, of course."

"Of course."

"The doctor was there finishing his psychiatric studies. He ate in my restaurant almost every night of the week until I shut down."

"Not profitable?"

"Very profitable. But I was placed under arrest."

Hazel tried to meet Villon's eyes but his were riveted on Malke. She heard him ask, "Why were you arrested?"

"I was accused of murdering three men who were having a re-union dinner. I recognized them from the war when they killed so many of my compatriots in a massacre of my village. They destroyed almost all my family. Only myself and a nephew escaped. Those men were from Himmler's SS squad."

"And how did you kill them?"

"I poisoned their borscht."

Eleven

Sacrilege," said Hazel, a borscht fancier.

Villon asked Malke, "You were acquitted? You didn't serve time?"

"The judge and the jury were French. The dead men were Germans. It was shortly after the war ended and the French were still smarting from the ruthless indignities they suffered under the German occupation. I had a superb *avocat*. He implored the court to see and understand my position. Prior to the trial, I was in the newspapers every day. I know it's hard to tell now, but then, I was very . . . how do they say . . . ?"

Hazel said, "Photogenic," and couldn't believe the smile of pleasure on Malke's face. Was this creature ever photogenic?

"If you have doubts, please realize that I am talking about an event that took place almost two decades ago. I know that over the years my features have coarsened, but one accepts that as a part of the aging process." Hazel sneaked a quick look at herself in a wall mirror. She was having none of the aging process. She thought she looked perfectly fine. "My mother taught us to realize there is more to aging than wrinkles and a weak bladder. So I stood trial and there was no need to throw myself on the mercy of the court. From the very first day when my *avocat*—my lawyer—told the court to see me as a Russian Joan of Arc, I could tell I would be acquitted. The judge and the jury embraced me with warmth and understanding."

Joan of Arc, thought Hazel, those people must have had very active imaginations to envision Malke Movitz on horseback and encased in armor.

Malke told them, "Romanov attended my trial every day. It wasn't a long trial. The prosecution did their best to send me to the guillotine. They were so impassioned in their demands that beheading be my fate that I think everyone in the courtroom suspected they had been German collaborators."

Villon said, "So Romanov proved to be a very good and loyal friend."

Her eyes widened. "But of course! It was he who instilled in me the desire to come to America."

If she's intimating that she and Romanov were lovers, thought Hazel, I shall throw myself from a window, though it's not much of a drop.

"He promised to help you find work? Perhaps open a Russian restaurant here?" There's something wrong somewhere, thought Villon. She wouldn't lie about standing trial because that's easily traced. It couldn't have been a love affair; Villon shuddered at the thought, photogenic or not photogenic.

"He suggested I cook for him and run his house. He treasured my cuisine. My pirogen, my blinis . . ."

Hazel couldn't resist. "Your borscht?"

Villon said, "What about Mordecai? I suspect he's your nephew."

"Why suspect? Is it a crime to be my nephew? He is indeed my nephew, my brother's son, a chirp off the old block."

"Chip," corrected Hazel.

"The *Boche* murdered his parents and his sisters and brothers. His father was very gifted. He sang, he danced, the whole family was musical."

Villon marveled at what a wealth of musical talent there must be in Russia. No wonder Hurok traveled there so often to search for talent. "And so Mordecai sings and dances," he said. "It must be very frustrating for him to be a chauffeur, and to be—or have been—the doctor's valet."

"It was good discipline for Mordecai. Mr. Villon, Mordecai is a very decent young man."

"And he's lucky to have a very decent aunt. Tell me, Malke, were you and Romanov acquainted before Paris? Back in Russia?"

Mallory was wondering when Villon would hit her with a zinger.

"I knew him in Siberia. In a prison camp. What we call a gulag, where I was falsely imprisoned for selling goods on the black market. I received a short sentence. I knew his wife. A little peanut of a woman, but the gulag was too strenuous for her. So she took ill and died."

Villon said, "Romanov said she was shot trying to join him in an escape."

"Oh yes?"

"That's what he said."

"Perhaps he told you that because it sounded more romantic." Villon turned his back on her and shot a "heaven help us" look at Hazel and Mallory. "Romanov made his escape the day she was buried. He helped carry her casket to the cemetery outside the stockade. It was a miserable day. There was a blizzard and one could hardly see a few inches in front of one, or so Romanov told me. There was a howling wind and in the distance Romanov heard howling wolves."

Howling wolves, thought Hazel as she examined her fingernails, what a lovely touch.

"And it was thanks to the blizzard Romanov made his escape. The snow and sleet blinded the guards. . . ."

"But Romanov was not hampered," said Villon.

"No, he wore dark glasses."

"He told you this in Paris?"

"Oh *da, da.*"

Yes, yes, thought Hazel, her heart belongs to *da da.*

Mallory looked at his wristwatch. He was impatient. Malke

and Mordecai had to be part of the spy network, most certainly Malke. Why doesn't he let her have it between the eyes?

"Malke," said Villon on a new tack, "you heard the coroner and I discussing the possibility Dr. Romanov was murdered. Poisoned. Poisoned over a period of time."

"But no! That is not possible!"

"Death in small doses is very possible."

"Death in small doses?"

"You heard me. Unlike the way you killed those Germans in Paris."

"I am a very impatient woman. Things must be done all at once. Small doses would take much too long. Ah! Ah! Ah!" She was pointing a beefy finger at him. "You are insinuating I poisoned the doctor!" She erupted with a stream of Russian for which none of the three needed translating. "Kill Romanov? I would sooner assassinate President Truman."

Hazel didn't doubt her one bit.

"I was devoted to Romanov! Mordecai and I were both devoted to him! He was so kind! He was so generous! He brought us to this country, to this free, wonderful country!"

Hazel was thinking, You're overplaying your hand, dear, slow down and possibly shed a tear, that's usually effective.

Malke didn't slow down, nor did she shed a tear. "He was generous to a fort!"

"Fault," corrected Hazel. Malke was breathing heavily and clutching her bosom as her eyes searched Villon's face for a sign of empathy.

Villon now led her up a simpler path. "Do you know any members of the Baronovitch company, that is, are you acquainted with any? For instance, I'm sure you know Romanov and Nina Valgorski were once lovers?"

"Nina Valgorski and everybody were once lovers," snorted Malke. "Her reputation covers the world. I heard plenty about her from Romanov."

"You were his confidante?"

She said with pride, "He had no other confidantes. He had only me. It was always 'Malke, did I tell you about me and the Iranian princess?' or 'Did I tell you about me and the Hungarian countess who was a chronic shoplifter?' or how he was pursued by Princess Margaret of Great Britain at a garden party and had to climb a tree to escape her? How women pursued him! Oh, how they pursued him!"

Villon decided to ask her the question that he knew would give Hazel indigestion. "Malke, were you in love with the doctor?"

Hazel thought she might sink through the floor. Mallory was trying to imagine Malke and Romanov having it off in bed and it made him giggle. Villon waved a hand at him impatiently by way of telling him to put a cork in it.

Malke had exhaled. Then she favored Villon with a look that should have told him she considered him to be a congenital idiot. When she spoke, she sounded as if she had chosen each word with the professional care a master jeweler took in assembling the precious stones for a queen's necklace. "Mr. Villon, do not talk to me like you consider me a fool. I have little patience for the precious time it would require to fantasize about obtaining the unobtainable. If I did, I would concentrate on Cary Grant for he is just as unobtainable."

"I'm sorry," said Villon. "I did not mean to offend you."

She stared at him for a few minutes. The silence in the room was deadly. She awaited his next question with a look she hoped told him she was prepared to accept all challenges.

"Are you and your nephew communists?"

That's my Herb, thought Hazel, take the offensive and batter away at it.

Malke hit the ball back in his court. "What does being a communist have to do with poisoning the doctor?"

"Are you communists?"

She held her head high. "I am a citizen of this country and I am a Democrat. I voted for Harry Truman. Mordecai is not a citizen, he hasn't been here long enough to apply for papers."

He could tell there was no point in pursuing the attack. He looked around the room, at the Picasso on the wall.

"Is the Picasso authentic?"

"It most certainly is. It is, of course, very valuable."

He indicated a Modigliani which hung over the bed. "And the Modigliani?"

"Also priceless."

Villon examined another painting, the style of which was unfamiliar to him. The subject was a man behind a desk who might have been a newspaper correspondent.

Malke didn't wait for him to ask her to identify the man in the painting. "That is Dr. Romanov."

"Oh really." He moved closer to the painting. "I suppose it could be."

"It was painted by Ginger Rogers."

Curiously, Hazel and Mallory joined Villon in studying the painting. Said Hazel, "I'm glad she has a day job."

Villon said, "There's a great deal of wealth in the house. Heavily insured, I suppose."

"I think so. The doctor's lawyer is Morris Synder. His office is on Beverly Boulevard." After a second she said, "He lives in Pacific Heights. I phoned and told him the doctor was dead. He offered to come over now but I told him I thought there was no reason to come now. So he will come tomorrow morning. He said the doctor's will stipulated Mordecai and I are to live here until his effects were inventoried and disposed of according to his wishes."

Hazel was busy manufacturing methods by which she could cash in on Romanov's murder, and in Malke Movitz she saw a promising potential. "Doesn't the doctor have any relatives?"

Malke shrugged. "If he did, he never mentioned them. In Paris, I remember, he had no contact with anyone in Russia, or at least he never mentioned it if he did. No, Romanov was, how do you say, ah yes, a lone wolf."

Said Hazel, "A wolf, yes, what with all those varieties of royalty pursuing him and nipping at his rear, but lone? Surely he had involvements here in Los Angeles."

"Whatever he did was ephemeral," Malke said somewhat airily. She sounded for a moment somewhat lyrical and Villon almost expected her to raise her hands over her head, hop on point, and do a few pirouettes around the room. On second thought, he dreaded the idea. If she did, it would be reminiscent of the dancing hippo in Walt Disney's *Fantasia.*

Hazel still held center stage. "So, in effect, you and Mordecai were, so to speak, his only near and dear ones." Villon let her alone. He didn't interfere. She was after something and whatever it was, it was in some way bound to be useful. "Imagine, Miss Movitz, if the doctor's entire estate was left to you." Malke said nothing. "Goodness, you'd be an heiress if you came into all his assets. Isn't that something nice to contemplate?"

Malke said with a smile, "In Russia we have an expression. My mother used it all the time in her sober moments. 'Do not roast the chicken until it is hitched.' "

"Hatched," corrected Hazel. "But the possibility is something pleasant to contemplate."

"Yes, if one is greedy. So my dear lady, if you are intimating that I knew the contents of Romanov's will and presumably he left everything to me, that I engineered his death"—she inhaled and folded her arms with head held high again   "you are barking up the wrong housekeeper."

There was a gentle knock on the door. Mordecai entered, eyes sparkling and face flushed while contemplating his possible appearance on the Ed Sullivan show. "Forgive me if I interrupt, but there is a great deal of impatience downstairs. The reporters and photographers wish to photograph the interior of the house and they wish to photograph you, Malke, and especially me, since my friends Fred and Ginger have told them they will try to arrange a sport for me on the Ed Sullivan show. 'Sport' is correct, no?"

Hazel said, "I think they meant a 'spot' on the show."

Mordecai was agreeable. "That would be fine too."

Herb assigned Mallory to hold the fort in the bedroom until he could send up another detective to replace him. "I want nothing touched in this room until it is thoroughly dusted."

Malke bristled. "I dusted the room myself this afternoon. It was spotless until the police tramped all over it."

Herb said patiently, "Your kind of dusting and our kind of dusting are different kinds of dusting. When the police dust, it is in search of clues, something that might be of use to use in solving the crime."

"I see," said Malke. "We do not have that expression in Russia. There is so little time between the committing of a crime and the execution of a suspect."

A grim-faced Herb led the procession out of the master bedroom downstairs to the reception room where Alida presided during the doctor's office hours. He instructed one of the detectives in the downstairs hall to go upstairs and replace Mallory in guarding Romanov's bedroom. The detective told Villon a forensics team was expected momentarily as dispatched by Edgar Rowe, and Villon dispensed a silent benediction on the absent coroner. Villon entered the reception room followed by Hazel, Malke, and Mordecai. He saw Theodore Varonsky and resisted the urge to raise an eyebrow. Ginger interpreted the look on Villon's face. "Mr. Varonsky and Alida are husband and wife," she explained in the tone of voice that might lead one to believe she had just invented the wheel.

"We are reunited after too many years apart." Varonsky's arm was around Alida's shoulder again. Their presence together confirmed Ike the valet parking attendant's information and Villon stopped suspecting he'd been swindled. Jim Mallory came into the room and was also startled at Varonsky's presence but Hazel quickly explained about Varonsky and Alida. Varonsky asked Herb Villon, "Alida has been Romanov's nurse for many years. Is there any reason to fear now that he has been murdered that Alida's life might also be in danger?"

"I can't answer that one," said Villon. "It depends on how much she knows about him. Likewise Miss Movitz and her nephew," indicating Mordecai, who stood next to Ginger and Fred proprietorially. "We suspect Romanov was a Russian secret agent." Hazel looked at Malke, whose face betrayed nothing. Clever lady, thought Hazel, very clever lady. "Likewise he was working for the

CIA. You don't look surprised, Mr. Varonsky. Neither does your wife and she was his nurse." His eyes locked with Alida's.

She said, "I had no reason to suspect Romanov indulged in espionage."

"Unless you were indulging with him," countered Herb.

Alida's face flashed anger. "I am loyal to the United States. I have applied for citizenship."

"Even though your husband lives in Russia?"

She took Varonsky's hand and said firmly, "He will stay here."

Now Hazel could read something in Malke Movitz's face. But she was having difficulty interpreting what it was that she was reading. She thought she saw surprise and shock and then thought maybe Malke was a bit bilious. Villon said to Varonsky, "You're planning to defect?"

"I don't have to. I have an exit permit."

"Don't all the others in the company?"

"Theirs is limited to the amount of time it will take to complete the tour. We are all thanking God Hurok arranged the television show as it adds to the time we can stay away. I speak, of course, of the remainder of the company."

"Why'd you keep your marriage such a secret?"

Alida spoke up. "It was for my sake. For my safety. We feared it might jeopardize my chance of getting citizenship papers."

"It wouldn't go well with the authorities if they caught you lying to them."

"I do not intend to lie," said Alida staunchly. "I do not have to lie. My lawyer assures me all will go well."

"Who's your lawyer?"

"His name is Morris Snyder. He came highly recommended."

"He's also Romanov's lawyer."

"Yes. How did you know?"

Malke spoke up. "I told him. I called to tell Morris, Romanov was dead."

"Oh poor Romanov," said Ginger as Fred recognized her impatience at not being in the spotlight. "I don't care if he was a spy, he was a wonderful psychiatrist. I shall eulogize him at his funeral."

Fred said, "You better not tell your mother." He responded immediately to the dirty look Ginger flashed him. "Be realistic, Ginger; according to your mother, to paraphrase Gertrude Stein, a spy is a spy is a spy."

Ginger said angrily, "Fred Astaire, where is your heart? Why, the poor man's wife was shot trying to escape with him. . . ."

Villon asked, "Who told you she was shot?"

"Why, Mr. Varonsky told us . . ."

Villon faced Malke. "You said she was taken fatally ill."

"That is the truth," said Malke. "She was not shot. Mr. Varonsky was misinformed. I was in the gulag when she died. It's like I told you—Romanov helped carry her casket to the cemetery in a ferocious blizzard and that is how he made his escape and that is the truth." She stared defiantly at Varonsky.

Varonsky said, "There are always conflicting stories about escapes from the gulag. I told you what I was told. And the housekeeper has another version. Perhaps a third will turn up and then you can pick and choose the one you find most acceptable."

Fred asked, "Is it all that important? The doctor and his wife are dead, let them rest in peace. I say we all go home and get some sleep."

"Just a minute," interrupted Ginger. She said to Villon, "I think I ought to tell you you've got a nut case working in your precinct."

Herb asked, "Which of the many do you have in mind?"

"A little man burst in here a little while ago shouting 'My idols! Fred and Ginger!' He sang a couple of bars of 'Change Partners' and then did us the honor, or so he said, of inviting us to watch Romanov's autopsy tomorrow morning. He wanted to know if we'd ever thought of doing a number in the morgue! Can you beat that?"

Twelve

$\mathcal{T}$he lead item on that night's television news was the suspected poisoning of Igor Romanov. Murder usually took precedence over any other news items as it had long ago been confirmed that American television viewers were a blood-thirsty lot. What made Romanov's death even more exciting was the fact that he was the most prominent psychiatrist in Beverly Hills. The commentator reeled off a laundry list of who were supposedly Romanov's patients, which was suspect by the knowledgeable, who knew the names of a psychiatrist's patients were privileged information. True, in Hollywood no such thing existed, everybody knew everything about everybody else. There was no such thing as privacy in Hollywood, where the hired help were notorious for ratting on their employers in return for monetary considerations. Every columnist had his or her own army of informants without whom the columns would cease to exist.

Lela Rogers gasped when she heard her daughter's name, not because she wasn't aware Ginger was a Romanov patient but because there were those nincompoops out there who chose to confuse psychiatry with insanity and if her public thought Ginger had a screw loose, acting jobs could become few and far between. And if they did, who would pay the mortgage on Lela's house? True, she had made a lot of money as the acting coach at the RKO studio when her daughter reigned as the studio's leading female star. Her greatest success had been with a pupil named Lucille Ball, but now Lucy was defending herself before HUAC who suspected her of subversion, the actress heatedly explaining that she adored and respected her grandfather, who gave her books and pamphlets to read to further her skimpy education and how was she to guess it was all communist propaganda because it seems grandpa was what was referred to at the time as a "parlor pink."

And then as Lela fumed at the television set, there before her very eyes were her daughter and Fred Astaire entering the Romanov house with Ginger pausing and addressing the microphones shoved in front of her face while the wiser Fred found refuge inside the house. "Dr. Romanov helped me survive a terrible personal crisis and I shall always be grateful to him. This is a terrible tragedy and I am here to comfort his staff as I feel it is my duty to do so. No, I do not in any way think the doctor was a communist, because he fled that country many years ago and if he was a communist, he wouldn't own this gorgeous mansion and two limousines. Yes, he was at the gala given by Sol Hurok tonight in the ballroom of the Ambassador Hotel where Mr. Astaire and I entertained to celebrate our forthcoming NBC television special in which we will be privileged to dance with this remarkable Baronovitch Ballet."

Lela was in the bathroom pressing a cold compress to her throbbing temples and taking some whiffs of smelling salts. Murder! Poison! Communists! A witches' brew if ever there was one! Ginger had said the doctor was taken ill at the gala. Ginger was there! Oh God have mercy. Now she might be a suspect. Lela rushed back into the bedroom and dialed the number of a trusted member of her Christian Science group. She might have some ideas as how to rescue Ginger. Ginger was a freelance, no longer under exclusive contract to a studio, so without a studio she had no protection, she was vulnerable.

She cried into the phone, "Elvira, this is Lela. I need . . . What?

You saw Ginger on the TV? Did you really think she looked wonderful? Why yes. I thought she handled herself beautifully too. Oh yes, for Ginger to rush to comfort the doctor's staff, yes, it's so like her. Well, she does take after me. I'm always quick to volunteer aid and comfort. What, dear? Why yes, I'd love to have lunch and read a chapter together. Noon will be fine. Just really fine."

In Caplan's kosher delicatessen on Fairfax Avenue, one of the few restaurants in Hollywood to offer late-night service, Mrs. Rogers' delinquent daughter was chowing down with Fred Astaire, Herb Villon, Jim Mallory, and Hazel Dickson. The place was unusually crowded with a lot of the guests from Sol Hurok's affair and Fred marveled how after the marvelous cuisine at Sol's party, so many people could repair to Caplan's for additional refreshments. The five had been discussing suspicions and suppositions and who was lying and who, if anyone, was telling the truth. Varonsky's version of Mrs. Romanov's death as opposed to Malke's. Villon held Fred and Ginger in thrall repeating Malke's story of poisoning the former SS men in her restaurant in Paris, standing trial and winning an almost instant acquittal.

Fred said, "If she's so well versed in poisoning and was in Romanov's employ for so many years, why wait until now to minister death in small doses?"

"Well, maybe everything was just fine until recently," reasoned Ginger, wishing there was less fat on her hot pastrami.

Fred said to Herb, "She's a prime suspect, isn't she?"

"They're all prime suspects," said Herb. "The housekeeper, the nurse, the nephew, the two prima ballerinas, Gregor Sukov, and the Ritz Brothers."

Fred asked, "How did the Ritz Brothers get into this?" The three Ritz boys were pals of Fred's for years. He knew the zany trio were very capable of mayhem but not murder, and he told Villon as much.

Villon said, "What's fascinating about this cast of characters is that none of them are really what they're supposed to be."

Fred made a flat statement. "They're all spies."

"If so," said Villon, "then what degree of spy is each individual? Somebody has to be giving the orders. Which one is capable of that?"

From out of left field, Jim Mallory brought up Ike, the valet parking employee who had been of use earlier in the evening. "Say, Herb, Ike did real good fingering Varonsky and the nurse." He then explained to Fred and Ginger about Ike and his function.

Villon said, "He also fingered Mordecai and Luba Nafka. But I can't see them as being married." Hazel Dickson, who had just asked a waiter for more pickles and celery tonic, picked up where Villon left off.

"It's obvious they knew each other way back when."

"How way back can when be?" asked Ginger. "Mordecai's awfully young."

"Luba isn't much older," said Fred. "She's also in her twenties. Hurok told me. The only one a bit long in the tooth is Nina, but don't anyone dare tell her."

"She made a pass at you." It was Ginger speaking. She hadn't asked a question, she was making a declaration. Fred's face reddened and Hazel thought he was even more charming when he blushed. "Well, didn't she?"

"Well, she sort of did," Fred admitted sheepishly. Fred was one of the few stars in Hollywood who could never be accused of extramarital affairs.

"What do you mean 'sort of'?" persisted Ginger.

"All right, she did. She invited me up to her room"—a fast glance at his wristwatch—"any minute now."

"Well, don't let us keep you," said Ginger, snaring a pickle as the waiter placed a bowl on the table.

"Now you cut it out," warned Fred, "you know I could never cheat on Phyllis. Besides, Nina is so obvious. She's just looking to add another notch to her belt."

From the depths of his private dream world, they heard Jim Mallory ask, "Do you suppose I could qualify?"

"Why of course you could, sweetie," said Ginger. "You're real cute and I'm sure Nina would go for you unless she's tough about accepting substitutes."

"From what I've heard," said Villon, "she's not tough about accepting anything."

Ginger said to Hazel, "What idiot said men were not gossips?"

Hazel said to Villon, "Herb, do you really think Malke Movitz might inherit all of Romanov's estate?"

Ginger said, "Well, if she does, then I think she deserves it. She has devoted her life to him."

Villon added, "She certainly presented a strong case for her loyalty. What's bothering you, Hazel?"

"What do you mean?"

"The way your hand is frozen in midair holding that pickle." Hazel stared at her hand and the pickle. She placed the pickle on her plate and then wiped her fingers on her napkin. "Is it something you suspect the woman of having done?"

"Well actually, Herb, it's something I suspect her of not having done." She paused, collecting her thoughts. "I don't think she cried." They all stared at her, mostly bemused.

"What have her tears got to do with it?" asked Villon.

"It's her lack of tears. Her face wasn't tear-stained. Her eyes didn't well up with tears when she spoke of her beloved Romanov. Her voice didn't even choke once with all the talking we did about him. Russians are notorious for their emotions."

Ginger suggested, "Well, maybe she's not one of your everyday run-of-the-mill Russians. I mean think of her past. She murdered some men. She stood trial. She served time in a prison camp. I should think by now she's all out of tears."

Hazel said, "Ginger, you never run out of tears. When I think of Vivien Leigh saying 'As God is my witness, I'll never be hungry again,' I always start to cry." Her voice choked and a tear trickled down her cheek. She wiped it away with her napkin.

Mallory said, "Say, Hazel, that was neat, do it again."

"Oh shut up. Let me tell you, if I was to hear Herb here was dead, I'd cry up a hurricane. I'd blubber up a flood and my eyes would get all puffy. . . ."

"Why Hazel, I'm touched." Herb bit into his corned beef sandwich.

"Sure, you would be, you bum. Well damn it, that woman's eyes were not all puffy from crying. Why for crying out loud, when they carried the body out of the room she didn't even let out a sob." Hazel paraphrased the famous Rhett Butler line, "Frankly, my dears, she didn't seem to give a damn."

Herb Villon sighed. "Well, I see there's a lot more on my plate besides the other half of my sandwich. Anybody want it?"

Hazel said with her usual practicality, "Tell the waiter to wrap it. I'll eat it later."

Around the corner from Caplan's delicatessen in a run-down apartment house that held two types of Hollywood denizens, those on their way up and those on their way down, one of the apartments was occupied by a middle-aged woman who was neutral. She had no place to go. Her name was Esther Pincus and she sat at her one expensive asset, a grand piano which had belonged to a wealthy aunt in Paris, who had shipped it to her favorite niece shortly before her death. Esther noodled at the piano while thinking over what she had seen on television an hour before, the news of Romanov's death.

She had met him in Paris many years ago when she was a hopeful pianist supporting herself playing in a café on the Left Bank so as not to depend on her aunt's largess. The café was adjacent to a modest little restaurant where the food was good, cheap, and plentiful. She remembered the ogress who owned it and did all the cooking and serving. She remembered the handsome Russian who ate there as often as she did, possibly more often because Esther only ate there on the nights she worked at the café and she only worked at the café four nights a week. He sported a monocle occasionally; she'd hoped it wasn't an affectation and now she would never find out if it was or wasn't. Occasionally he would chat a bit with her and she found his Russian accent charming.

She learned he too played the piano but no longer played professionally. In time she came to fantasize that perhaps he would come to her flat and they would play duets but this was not to be.

The morning after a night she had not dined there, she read in *Paris Match* that she had missed all the fun. Several German men had been poisoned and the ogress proprietor had been arrested, accused of the crime. The restaurant was closed and Esther would never see Romanov again and also never learn the outcome of the trial as her aunt gifted her with a long-desired trip to the United States. Esther never returned to Paris. She met a violinist who after fiddling around, wooed and won her and spirited her away to Hollywood, where he succumbed to a fatal illness. His young widow soon rallied and found work in the studios as a rehearsal pianist.

For many weeks now, Esther had bemoaned to herself that she had nothing to look forward to, no future worth considering, just the endless drudgery of piano lessons at bargain prices. But today, there suddenly was a future, a gift from heaven, a phone call from the highly respected dance director Hermes Pan. If she was free, he wanted her to be the rehearsal pianist for a television special starring the highly respected Baronovitch ballet company, in which the special guest stars would be Fred Astaire and Ginger Rogers. Mr. Pan would be assisting Mr. Astaire in choreographing a ballet for the program.

Gaily and with a *joie de vivre* long absent from her life, Esther Pincus began pounding out "I Won't Dance" until the banging on the wall of the opposite apartment was a warning to her to cease and desist—it was past midnight. She left the piano, sank into a lumpy easy chair, lit a cigarette, and poured some wine from a decanter on the end table next to her. It was a red Valpolicella, the wine Malke Movitz had introduced her to in her Parisian restaurant and which she had occasionally shared with Romanov.

Malke Movitz! Of course! That was the name of the ogress! Now Esther rebuked herself. Not nice referring to Malke as an ogress. That she was so large and so homely was an accident of birth, a cruel stroke of fate. She was always kind to her clientele.

The place was like a clubhouse, a hangout. Herself, Romanov, several cab drivers, some clerks from a nearby department store—and oh yes, that young man, an attractive American who was strangely aloof, joked with Malke Movitz, and was very friendly with Romanov. Esther was never introduced to him, as it seemed to be an unwritten law that his privacy be respected. That was fine by Esther. She recalled the things about him that made her uncomfortable—his forced laughter, his pipe, the way he always made sure he sat with his back to a wall, his furtive glance at the door when someone entered. Subconsciously, Esther stared at her arm where some years earlier she had worn a yellow band signifying she was of the order of an inferior race. She had escaped the horror of a concentration camp, again thanks to the aunt who had shipped her the grand piano. Her aunt had friends in high places and cultivated and utilized them ruthlessly. Esther suspected she was somebody's mistress, a powerful somebody this mistress had successfully mastered. Dear Aunt Rosa, a mediocre actress but a brilliant courtesan. Her mother's sister, her long dead mother's sister.

She poured herself more wine and lit a fresh cigarette with the stub of the one she'd been smoking. She went to the window, which overlooked an alley with its population of garbage cans. She looked at the sky, a typical Hollywood sky filled with stars. She sighed and lowered the shade.

Astaire and Rogers! The big time! And even better yet, a very generous salary. And she would meet Sol Hurok, America's greatest, most influential, most powerful impresario. The man could move mountains! He would come to rehearsals and admire her virtuosity. He would ask in astonishment, "But why are you hiding your light under a butcher?"

"A bushel," she would correct him and he would gently tweak her cheek and arrange her debut at Carnegie Hall.

"Oh Christ!" she cried to the ceiling, "why is there no fairy godmother for someone like me?" Her French accent echoed across the room, the accent that Romanov had told her was sweetly charming. And for about the two-hundredth time she regretted not having gone to bed with him when he asked her to. She stared into the mirror that hung above the piano. Not bad, not bad at all. Esther Pincus was still an attractive woman despite the gray hairs, the lines under her eyes, the heavy eyebrows. Tomorrow, she promised herself, I will make an appointment with Fairfax Avenue's most popular crazy beautician and hairdresser, Mr. Eloise. Walking past his establishment earlier in the day she had been transfixed by a woman emerging from Mr. Eloise's establishment, her hair so flaming red it looked like a conflagration. Esther Pincus admired that woman. Her courage to dare to venture out in public with that hair, her devil may care attitude as she smiled at the world—that hair obviously made her feel good, and feeling good was all that mattered.

She raised her glass of wine in a silent, lonely, but very sincere toast. She drank to Hermes Pan, to Astaire and Rogers, to the memory of Igor Romanov, and to Sol Hurok, and then flopped backward onto her couch and passed out.

Gregor Sukov sat up in the bed in Nina Valgorski's suite and asked the reclining ballerina, who was also not asleep, "Why does making love to you always make me thirsty?"

Nina was lighting a cigarette as Sukov got out of bed and found one of the several bottles of champagne he and Nina had retrieved from the ballroom. He poured himself a glass as Nina said, "Pour me one too."

Gregor said, "It's warm," and made a face.

"Warm it works quicker," said Nina.

He poured the second drink and carefully brought them back to the bed. "It's late," said Gregor, his eye catching the attractive timepiece on the desk.

"It is always late," said Nina darkly. She took a glass from Sukov and sipped and made a face and then sipped again. She shrugged. One always gets used to champagne, warm or cold. "Champers," she said.

"Champers? What is champers?"

"The British call champagne champers. In many ways, though

both countries speak English, British English is very different from American English."

Gregor was back under the covers with Nina, who wished he'd go back to his own suite. She was tired and he was hyperathletic and she knew he would soon expect an encore of the sexual act they had just completed, which, because of the hullabaloo caused by Romanov's death, they had found hard to give their best performance.

"Who do you suspect?"

Nina groaned. "I told you, no one in particular."

"You don't have to be particular. Just speak a name."

"Gregor Sukov."

He boomed in Russian, "We are not amused!"

His speech was still as guttural as when she had first met him some ten years earlier. How fortunate he was blessed with the body of Adonis and the face of an angel, a magical combination he dissipated by opening his mouth.

"Gregor, leave me alone," she said wearily. "I must get some rest if I'm to look my best for the photographer's tomorrow."

"You are dismissing me?" He was indignant.

"We have a long tour ahead of us. Don't expect to accomplish in one night. . . ."

He slammed his glass down on a night table and leapt out of the bed. She had insulted him and his manhood and if she was a man he'd challenge her to a duel. Nina yawned lavishly as he struggled into his clothes. The tirade in Russian continued but fell on deaf ears. Her mind was on Villon, who she thought suspected her and several others of espionage. There was Don Magrew to think about. Several times she danced with him and he was quite good. For a brief moment she wished Gregor Sukov would turn into Don Magrew and she scrubbed that, preferring to wish Sukov would turn into a pizza, an American delicacy she had come to adore the past six weeks of the tour.

The door slammed behind Sukov.

Nina exhaled and sat up. *Who do you suspect?* The fool. The bloody fool. She got out of bed and went to the bathroom and bravely took a cold shower. As she rubbed her body with a large raw sponge, she berated herself in a variety of languages for not having married years ago when she had many opportunities, given birth to at least three children . . . *Three* children . . . my God! Think of what that would have done to my gorgeous figure.

"For crying out loud, Hazel," muttered Herb Villon, "will you please go to sleep. It's almost daybreak."

Hazel tugged at the blanket ferociously.

Herb sat up. "What the hell are you doing?"

"You're hogging the blanket. Look at my skin! Gooseflesh!"

"Very becoming," he said and fell back on the pillow.

"Okay, okay," exasperated, "you weren't asleep. You've got someone on your mind."

"I've got a lot of someones on my mind. They're all in a jumble."

"So just line them up in a row and let's take them one at a time. Malke Movitz comes first."

"You're so sure." He sat up and lit a cigarette.

"Light one for me too," she said cozily, "like Paul Henreid did for himself and Bette Davis in *Now, Voyager.*"

He placed two cigarettes in his mouth, inhaled, and almost choked on the smoke. "Christ, Henreid must have had a double."

"He had no double. It's just that you're not suave and smooth. You got no class, Herb."

He let that one pass. He could have challenged her remark with a snappy line about her phony red hair, but he preferred to keep the peace and discuss the murder. "Hazel," he said.

"What?"

"Malke Movitz is waiting."

"For what?"

"To be discussed. You wanted her first on line, she's first on line."

Hazel puffed her cigarette. "Why wasn't she shattered by Romanov's death?"

"Maybe because someone her size doesn't shatter easily. Okay, so no puffy eyes or cheeks, the look most women get when they're peeling onions. Hazel, she wouldn't decide on her own to kill him."

"Why not?"

"Why yes? She's been away from Russia over fifteen years. On the surface she no longer has an allegiance to Mother Russia."

"Never trust what's on the surface. Look beneath! *Dig.*"

"For what am I digging? Look, I think the woman is involved in Romanov's murder, but she wasn't the only one with access to him. There's the nurse and the nephew."

"Mordecai's not very bright."

"You don't need brains to poison anyone. All you need is poison. And Ginger just about bust a gut giving us the layout of Romanov's house, leading up to the potting shed and the weed killer to be found there. And for *weed killer* read *cyanide*, which is very, very popular in certain circles. What I think is that Romanov managed to keep his double-cross of the Russians quiet for a long, long time until he slipped up someplace and the KGB in Moscow decided he needed to be eliminated, but subtly, slowly, not all at once the way she did in those Germans in Paris. Neither side has any use for moles but somehow they keep turning up."

"Who's next in line?" She stubbed out her cigarette.

"Alida Rimsky, or Varonsky, if those two are really married."

Hazel's eyes widened. "You have your doubts?"

"I always have doubts, you know that. Just because they say they're married doesn't mean it's so. They haven't shown us a marriage certificate, have they?"

"I doubt if they carry it on them," said Hazel. "Though I would keep mine close to my heart forever."

He ignored the remark. "What bothers me are the two versions of Mrs. Romanov's death. Varonsky and Malke are at variance there. Somehow Malke sounds like the most likely." He stared at her. "Now where are you?"

"I'm in the ballroom where Varonsky and Alida were dancing and you remarked they looked like an old married couple."

"Well, they did! Looks can be deceiving." He frowned. "They

seemed pretty devoted back at Romanov's. Oh the hell with it. Whether they're married or not won't deliver me Romanov's killer."

"Or killers," said Hazel. "This could have been a group enterprise. You know"—she addressed imaginary suspects—" 'I'll give him a dose now. In a couple of days you give him one and then a few days later *you* take a hand in it. . . .' "

"Oh shut up. If Varonsky and Alida aren't deeply in love, then they're superb actors."

"You don't have to be married to be deeply in love."

Villon again sidestepped Hazel's implication by saying, "Alida could have been sent here by the KGB to either assist Romanov or ride herd on him."

"Maybe she unmasked him as a two-header."

"Possible."

"And maybe the Baronovitch tour was really arranged to get more spies into the country. Set up a network with fresh blood. Herb, the Russians are very clever with that sort of thing. Remember the circus they sent here a couple of years ago where one of the great routines consisted of a boy or girl disappearing from one side of the ring in a puff of smoke and only seconds later reappearing at the other end of the ring in another puff of smoke."

"That's an easy one," said Herb. "They used sets of identical twins."

"Exactly, but the tour was suddenly canceled and not for lack of business. The CIA soon figured out which twin had the Toni"—an advertising campaign for a popular home permanent—"and deported the whole bunch of them. Along with their cameras, their invisible ink, their sophisticated listening devices, and so on."

"Well, they're not kidding us with the Baronovitch. That's why Don Magrew has been on their tail, following the tour so closely."

"Cute."

"Who?"

"Don Magrew."

"Mordecai is getting impatient."

"Mordecai?"

"He's the next one up at bat. Malke says he's her sister's son. I should think Malke's sister would bear some resemblance to her."

"Logical. So?"

"Malke and Mordecai look about as much alike as Laurel and Hardy."

"And they're nowhere near as funny," said Hazel.

"Mordecai is funny," said Herb.

"I don't see it."

"The Ed Sullivan show bit. I wonder what he'd do if Fred really got Sullivan to give Mordecai a spot."

"Sport," said Hazel, now whimsical. "You know, Herb," she said with a faraway look in her eyes, "the kid just might knock them dead and surprise us all."

"Do you suppose he knocked Romanov dead?"

"Did you ever see a Dietrich movie called *Shanghai Express*? Dietrich was a whore named Shanghai Lily, and she had a great line of dialogue." Hazel spoke the line in a ghastly imitation of Dietrich, " 'It took more than one man to give me the name Shanghai Lily.' It took more than one person to put the final nail in Romanov's coffin."

"And who was that?"

"Search me."

"I don't have to. Nina Valgorski got Romanov a glass of soda water."

"You mean she slipped him the fatal mickey?"

"I think she did."

"In a crowded ballroom? But how? That gown she wore was plastered to her body! Oh, of course she might have been hiding a vial in her cleavage." Hazel gave it some thought. "You could hide a motorcycle in that cleavage. It's a wonder she doesn't keel over when she pirouettes."

"I doubt if she had anything in her cleavage except maybe a dainty handkerchief bordered with lace."

"Then for crying out loud, is she a magician?"

"Did you notice what she was wearing around her neck?"

"A necklace?"

Villon rubbed it in. "Not as observant as you claim to be. She wore a chain from which dangled something resembling a whistle. She kept touching it as though she didn't want to lose it."

"Well, knowing Nina, it is probably very valuable."

"I'm not sure what it might bring in a hock shop, but I think that whistle has a hollow center. And in that center was a dose of poison. Probably cadmium. You know, what Nina was pushing as the most popular poison in Russia. That's how I think they got him. I'm pretty sure he was a goner by then, but that final dose was necessary for the *coup de grâce*. Because maybe Romanov was finally wising up he was being done in and would tell the CIA . . ."

"Like the snatch he had been for years."

"Snitch," corrected Villon. "Snitch, Hazel, rhymes with Witch Hazel."

Thirteen

$\mathcal{V}$illon got out of bed and staggered to the kitchen for a glass of water. He was always unsteady on his feet in the morning, whether suffering from a hangover or a guilty conscience. Often he wished he was on the loose like Jim Mallory, unencumbered by an albatross around his neck, playing the field. He gulped the water. What field? Where was there a field for him to play in? He had never been any good at flirting, though he usually recognized when some woman had him in her sights. Ah what the hell, he'd been attached to Hazel for fifteen years, he was used to her, how would he get along without her—though he often thought of trying.

Hazel shouted from the bedroom, "What about Luba? Varonsky? Bochno?"

"They were either not in the country or on tour when Romanov probably started getting the deadly infusions." He emerged from the kitchen scratching his belly and yawning. Another sleepless night. Another case loaded with crackpots. He wondered if all Russians were as crackers as the bunch he was now dealing with. He was back in the bedroom and at the closet examining his meager wardrobe. When, he tried to remember, had he last bought a new suit? When, he tried to remember, could he last afford to buy a new suit? Why didn't he get into a more lucrative profession and make some real money? Such as what? he asked himself and received no answer.

"Such an awful sigh!" said Hazel. "What's troubling you, sweetheart?"

"Hazel, a policeman's lot is not a happy one."

"Gilbert and Sullivan," said Hazel.

"What about them?"

"They wrote that line. Or at least one of them did."

"What line?"

"A policeman's lot whatever."

"My my! So I can quote Gilbert and Sullivan. Now how do I lay my hands on that whistle thing?"

"Subpoena it."

"It's a thought. Yes, it's a thought."

An hour later, freshly bathed and wearing a jaunty blue blazer with a pair of gray slacks, Herb Villon was at the desk of the Ambassador Hotel, asking for an audience with Nina Varonsky. For emphasis, he flashed his badge. The clerk, who bore a slight resemblance to the character actor Hans Conried stared at the badge and asked, "What's she done?"

"She hasn't done anything." He almost added, "Not anything I can prove," but decided caution was the watchword—this might be one of the many informants in Hollywood with direct lines to gossip columnists.

"Then why'd you show me your badge?"

Villon asked the desk clerk, "Would you rather I flashed something else?"

"I'll see if she's in." The clerk's look was deadly but not fatal. In response to Nina's "Yes?" he told her Detective Villon would like to see her.

Nina rubbed her cheek and studied her reflection in a wall mirror. Herb Villon. Ah yes, she reminded herself, the taciturn one. Very much the he-man. Yes, he would do just nicely at this hour of the morning. The detective would like to see me indeed. Romanov's death. Why else? "Ask Detective Villon to come to my suite, and then find out if the breakfast I ordered for half an hour ago is coming by way of Mexico."

"I'm sorry, madam. Room service is terribly busy this morning. The hotel is heavily booked with Elks. They're having a convention here."

"Elks? Animals? Indeed, what a strange country." She slammed down the phone and slipped out of a housecoat and into a very revealing and seductive negligée, a Chanel original. She hurriedly brushed her hair for the fifth time that morning and then struck several poses before deciding which one would appeal to the detective. She did not know Villon was immune to seductive poses. A few minutes later when she opened the door to admit him, she was delighted to see behind him a waiter wheeling a cart on which reposed her breakfast.

"Ahhhhh! Two most welcome sights! A handsome detective and my breakfast." Villon stood to one side as the waiter rolled the cart to an area indicated by the ballerina, a table between the sofa and an Eames chair. "Mr. Villon, how nice of you to come calling. May I offer you coffee? A little Danish pastry? Oh do have coffee. There are two cups and two saucers. I ordered my breakfast last night when I thought there would be someone to share it with me. And so there is! You!"

She signed the waiter's chit and he hurried away for fear of asphyxiation from her powerful perfume. She sat in the Eames chair and invited Villon to sit opposite her on the sofa. He asked if she'd mind if he opened a window; the perfume was overpowering. "But of course! Open the window! Let us breathe of your magnificent California air!"

While he crossed to a window and opened it, she poured two cups of coffee. "You have come to question me about the unfortunate Romanov?" She laughed at the look on his face while uncovering dishes and greedily sniffing them. "Maybe I told you last night that many years ago when we were teenagers we were lovers and if I haven't told you, now you know. Milk? Sugar? Pastry?"

He refused all three. "Black! You drink it black! You are a man's man!" She sipped her coffee. "What is wrong with you Americans? Coffee needs chicory! Oh well, our coffee is also thicker but then, we don't have Danish pastries and they are so delightful." She held up a plate of miniature pastries and again he rejected them. He refused her offer to share her mammoth breakfast of wheat cakes, sausage, bacon, ham, eggs sunnyside up, hominy grits, home fried potatoes, toast, jam, and a slab of unsalted butter. Madame, he thought, undoubtedly dances like a sylph in heat, but eats like a longshoreman.

She slathered the wheat cakes with butter and maple syrup and Villon hoped he wouldn't take ill. He sipped some coffee and happily for him, it was excellent. When he replaced the cup on the saucer, he found her looking at him seductively despite her mouthful of food. She said, "You detectives do things so differently from my country. Here you present yourself to the desk clerk, giving me plenty of time to escape down the rear elevator if I am so inclined. In my country they kick in the door, grab you by the hair, force you down on your knees, slap your face a few times, and *then* ask questions." She reloaded her mouth and smiled. "I prefer your method. You remember I told you I was a student of criminology?" He remembered and wondered if this meeting would end up with her doing all the questioning. "But your only interest in me at the moment is Romanov, and do I in some way relate to his death. They said on the television it was death by slow poisoning. You will explain that, please?" He explained it briefly. "Ah yes!" She thought for a moment and then pointed her fork at him. "Madeline Smith."

"Who was she?"

"What? You are not familiar with Madeline Smith? Shame on you." He half expected her to make him stand in the corner. "British. A classic case. She poisoned her little brother. She was acquitted. She had a very smart . . . How did Dashiell Hammett put it . . . ?"

"Shamus."

"Yes! Yes! A shamus lawyer! You have read Hammett! Good!"

She laid waste to ham, eggs, potatoes, and grits washed down with more coffee. Suddenly she said, "Now why do you suppose Romanov was removed?"

He knew now she knew more about Romanov's murder than she would ever tell, but he persisted. She was bound to slip up sooner or later; all such self-assured people did. "He was a mole."

She laughed but fortunately did not spray her food. She was obviously determined not to squander any of it. "A mole! Of course! Two spies for the price of one. He spied for both the Soviets and your people. A very dangerous occupation, very dangerous." She smiled as she dabbed at her mouth with a napkin. "You are here because you suspect I too am a spy. Why? Why do you suspect I am a spy? Does Hurok share your suspicion?"

"I doubt if Hurok knows I'm here with you."

"He knows." Very self-assured. "He tips the staff well and they supply him with tips in return. Everyone is greedy." Now she was lighting a cigarette. "I only arrived in this city a few days ago. If I poisoned Romanov, it would have to be quick. And I don't know where he lives, so how could I have gotten to him?"

"I didn't say you poisoned him."

"Ah? So I have not been understanding you?"

"You've been understanding me," said Villon. "You're a very smart ballerina."

Again she laughed. They were playing a game and she enjoyed it. "Ballerinas are usually very dense, but they know how to make their own costumes. I am very smart, how else could I study criminology, but I am a very poor seamstress. So what do you think I had to do with my poor Romanov's death." She had moved to the double doors that opened on a balcony and pushed them open. She then struck a pose in the doorway, in which her negligee revealed everything except unexposed film. Villon appreciated what he saw but was not about to be sidetracked. "My poor ill-fated, star-crossed, doomed Romanov. He was such a wonderful lover. He was nineteen, when men are said to be at the height of their sexual power. For women the age is forty. I still have time." She cleared her throat and waited for a compliment but none was forthcoming. Villon realized time was running out. He wanted to get to the precinct. Edgar Rowe was sure to have performed the autopsy and Villon was anxious to read his report.

"Last night you wore a very attractive trinket."

"Trinket? I do not wear trinkets."

"I used 'trinket' for want of a better description."

"Ah! You mean my good luck charm. I'll get it for you, it's in my jewelry case in the bedroom. Have some more coffee. I assure you it's not poisoned." The sound of her laughter trailed her out of the room. Villon studied the remains of her breakfast. This was indeed a woman of ravenous appetites, an appetite for food, for sex, and most assuredly for intrigue. She returned, her closed right fist obviously holding the object of Villon's interest.

She said with remarkable self-assurance, "I will not offer you a ruble for your thoughts for obviously they are much more valuable. And do you know why I know this? Because"—she leaned forward, offering him what she knew to be an exciting view of her fascinating cleavage—"you are thinking of me. I am right? Yes?"

"I am thinking you seem to take a special delight in playing games."

She straightened up and extended the right fist to Villon. She opened her hand and Villon saw what he was after. "Take it," she said, "it will not harm you. It is very expensive." He took it and examined it. "It is modeled after a whistle. It is made of platinum. It was a gift from Stalin himself. It was made by a grand duke for his grand duchess. They are both dead. Stalin adored me. He had pictures of me but he could not display them because his wife, the cow, was very jealous." Her laugh tinkled. "And let me tell you she had every reason to be. When Valgorski plays, she plays to win." Villon had no reason to doubt her and he was busy deciphering the whistle. "Yes," she said, "it is hollow. It is an object the Borgias would have appreciated."

"And what does it usually hold?"

"Slivovitz." She folded her arms. "You know Slivovitz?"

"Not intimately."

"It is a strong and very delicious liqueur. It is the most popular drink in Russia among the upper classes."

"I thought Russia was a classless society."

"Propaganda. Don't believe everything you read about Russia. We are a very complex people."

Silently, Villon agreed with her. He had not solved how to open it. She told him, "Lightly press the tip. The top will pop open." She was right. He sniffed it. "You will smell nothing. I have washed it. I always wash it after I have used it or else there will be a very unpleasant stale smell."

He popped the whistle shut. "You carry slivovitz all the time?"

"No, because I do not wear it all the time. Only special occasions when I think I will require a few drops to refresh me."

"And last night you required a few drops. And I was under the impression last night champagne was your favorite tipple."

"Such an amusing drink, champagne. Did you know the British call it champers? But then, they call lamb patties faggots, which I positively do not understand. At several points last night I sipped some slivovitz. Now I am sorry I rinsed it."

"Why?"

"Because I can see you are disappointed."

"I didn't know it showed."

"You were thinking perhaps I carried poison." The laugh tinkled again. He wondered if she guffawed at funerals. "And why not. I was seen carrying a glass of soda water to Romanov. I could see he was burning with fever and was parched, which was why I volunteered to fetch him the soda water." She paused and then said, "I poured some slivovitz into the glass, because we Russians feel it has medicinal powers. Actually, Romanov looked a little better for having drunk it."

"He didn't comment on the taste?"

"He said he wanted to go home. His nurse and chauffeur were rallied and they took him home. You are thinking I have covered myself well by telling you I poured the liqueur into the soda water, in case I was seen doing it." She shrugged. "Has anyone come forward to accuse me of doctoring the drink?"

"Nobody. But you covered yourself." He stood up. He handed her back the whistle.

"You aren't confiscating it?"

"There's no reason. It's clean. It will tell my forensics people nothing. Why waste their time?"

"You are going?" She looked like a stricken fawn. She had a wide variety of poses and attitudes, all exaggerated and overwrought from Villon's observations. He couldn't wait to tell Hazel, who had vociferously warned him Nina was more dangerous than a man-eating tiger and would use every wile in her book to lure him into bed.

"I have to get to the precinct and read the coroner's report. Romanov might have been poisoned by cyanide. But I also told the coroner to watch for traces of cadmium."

A hand flew to her bosom. She said archly, "Cadmium. *My* cadmium."

"That's right. I suggested he look for traces of your cadmium. I'm sure we'll see each other again. Thank you for giving me this time. And for letting me examine your whistle." And he was out the door.

Nina went back to the bedroom, sat on the unmade bed, and asked the operator to connect her to another room in the hotel. Her party responded and Nina spoke rapidly in Russian. "He is very clever, this Villon, very, very clever. Of course he was here, he just left. He goes to his coroner to find out if there was a trace of cadmium in Romanov's body." She listened and then said, "Last night I didn't think before I spoke. I mentioned cadmium was a very popular poison in the Soviet Union. Don't ask me why, it came up in a conversation. Don't scold me, damn you, don't scold me! *You* devised the method of Romanov's death!" She listened. "You are boring me! I must go to the theater and make faces. The company is to be photographed and that's all I can tell you. I must hurry or I will be late." She slammed the phone down. She lit a cigarette. She walked to the dressing table where she had left the whistle. She stared at the whistle. She castigated it in a stream of gutter Russian. Then she spoke to her reflection in the mirror.

"So, Nina Valgorski, you have almost outsmarted yourself again. You overestimated yourself and underestimated this detective Herb Villon. But you covered yourself beautifully by using slivovitz as a metaphor for cadmium." She took a long drag on the cigarette.

The phone rang. She crossed back to it. "Yes?"

"It is Hurok here," he boomed in his room, where he and Mae Frohman had shared his usual breakfast of stewed prunes, Wheaties, and warm milk and cocoa. Later, Mae would repair to the coffee shop for more substantial fare. "What did the detective want?"

"How did you know I was visited by a detective?" And why had she bothered to ask? She knew he was tipped off by the desk clerk.

"I know everything!" Mae winced at his booming voice and refreshed her coffee cup.

"Then you know what he wanted to know!"

"Nina, don't be difficult. Tell me, my dear, is there a connection between the company and Romanov's murder?"

"I knew him when I was in my teens, but that's hardly much of a connection, don't you agree?"

After a few seconds he said, "If you say so." She told him she was in a hurry to get to the photo shoot and they both hung up.

"Mae?"

"Yes?"

"There is something going on behind my back. I must move it to the front."

"You will, Mr. Hurok, my money's on you."

"You know what Sherlock Holmes always says." He raised a finger and pointed it ominously as he misquoted, "There is something underfoot!"

"Afoot," Mae corrected, *a*foot.

Fourteen

Theodore Varonsky was at the wheel of a car provided by NBC and was driving Alida to the Romanov house. He had spent the night with her in her modest West Hollywood apartment. They had made love and then she brewed tea. They were driving in silence and it gave Varonsky time to measure Alida against the girl he had married seven years ago and had not seen for over five of them. Then she was staid and stoic, the model of a young Russian bride trained to be a good and obedient wife. Last night in bed he found her a bit frivolous, like the ditsy French ballerina in Anthony Tudor's delightful ballet *Gala Performance*. Then when they settled down to tea and slices of babka, the popular Russian cake, she was so animated and bubbly, he suspected she must have had many lovers in Hollywood. He'd been told by a KGB spy who had spent several years in the Russian embassy in Los Angeles that lovers of both sexes literally grew on trees. On the other hand, he had not lacked for female companionship during their long separation, either. They had agreed before parting that each was free to pursue sexual adventures but each also was to try not to take any liaison too seriously. They did not ask each other questions, a rule that had also been agreed upon, but Varonsky had little doubt that Alida had provided Romanov with a certain degree of comfort. He caught a glimpse of her looking out her window as they drove along Sunset Boulevard in Beverly Hills, past the many lovely mansions with their well-manicured lawns and beautiful landscaping.

Varonsky commented, "There is much wealth here. How seductive it must be. Romanov, I assume, was easily seduced."

Alida rose to the late psychiatrist's defense. "He worked very hard for his wealth. Sometimes seven days a week, ten hours or more a day. It was very grueling. I know because I was there with him."

"You should have resided in his house. It is a long drive from your apartment."

"My darling Theodore, everything is a long drive in Los Angeles. Los Angeles is thirty suburbs in search of a city. You must have wheels to survive in this place."

"You never learned how to drive."

"I am terrified of driving. Especially here. They are maniacs. They ignore speed limits and if they are trapped they think little of offering bribes. It is a very corrupt city. The police here are notorious for their corruption."

"Yes? Policemen must be very wealthy."

"Not all, of course, but a good proportion."

"This Herb Villon and his partner . . ."

"Jim Mallory."

"Ah yes, Jim Mallory. They too are corrupt?"

"I don't know. I hope not. I like them very much."

"You know them? You've met them before?"

"I've never met them before last night. But I couldn't help noticing they had good manners."

"And the lady with the terrifying hair?"

"Hazel Dickson. She is what they call in this country a 'yenta.' " He repeated the word. "A yenta is a loud-mouthed, nosy gossip."

"I have been told gossip is a very big industry in this country."

"Especially in this city. Hazel is almost a celebrity in her own right. She gathers gossip from various sources and sells it to the people who write gossip columns."

"Was there much gossip about Romanov?"

"Not as much as about his patients."

"I see. What do you know about Fred Astaire and Ginger Rogers?"

Here it is, she thought. The cross-examination. She knew it was inevitable, and had expected it last night. But he was so hungry for her sexually that he tabled the cross-examining and busied himself teaching her a few things, several of which she could have happily done without. Even after they were spent and settled down to tea and cake, he surprised her by talking only of Russia and the friends and family she had left behind and how his career as a *maître de ballet* had thrived from the moment he'd been assigned the much sought-after position.

"I asked you about Astaire and Rogers."

"Yes, my dear, I was wondering what took you so long to get around to it."

"My wise Alida, you are prepared for me."

She shrugged. "What is there to prepare? It isn't as though you gave me a list of questions. Certainly you read my communiqués, which I fed to the KGB quite steadily."

"I read them indeed. Very good too. You will be commended officially." Then he snapped the names. "Astaire and Rogers."

She resisted an urge to salute him. "He is a superb artist. He is highly respected. He has no particular political leanings, he is only interested in dancing and composing songs that nobody publishes or sings. He has a very few friends but he treasures them zealously. He is devoted to his wife, Phyllis, a product of what in this country they call high society, the upper classes."

"The upper classes despise communism."

"Oh my dear, innocent Theodore, just about all classes in this country despise communists. They think we run around in black cloaks under which we carry bombs with which to blow up bridges and factories and cause all sorts of disruptions."

He laughed. "What a country! We haven't blown up anything in a long time. Bombs are so expensive. You know, we have strict orders now to tighten our belts. Fortunately, the Baronovitch company is proving to be highly profitable. Sol Hurok is a very clever partner. Now what about Ginger Rogers?"

Alida asked shrewdly, "You want to hear about her or her mother?"

"Both."

"I'll begin with the mother. She is very bossy, very pushy, an extreme rightist, and I'm told plays a rotten game of bridge. She once dominated her daughter but as Ginger's fame grew, she eased herself out from under her mother's thumb. One of the few things the two have left in common is the practice of Christian Science."

"We banished those people from Russia!"

"I know. Don't shout, I'm sitting right next to you. They seem more or less devoted to each other though the mother, Lela—"

"I know her name."

"—Lela never approved of Ginger's husbands. Her first was a vaudeville performer, Jack Pepper. He taught Ginger, who was still in her teens, the ropes." She explained *ropes* as gaining from experience as opposed to tying one around a neck and hanging someone. "Then she married a very fine actor, Lew Ayres, who is still popular. He is a pacifist, but survived the slings and arrows when he refused to carry a gun during the war. Instead he drove an ambulance or something like that. Her third husband was Jack Briggs, a marine. She married him during the war. I think it was an act of patriotism on her part; it seemed that all he had to offer her was a magnificent body. She was with RKO then, and she got them to give him an acting contract. He couldn't act. Now she just married a French actor, Jacques Bergerac. Beautiful body, beautiful face, I knew nothing about his politics. And there you have it."

"I don't have enough."

She was finding his line of questioning tiresome. And he was driving much too slowly for her taste. Other cars passed them after honking horns ferociously, forcing Varonsky to give way. It didn't seem to bother him at all. When they did it to Ginger Rogers she offered them the raised middle finger of a hand and it was days before Alida learned that it was a very offensive gesture.

"Well, Theodore, I have sent many communiqués on Ginger and her mother and Romanov's other patients—"

He interrupted her. "There was nothing to indicate she had the potential to be converted. She gave you lifts many times."

"So?"

"Were there no opportunities to feel her out?"

"You don't bother when a person refers to us as 'Them there commies.' "

"Yes. You are right. And I'm beginning to think that perhaps we misunderstood Fred and Ginger."

Alida was a bit at sea. "Misunderstood? What was there to understand?"

"Don't be so dense." She felt the blood rushing to her cheeks.

"I am not dense!"

"We assumed if Fred and Ginger agreed to appear with us they were *sympathetic*!"

She erupted and shouted, "It is you who are dense! They are major film stars. They don't need Baronovitch and they hardly need to be sympathetic to appear with them. Astaire said yes because he respects the tradition of Russian ballet, and so does Ginger. They feel honored to dance with the Baronovitch, and Ginger swallowed her pride to dance the part of a mother of five children, one of which is about as old as she is! Hurok gives Fred the opportunity to choreograph, his lifelong dream, and you expect them to be sympathetic? And the dream has become a nightmare—if not for them, then for me! Now Ginger and Fred are embroiled in murder! Murder! And it isn't even *their* murder, it's *our* murder!"

"Shut up! You might be overheard!"

"By who, for God's sake! We are motoring!"

Momentarily, he looked sheepish, then he said, "It is not good that Fred and Ginger are working with the police."

"Where did you hear that?"

"They were with the police last night!"

"Please, Theodore, don't make life any more difficult than it is. Ginger came to the house to give comfort to Malke Movitz and me."

"Ha!"

"You are being very difficult."

"We are in a difficult situation."

"Theodore, Romanov's death will remain a mystery."

"American forensics teams are brilliant, highly sophisticated."

"Yes, that was understood when we were instructed to kill Romanov by the slow death. The autopsy will show there was cyanide in his system, built up over a period of months. So what? It has happened before. It is commonplace, like chewing gum."

"Quite true. But not when they also find cadmium in his system. And cadmium is commonplace only to Russians. Put that in your samovar and boil it." He explained about Nina Valgorski's administering the final fatal dose.

Alida said, "Theodore, we may have outsmarted ourselves."

Edgar Rowe, the coroner, was scampering about like the White Rabbit in *Alice in Wonderland*. "I'm late! I'm late! I'm behind schedule. The bodies are beginning to pile up." Herb Villon and Jim Mallory watched without flinching as he made another incision in Igor Romanov's body. "There was a pileup on Hollywood Boulevard. Six cars, five dead." He turned to his assistant, who was in the eighth year of the job, and said, "They'll have to wait their turn." As he probed and dictated, he whistled between his teeth.

Jim said to Herb, making no effort to mask his distaste for their environs, "The son of a bitch really enjoys his job. I mean talk about whistling while you work."

"He also teaches Sunday school."

Edgar Rowe was standing back, admiring his work like an artist standing before an easel. He dictated some more to the young man who was his assistant. "A very fine specimen, very fine. One of the best we've had here in months." He said to Villon, "There was enough cyanide in him to kill a dozen men."

"Then the cadmium was overkill."

Hands on hips, the coroner said, "Poisoners always go too far. Especially the ones in slow deaths like this. They're so impatient. I mean if they know it's going to take time to polish off the bugger, then wait for the poison to accumulate in the system. I miss the good old days of belladonna and cyanide. Those are really nifty poisons, but they were hard to come by. You needed a prescription. Cyanide of course is in a weed killer, easier to get hold of." He said to his assistant, "Cover him and refrigerate him. Anybody claiming the body?"

"His housekeeper," Villon told him. "Deliver the corpse to Utter McKinley on Hollywood Boulevard." McKinley's was Hollywood's busiest funeral parlor, with an excellent reputation.

While removing his smock, Edgar Rowe lifted his voice in song. " 'Lovely to look at, delightful to knowww . . .' " He did a little tapping, then indicated for Villon and Mallory to follow him to his office where there was always a pot of coffee brewing. "What a thrill meeting Fred and Ginger last night! Weren't you thrilled?"

"Enchanted," said Herb.

Once the coffee was poured and the three were settled in chairs, Rowe asked Villon, "So who did him in? You must suspect someone. I know you, Herb. We've been together a long time. Come on, who done it?" He slapped his knee and laughed. If it was one thing Herb Villon could live without it was a jocular coroner, although he made an exception for Edgar Rowe. Without his sense of humor, Herb suspected the little man might be suicidal. When his wife died unexpectedly several years earlier, his despondency was so acute he was given a month's leave of absence for fear he'd have a nervous breakdown. He spent the month touring European graveyards and becoming acquainted with the final resting places of the great scholars, poets, playwrights, heads of state, and politicians. He came back to Los Angeles refreshed and revived and a delightful source of European necrophilia.

"Now don't go silent on me, Herb, who's your prime suspect?"

Herb crossed one leg over the other. "I suspect a small group of friends murdered Romanov."

"*Friends?* You call them friends?"

"That's right. Friends who were following orders from the evil ones in the Soviet Union."

"Evil ones. How quaint. I thought once they were rid of the monster supreme, things might slacken up a bit. Stalin was a monster and in spades."

"I get the feeling his successors are out to go him one better. Here's the scenario I've constructed so far. It's a little rough because I haven't had all that much time to think."

"Come come, Villon. You're much too modest. You probably have an idea who the killer is, you can't kid an old friend like me."

"Killers. Plural."

"Plural! Heavens! The old safety in numbers bit."

"Romanov had a tough assignment."

Rowe held up a hand. "Wait! Are you telling me Romanov was a spy?"

"Of a very sophisticated denomination."

"Well, I'll be damned." He clapped his hands together. "I've autopsied my first spy!" he said joyously to the ceiling. "All things come to him who waits! Think of it! My first spy!"

"Hold on to your patience and you might be entertaining a few more."

"Really?" He was ecstatic. "Oh, how my cup runneth over!" He thought for a moment. "Who's supplying us with all these spies?"

"The Baronovitch Ballet."

"No! Oh my dear, Herb! Are Fred and Ginger aware of this?"

"I think they're beginning to catch on."

"And they're not afraid of the danger? Oh, they are so brave."

Jim Mallory suddenly spoke up. "You know what show people always say—the show must go on."

"Jim," said Villon.

"What?"

"Not too much caffeine. It can overstimulate. Where was I? Oh yeah. Romanov's assignment." He explained to the coroner Romanov's training and induction into psychiatry with Hollywood as his assignment.

"Keep in mind, Edgar. Hollywood was hyperactive during the war. USO tours, a big number in service, a lot of them given commissions and in a position to hear things that would be of use to a foreign government."

"Still? All these years later?" The little man was fascinated.

"I should think there are secrets lying dormant which, once revived, examined, investigated, and analyzed carefully, would reveal a whole new secret that could be of inestimable value to the Soviets."

"Sure," said Mallory, getting into the swing, "more new kinds of bombs."

Rowe asked, "Are you bored with the ones we've got?"

Said Villon, "Jim's thinking's on the right track, if a little muddy. We've probably got secret weapons that have yet to make it to the toy stores."

"And deadly gases," Jim reminded them.

"All the actors who were active in the war met a lot of people. They ate and drank together, and heard things that may have meant nothing to them at the time. But when they repeated them years later while lying on an analyst's couch those things could mean a hell of a lot to the analyst, especially one like Romanov, who I'm sure sent much of what he learned and thought was important back to the Soviet. And Romanov has been treating some pretty important Hollywood people."

Rowe sat up, looking like a puppy begging a treat. "So the CIA caught on and arranged for him to be killed!"

"Close," said Villon, "but no cigar. When the CIA caught on, which was quite a while ago, they forced Romanov to work for them. Romanov became a two-headed spy to save his skin. Except once the Russians wised up to the situation, Romanov's goose was cooked. The old familiar recipe."

"You said friends murdered Romanov?"

"I call them friends. Three of them worked for him. His nurse, his housekeeper, who was also his cook—"

"Aha!" aha'd Rowe. "She had the easiest access to the skull-duggery!"

"—and his valet who was also his chauffeur and is the house-keeper's nephew." He lit a cigarette. "They all fed him cyanide in carefully measured doses. But now Romanov had to die a little faster than originally planned. Nina Valgorski took care of that."

Edgar Rowe's chin dropped. "A prima ballerina *assoluta* a poisoner?"

Jim Mallory said, "She's been killing audiences for years," and then wished he hadn't after the deadly look Villon flashed him. Villon told them how the dancer had accomplished her contribution to Romanov's death.

The coroner's eyes sparkled. "Our own Lucrezia Borgia! When are you collaring them?"

"I'm not."

"You're letting them go scot-free?"

"I've got no proof and I've got no evidence. So now I wait, and soon my pigeons will come home to roost. Soon they'll give themselves away. They've been telling lies left and right. And they'll soon start tripping over them. You see, the four who poisoned Romanov are small fry."

"But Nina Valgorski is an international star," said Rowe.

"A tool, like the other three, all tools. And I'm after bigger game."

"Come on, Herb. Stop being so obtuse." Rowe was sitting on the edge of his chair, leaning forward.

"All in good time, Edgar." Villon extinguished his cigarette.

"In other words, you don't know."

"There's a lot I know and suspect that I'm not sure about.

Frankly, Edgar, I'm dealing with people who as far as I'm concerned are from outer space. And then there's Don Magrew."

"Ah! Another country is heard from! And who is Don Magrew?"

"He's CIA. Assigned to the ballet company. Been with them since they began touring, but seems to keep a very low profile. So far he's not been underfoot, which is the way I prefer it." Villon looked at his wristwatch. "Come on, Jim. Let's go to my office and order some lunch. I've got notes to type up while you, Edgar, get your report to me in triplicate. And get somebody to phone Romanov's housekeeper and tell her the cold cuts are ready for delivery to the mortuary. The company starts rehearsing this afternoon and I'm interested in seeing how far Fred gets with this bunch before artistic temperaments start exploding all around him." He had the door open to leave.

"Wait!"

Villon and Mallory turned to face Edgar Rowe. "Promise me Fred and Ginger aren't in danger!"

The little man was truly concerned. Villon asked, "Now who would want to kill either Fred or Ginger?"

Fifteen

At the same time Edgar Rowe was probing into Romanov's body, Theodore Varonsky pulled into the doctor's driveway. Alida led the way into the house and they could hear Malke Movitz laughing heartily. The laughter came from the library, which was in back of the house, adjoining the kitchen. The laughter, Varonsky thought, was hardly appropriate to a house supposed to be in mourning. He and Alida heard a car pull into the driveway and park behind them. It was the doctor's limousine and Mordecai Pfenov got out of the car, paused to breathe deeply of the air rich with the scent of the flora that surrounded the house, and then examined the car on loan from NBC. Then he went into the house where he too wondered what was the cause of his aunt's apparently uncontrollable mirth. He too followed the laughter into the library where Malke sat facing a man who sat behind the desk on which was a briefcase from which spilled some important-looking documents.

The man behind the desk, whom all three recognized as Romanov's lawyer, Morris Snyder, signaled hello and then suggested Mordecai get his aunt a glass of water.

"Seltzer!" countermanded Malke between hiccups, and then

began laughing again like a calliope out of control. Snyder was a middle-aged man in a business suit, something rarely worn or seen in Beverly Hills, where men's wardrobes were expensively casual. He had a bald spot, which he carefully attempted to camouflage with hair combed expertly over the bare skin, but to little effect. Mordecai had hurried to the kitchen in fear that his aunt might be suffering an apoplectic fit. Alida and Voronsky were perplexed and stared at Malke, who now had two streams of tears coursing down her cheeks, unlike the night before when the tears would have been more appropriate but were noticeably absent.

"What is it?" Alida asked the lawyer. "What is she laughing at?"

"Please sit down, Miss Rimsky," said Snyder in the voice he usually reserved for the courtroom.

"Mrs. Varonsky," corrected Alida. "This is my husband. He is newly arrived in the city. He is the *maître de ballet* of the Baronovitch ballet company." The men shook hands.

The lawyer didn't know what the hell she was talking about but accepted it on face value. After all, Alida was now a client of his and he rather liked her. The sudden materialization of a husband was like an arrow to his heart, as he had long fancied an affair with Alida as soon as his wife, who was fatally ill, made her long-awaited departure.

Malke's laughter was beginning to subside. She had rummaged in her cleavage and found a handkerchief which she now used to dab at her face. Mordecai had returned from the kitchen with the glass of seltzer, which Malke downed in one sustained gulp.

"Are you feeling better now, Malke?" asked the lawyer. Malke blew her nose with such force her nephew thought the room trembled. "Sit down, Mordecai," ordered the lawyer and Mordecai willingly complied. He'd had quite a night with Luba Nafka in her suite at the Ambassador Hotel and both were so exhausted she barely made it to the photo shoot, and he ached to soak in a hot bath.

Malke looked at Mr. Snyder and then at Alida and finally at Mordecai and her body began to shake in prelude to another fit of laughter.

"Please, Malke, please!" pleaded the lawyer. She managed to gain control of herself and then sat back with a sigh, moving her head from side to side, disbelieving something the others would soon be hearing.

The lawyer cleared his throat and explained to Alida and Mordecai, "I made this appointment last night with Malke when she phoned to tell me of Dr. Romanov's sad and unexpected demise."

"Unexpected!" And Malke was laughing again.

"Malke!" shouted Snyder and it was effective. The laughter strangled in her throat and this caused a fit of coughing during which Varonsky said to Alida, "I must get back for the photographs and then the rehearsal. Fred has blocked his preliminary movements and this morning he phoned bubbling with enthusiasm. Hermes Pan was even able to secure the services of their favorite rehearsal pianist, whom Fred says they expect to adapt the Khrennikov symphony for them. This, of course, is great progress. Americans move so fast!"

"Oh we do move fast, indeed we do," said Snyder who had overheard Varonsky now that Malke's coughing had died like the stalling motor of a Mack truck. "All better now, Malke?" asked the overly solicitous lawyer.

"Yes, yes, I am fine. I am sorry." She asked Varonsky, "You will forgive me, please." Then she looked at Mordecai and chuckled.

Mordecai was annoyed. "What is so funny about me?"

"Not you, all three of us. Me, Alida, and you. Wait till you hear!" She urged the lawyer, "Go ahead, Mr. Snyder, tell them."

Snyder folded his hands on the desk. "Mordecai, Mrs. Varonsky . . . did I get that right?"

"Very good," complimented Varonsky while Alida smiled weakly. Her intuition warned her a bombshell was about to be dropped.

"I've already congratulated Malke, now I have the pleasure of congratulating you, Alida, and you, Mordecai. On the desk are copies of Dr. Romanov's will. One for each of you and I'm anxious to file it for probate, which was the doctor's wish and officially documented and signed elsewhere." He held up a sheet of paper. "I won't read the entire will as it has all those dreadfully boring whereases and wherefores and the rest of the deadly legal phraseology, which I loathe and I'm sure you would too if you had to listen to as much of it as I do every day."

He riffled the pages and Alida was beginning to feel giddy. *He has left me something. A keepsake. A memento. His appointment book.*

The lawyer was clearing his throat again and riffling papers. Mordecai was perspiring with anticipation. *What could Romanov have left him? The cars? Oh yes! Probably the cars. He would keep one and sell the other two. How many could he drive at one time?*

Snyder was speaking. "The house and its contents will have to be completely inventoried. I will leave that to you three. Of course one of my assistants will work with you to make sure everything is in order. It's not that you aren't trusted, it is required by law."

Alida sat forward and spoke up. "Mr. Snyder, exactly what are you supposed to be telling us?"

"Oh my, do forgive me, I'd already told Malke."

"We're rich!" boomed Malke. "The three of us are loaded! He's left us everything! Everything!" She boomed the word again. "Everything! This house with all its acreage! The contents! The furnishings! The paintings! His bank accounts! And you want to know why I am laughing? Because it was the bastard's little joke. He guessed what was going on and now he exacts his revenge from the grave. Because with all this wealth, how can we go on being communists?"

He guessed what was going on and now he exacts his revenge from the grave.

Snyder considered himself a true Hollywood sophisticate. He belonged to a country club. He played golf and tennis. He drank martinis with three olives, and he was in his third year of trying to read *War and Peace.* He enjoyed watching television tremendously but told everyone he loathed it. In his household there were three in help, a cook, a maid, and a man of all work. There was a part-time gardener and a part-time pool man. But what had Romanov suspected was going on and what kind of revenge was he exacting from the grave? Leaving this trio in a financially advantageous position was a form of revenge? Such revenge should befall him. He held his peace. He asked no questions. With all this money, Malke had asked, how could they go on being communists? Though they were of Russian origin, it had never occurred to him they might be dyed-in-the-wool dedicated communists. And therefore, would he be guilty by association?

Alida asked, "Supposing the will is contested?"

"Who by? He has no known relatives, unless—do you know of any relatives?"

None of the heirs did. "So you see, the three of you are home free."

Varonsky was on his feet hugging Alida, Malke dabbed at her eyes. The tears now were genuine; she now found it affecting to be an heiress and she was already planning how to stash her inheritance so that the Soviets couldn't possibly demand a share if not all of it. Mordecai was planning the wardrobe for his debut on the Ed Sullivan show and whether to permit Luba Nafka to hitchhike a trip to his future success by riding on his coattails. Last night she spoke of commitment after five years of separation, the plan to defect and find a worthier international career. He wondered what the strange look on Morris Snyder's face meant. Then he nursed the chilling thought that Snyder was now harboring suspicions about Igor Romanov's death. He would discuss this with Malke at the first opportunity. Determination was reflected in his face but recognized by no one because no one was looking at him.

Varonsky asked Morris Snyder, "Will there be a mention of the inheritance in the newspapers?"

"I don't see why, unless you want one. I can have my friend Hazel Dickson spread the good news if you want it publicized." They all had met Hazel Dickson and preferred she not be involved. All agreed a cloak of silence should be the fashion for their windfall.

Snyder reminded them, "There is no avoiding taxes, you understand." He chuckled. "Perhaps you've heard the expression 'Nothing is inevitable except death and taxes.' "

Malke thought in Russian, "*Da,* this death has certainly led to taxes." She said in English, "We shall certainly not avoid paying taxes. I, after all, am an American citizen. And soon also Alida and Mordecai." And like all good Americans, thought the lawyer, you'll bust your gut setting up a scheme to defraud Uncle Sam. "I have an excellent tax lawyer in my office, and he'll be of great help to the three of you."

Varonsky consulted his pocket watch. "I must fly! I will be too late for the photographs. I shall go directly to rehearsal. Alida, you will have no transportation problem?" She assured him she wouldn't and walked him to the door. He took her hand and led her outside to his car where he said, "You heard what the cow said? Romanov exacts his revenge from the grave. The lawyer must be wondering what she meant by that."

"No, no," Alida reassured him, "I didn't see him react. He would have asked a question if she had aroused any suspicion. He and Romanov were good friends. Snyder's wife is dying and Romanov has been his rock of Gibraltar. Don't worry, Theodore." They kissed. "Have a good rehearsal. Tell me, my darling: do I taste any different now that I am an heiress?"

After a conference with the head of his department, it was agreed that Villon with Mallory's assistance would spend as much time as he deemed possible with the Baronovitch company. Silently, Jim Mallory was elated. He moved onto cloud nine and looked forward to a delightful and fruitful tenancy—all those nubile ballerinas—except for the few who had already been claimed by the male dancers. When the detectives arrived at this first rehearsal, they weren't surprised to find that Hazel Dickson already had staked out the territory half an hour earlier. Though the company hadn't had much sleep after the previous night's gala and the early photo call, they all were in high spirits and mentally alert, listening carefully as Fred and Hermes Pan blocked the opening scene. They were amazed at the resemblance Pan had to Astaire, insisting they must really be brothers. Ginger reassured the company they weren't, and was beginning to live her role of the empress, taking the younger dancers under her wing and being generous with her time. She knew she looked quite fetching in her rehearsal clothes, simple shorts and an even simpler blouse, the shorts sky blue and the blouse ivory white.

Esther Pincus, the rehearsal pianist, holding a container of black coffee, was pleased and flattered Ginger took the trouble to introduce herself, knowing Fred and Hermes swore by her. A rehearsal pianist could make or break you and although Ginger didn't shatter easily, she had to be sure Esther was an ally. In two seconds flat Esther adored her and assured her she would provide the right beat at the right time. "I'm amazed I've never played for you before."

"I know. Isn't it crazy? But I haven't done a musical in years."

"Which is a crying shame. Look, I think Fred is signaling you."

Ginger turned and saw Fred at the opposite end of the large rehearsal room and shouted she'd be right there. And then she smiled, delighted to see Villon and Mallory were with Fred. Of course! He had the results of the autopsy.

She passed Sol Hurok and Mae Frohman who were at a table with the designer, poring over the costume and scenic designs he'd spread across the table. "Very good," said Hurok, "I admit I am very unpressed."

"Impressed," corrected Mae.

Hurok, as always, ignored her interruption. There were those who suspected Hurok deliberately mangled the English language when Mae was present to give her the pleasure of correcting him. Little did he know she found correcting his speech tiresome, and frequently thought of telling him. It was the way he mispronounced names that frequently came close to driving her around the bend. Miss Heartburn was Katharine Hepburn. Helen Herz was Helen Hayes. Josie Furrier was Jose Ferrer. And when it came to Rabindranath Tagore, forget about it.

Villon told Fred and Ginger the result of Romanov's autopsy.

Fred insisted Romanov had to know what was being done to him. Ginger had some doubts. "Remember, Fred, when they'd give a mickey to obnoxious drunks in speakeasies, those guys keeled over faster than a whore landed on her back."

"Mickeys," Fred reminded her, having in his time bribed a waiter to slip one to an offensive character, "work right away, when they work, but Romanov was a long-term proposition. Why, I'm not quite sure, but I'll bet his killers thought they knew what they were doing."

"They knew what they were doing because it was an old Russian custom. Death in small doses. If the victim takes a long time dying, it's less suspicious than if he keels over right there on the spot." Villon accepted a container of coffee from Mallory, who had ordered them for himself and Villon. "It would have worked with Romanov because he might have had the occasional discomfort that goes with an intestinal disturbance, but for some reason, the process had to be hurried up, so Nina Valgorski did the honors."

It was the first time her name had been mentioned by Villon in connection with the murder and the stars were dumbfounded. Ginger gasped, and Villon quickly placed an index finger on his lips warning silence. He told them how she had placed the cadmium in Romanov's soda water.

"And to think I admired that whistle," said Ginger. "Boy, them there commies sure do think up some bizarre ways to knock a person off."

Villon asked, "Are you frightened?"

"Speaking as a one-time girl scout and a girl guide, hell no. Speaking for myself thirty years later, don't you dare let me out of your sight!"

"Now, Ginger," asked Fred, "who would want to kill you?"

Ginger snapped, "I can think of half a dozen actresses and as many leading men, with equal time for as many directors."

"Ginger," Fred reminded her, "they are none of them in this company."

"Just don't share your thoughts with anyone in the company," advised Villon, "and you'll make it past New Year's Eve."

"Thanks a bunch," said Ginger morosely. "So Fred and I are the only ones who know the autopsy result."

"Right," said Villon.

"Would it bother you if I told you I don't feel privileged?" She borrowed Villon's container of coffee and took a much needed swig. "Awful! No sugar!"

"But plenty of Ginger!" exclaimed Mallory, who was chagrined by the moans with which he was rewarded.

Ginger patted his hand. "It's okay, cutie, I get it all the time." She asked Villon, "Will the autopsy results be published?"

"Not unless you don't lower your voice," said Fred. Hazel was headed toward them. She wore no hat and her hair was back to its natural brown color. Only Villon noticed the absence of gray hair.

"Now you look like Hazel Dickson," said Villon.

Hazel said swiftly, "The four of you look like you just partook of a mouse. Okay, Herb, what's being kept from me?" She didn't wait for an answer. "Edgar Rowe confirmed your suspicions. I knew it!"

"You know nothing," said Villon, not attempting to hide the threat in his voice. "I don't want to see a line about it in the papers, you get me?"

"Why not?"

"Because I say so."

Ginger leaned forward conspiratorially and said to Hazel, "You don't want to give the game away, do you?"

"What game?"

Fred said, "The four killers shouldn't guess Herb knows who they are and what they did."

Ginger added, "Or Herb might blow the whistle on you!" They probably didn't get it because there was no applause. Glumly she asked Fred, "Shouldn't we be rehearsing?"

Fred actually wore a whistle around his neck as did Hermes Pan. Whistles were necessary at rehearsals, especially for a group as large as this one. They were plain, ordinary, five-and-dime-store whistles of the kind worn by gym instructors. The company rallied at Fred's signal and stood in varying poses and positions, waiting for Fred's words.

He said in Russian, "Welcome, my comrades!" Sol Hurok beamed. He had taught the words to Fred earlier, and the company exploded in laughter and applause.

"Showoff," said Ginger under her breath.

"I don't have as much time with you as I would like," said Fred, "but we're going to make the most of what we've got. This gentleman"—he put his arm around Hermes—"is my partner and if I'm not available, he will help you. His name is Hermes Pan."

"Pan?" Nina Valgorski asked Theodore Varonsky, who arrived late because Alida's instructions to get him to the rehearsal were secondhand from Mordecai. "Pan?" repeated Nina, "that is all? What a terribly strange country with terribly strange names." She was a vision in imitation leopardskin leotards even while eating a tunafish salad sandwich. She explained to Mikhail Bochno, the *régisseur général,* "I had very little breakfast."

Fred said to the eager company, "We're going to have a lot of fun with *Rasputin.*"

Gregor Sukov said gloomily, "There was nothing funny about Rasputin."

"There is now," said Fred with determination, "because I see him as funny. I'm sure they have this expression in the Soviet Union, 'One man's meat is another man's poison,' " and from the look on Villon's face, he wished he hadn't said it.

"Fred, I have this gut feeling that *Rasputin* is going to be one of the most delightful ballets ever." Ginger hoped Fred appreciated her support. The ballet dancers weren't exactly madly enthusiastic. They stood staring at Fred, Ginger, and Hermes Pan as though they were candidates for a firing squad.

A nervous Sol Hurok said to Mae Frohman, "What did Shakespeare write about the quality of moishie?"

"Mercy," corrected Mae.

Nina asked Fred, "You will dress like Rasputin dressed? Unclean, unwashed, unappetizing?"

Fred felt a surge of impatience. He sensed the hostility of the troupe toward an American upstart daring to choreograph for Russian dancers, famous movie star or no famous movie star. He decided to grab the bull by the horns. "Now, look, let's get one thing straight. I was asked by Mr. Hurok to choreograph this ballet and dance in it with Miss Rogers. You see, there's an institution in this country known as Box Office. On your tour to date your box office was better than expected because you had no competition from other ballet companies. Am I right, Sol?"

"Positively!" cried Hurok.

Fred continued, "On television, it's quite another story. Television viewers in this country have a choice of several channels. The other channels might have opposite us a baseball game, or a popular comedy series or a drama. Well, it's up to us to draw as big an audience as possible. On its own, I can easily predict the Baronovitch Ballet will be a big loser." Now the company was uneasy. "That's why Mr. Hurok enticed Ginger and myself into appearing with you. We draw big audiences, we are Mr. Hurok's insurance that you will have a very big percentage of viewers. Face it. You are not known in this country and we are a very big country. But after one successful appearance on television, the name Baronovitch will be on everyone's lips. And I don't think you will find anywhere in the world audiences as enthusiastic as you will find in this country!"

Carried away, Esther Pincus began playing "Anchors Aweigh." Fred hushed her.

He asked the company, "Do I have your cooperation?" There was a smattering of applause. "And if you want to know what we'll all be wearing, there's a display of the costumes we'll be wearing on that table." He made a vague gesture to the right of him. He then began with renewed enthusiasm to reel off what he hoped would be the highlights of the thirty-minute ballet which would close the program, forcing viewers to hang in past highlights from such ballet warhorses as *Firebird, Swan Lake,* and *Coppélia.* He knew Hurok preferred the finale to be a song and dance number by Fred and Ginger, and if he and Ginger agreed, Fred thought of using one of his own songs, "I Need a Shoulder to Cry On."

"Of course everybody in Russia knows Rasputin was a sexual pervert, but Americans know very little about him so we'll have to treat his perverted side delicately."

"Why?" asked Nina.

"Well you see, Nina, we are very puritanical. I mean, we can't depict Rasputin raping women and seducing young men."

"So show him seducing old men!" said Nina, which drew her a laugh.

"Miss Valgorski, why do I get the feeling you'd prefer not to participate in my ballet?"

She took a few steps toward him with her hands on her hips. "Who says I will not participate?"

"Your very weak little jokes tell me you are hostile toward me."

Mae Frohman beamed with approval. Hurok mopped his brow. Hazel Dickson had already decided she'd sell this slight contretemps to Hedda Hopper, who wanted the show to be a loser.

From the sound of Fred's voice and the look on his face, Nina knew he was prepared to take her on and she also knew he would have to be victorious or the ballet was in jeopardy, and no Fred and Ginger, there would be no NBC. The project had been widely publicized in the USSR, where it was promised a television showing by way of a kinescope. "Forgive my very weak little jokes. Weak little jokes are one of my very little weaknesses." Her voice encompassed the company. "Forgive me, comrades. I offer our dear Fred Astaire my complete cooperation, and I expect the same from everyone in the company. But it is a historical fact that Rasputin was a filthy slob!"

"Don't worry, Nina. I'm cleaning him up." Fred blew his whistle hard. Ginger expected him to announce a football formation. The whistle was Hermes Pan's cue to move the dancers into position for the grand procession which would open the ballet. Nobody had seen her change into it, but Luba Nafka suddenly pirouetted into their midst wearing a white tutu. She halted with practiced precision in front of Fred.

"You like it?" she asked coquettishly.

"Tutu divine, now get into a leotard and make it snappy." Luba slunk away.

Sol Hurok shook his head and clucked his tongue. "What has gotten into them today!"

Mae said by way of explanation, "Mr. Hurok, you've been around ballet companies long enough to recognize they're testing the authority of the fledgling choreographer."

"They wouldn't dare do this to Balanchine!"

"I don't think Balanchine would consider a ballet about Rasputin. I'll get us coffee." She marched across the room toward a table near the piano where the coffee urn had been placed. Hermes Pan had joined Esther Pincus at the piano and was making notations in her score as ordered by Fred.

While Mae filled two cardboard containers with coffee, she overheard Hermes Pan ask Esther, "What's the matter, Esther, you look as though you've seen a ghost." He expected her to cross herself from the weird look on her face, but then remembered she was Jewish.

Esther replied to his question in a strained voice. "I think I have."

Sixteen

*H*azel said to Herb Villon, "Are you deliberately ignoring Don Magrew?"

"Magrew? Where is he?"

"Yonder," she indicated with a toss of her head. Villon saw Magrew standing beyond Hermes Pan and Esther Pincus and
crossed to greet him. They shook hands and Magrew led Villon
to a spot where he felt they'd be out of earshot of anyone.

"Your precinct told me where I could find you."

"Something urgent?"

"Herb, it's like this. Romanov's poisoning poses some prob-
lems."

"Oh yes?" asked Herb.

"Look, I'm leveling with you because I have to now. I kept some
information from you because we didn't think it necessary to let
the police know too much."

"Magrew, I never can know too much. But I know a lot more
than I did yesterday. And there's a hell of a lot more I need to
know and intend to find out, with or without your cooperation.
You want spies and I want killers. Damn this noise!" The opening procession featured a lot of foot stomping accompanied by

Fred and Hermes Pan imitating the blaring of trumpets. Esther Pincus pounded the piano ferociously while Sol Hurok was beginning to feel optimistic. He could envision the majesty of the great entrance once the company was in full regalia, and bemoaned to Mae Frohman how sad it was that color television was years away from being perfected.

Villon and Magrew had moved to the hallway where they still could hear the sounds of the rehearsal, although they were now somewhat deadened. Villon told Magrew, "Let me tell you what I've deduced so far and then I'll give you equal time to pump me."

Magrew nodded. The inevitable pipe was in his mouth and he applied a match to the tobacco in the bowl. Villon hated pipes as much as he hated cigars. He wondered if Magrew had left it in his will that he was to be buried with his pipe in his mouth. Magrew asked, "So? What have you deduced?"

"Romanov was a Russian agent. You guys caught on and rather than put him behind bars you kept him in front of them, bending elbows with Hollywood's best when he had the time away from his very busy practice. If he thought he learned anything useful from a patient, he turned it over to the reds for dissemination."

Magrew continued, "We fed Romanov what he fed the reds. They got suspicious and therefore he was a very likely candidate for the slow death."

"Why didn't you guys warn him?"

"We did."

"And he did nothing to save himself?"

Magrew was finally content with the glow in the pipe bowl. "He only had a short time left anyway. Bone marrow disease. Something like that."

"No options for the poor bastard. I kind of feel sorry for him." It was obvious to Villon that Magrew didn't. Cold-hearted buggers, the CIA. "The small doses were fed by his household staff. The housekeeper, her nephew, and the nurse." He waited. Magrew didn't comment. His face was neutral. No mention of Nina Valgorski. Odd.

"And you haven't sufficient evidence to bag the three."

"That's right. I'll get them in time."

"I admire your confidence." Villon would politely admire some of his but Magrew didn't seem to be confidant of anything special, and Villon knew he was holding back. Sneaky devil.

Villon said, "You know the nurse Alida is married to Theodore Varonsky?"

"We sure do. She's been busting a gut trying to get him out from behind the iron curtain. We finally got Hurok to make a bid for Baronovitch so we could get him here."

"Hurok is a tool of the CIA?" Villon couldn't see the impresario wearing a cloak or wielding a dagger, but apparently he did and quite deftly.

"It's been highly profitable for Hurok. He's amazed the company's been doing so well at the box office. And we're delighted because the deal is that Uncle Sammy covers his losses. Then of course up popped NBC with their offer and so now we're home free."

"Varonsky doesn't have to return to the Soviet when the company does?"

"He's defecting, along with Luba Nafka and Gregor Sukov. Nafka and Sukov are planning a company of their own along with Mordecai Pfenov. They all share the big dream of easy capitalistic money. They're so innocent, they just might make it big."

"Malke Movitz," said Villon.

"What about her?"

"She's the real head of the ring here."

"You think?" asked Magrew.

"Haven't you guys considered it?"

"Not really. We've actually had no reason to."

"Now don't shit me, Magrew."

"I swear!"

Villon didn't believe him, but didn't tell him. Instead he chose a different path, the long way around. "She seemed to have little difficulty escaping the Soviet Union to Paris and her quaint little café. Seems to me she was given the same route as Romanov. Stands to reason they were set up to operate as a pair. I learned long ago that's the way the reds operate. In pairs."

"I have to admit, that's a very sound observation."

"You going to let the three stay if they defect?"

"Oh, they'll definitely defect. Gregor Sukov and Luba Nafka are harmless. She's in love with Movitz's nephew; Sukov is still continuing his undying romance with himself. Varonsky will get special treatment. We suspect he knows a hell of a lot about the locations of Russian nuclear stations and warheads, privileged information that's come his way over the years. Once we get it out of him and where he can do us no harm, we'll give him a hot dog stand in Coney Island where undoubtedly he will thrive."

"Magrew, why do you suppose I keep nursing this cockamamie idea that somewhere in this country there's somebody who's really calling the shots for the Russians?"

"Herb, that's always a possibility. Look at the Rosenbergs."

"I have. Expendables. Small fry. Not worth spending the money to jail and fry them. They ought to free them and set them up with a chicken farm in New Jersey."

"They won't." He thought for a moment and then asked Herb, "This theory of yours that there's an X factor secretly running the espionage ring—got any suspicions?"

"I haven't gotten that deeply into it."

"When you do, let an old buddy in on it, okay?"

"Why sure, old buddy. I'm enjoying this game of give and take."

"I'm going to let you in on something else. I don't know what it will mean to you, but on the other hand, you never can tell." The light in his pipe bowl was dimming and he applied a match to the bowl. As he sucked on the stem of the pipe, he told Villon, "Romanov accumulated quite a fortune."

"Yes? All from his practice?"

"And some shrewdness on his own part. Stocks, bonds, real estate, you name it. He left it equally to Alida Rimsky, Malke Movitz, and her nephew."

Now Villon was astonished. "He's not dead twenty-four hours and you know this for a fact?"

"His lawyer was a help." He winked.

"So now Varonsky has every reason to defect and if he has to, live off his wife and you know what you can do with your hot dog stand." Villon was quiet for a moment. "There's no more noise from in there." He led the way back into the rehearsal hall. As they walked, "I suppose the contents of the will are top secret for now."

"I'm sure the heirs prefer it that way. The KGB is notorious for attempting to confiscate what they consider ill-gotten assets. After all, they trained Romanov. They set him up here. Without them, he might be playing piano in some Moscow cocktail bar. Except you won't find many cocktail bars in Russia. He might be a re-hearsal pianist like the lady over there." He was referring, of course, to Esther Pincus.

Villon asked Hazel, "What's going on?"

The entire company was sitting on the floor, each in the lotus position, arms folded across their chests, eyes shut. Hazel said with a note of whimsicality, "They're meditating."

"Meditating?"

"Yes, Herb. Meditating. It's to relieve tension. Fred thought they were all too tense. Look, even Hurok's joined in."

Hurok whispered to Mae meditating next to him, "Do I look like the god, Butter?"

"Buddha," corrected Mae, "and you're not meditating."

"Meditating! What kind of *mishagoss* is meditating?"

"It's good for the soul," whispered Mae.

Hurok's eyes flew open. "Better it should be good for the show."

Esther Pincus sat on the piano seat. No sitting on the floor for her, not with her arthritis. She was tired of meditating. She was thinking of old ghosts, ghosts she had tried to lay to rest for many years. She thought again of Paris because she would always think of Paris. So much of her past was there. She opened her eyes. She reached for her container of coffee, and sipped. It was cold. She went to the table that held the coffee and the containers and poured herself a fresh cup. She carried it back to the piano on tiptoe, as she usually set up a clatter with her heels when she walked. She saw Villon and Hazel with Don Magrew. She sipped her coffee. She tried to remember a name. She played the alphabet game with herself. A for Aronoff, B for Beauregard, C for Colman, hoping to remember a name for which she was probing about in her brain. She had chatted briefly earlier with Hazel Dickson and now considered her an old friend.

Stifling a yawn, Hazel saw Esther trying to catch her attention. Maybe she wanted Villon or Magrew. Hazel pointed to herself. Esther nodded her head. Hazel had asked her half an hour ago to keep her eyes and her ears open for any tidbits of gossip Hazel might use in her line of work, which she had explained to Esther with a promise of ten bucks for anything of value. My God, thought Hazel, she can't have come up with something already.

With caution she picked her way through some of the meditators. As she passed Nina Valgorski, she saw the whistle hanging from the chain around her neck. She remembered at once what Villon had told her about Nina and the whistle. Nina had told him last night the whistle was filled with slivasomething. She couldn't remember the name of the liqueur. Hazel sat on the piano bench next to Esther.

"What have you got for me?" asked Hazel.

"I'm sorry. I have nothing so far."

"Oh."

"But perhaps you can help me."

Hazel awaited the worst. The last woman who had said that was desperately in need of an abortionist and Hazel was able to oblige with a list of six. "What's wrong, Esther? Are you in trouble?"

"That man you and Mr. Villon are talking to."

"Don Magrew?"

"Don Magrew?" Esther ran the name through her mind while watching Nina Valgorski get to her feet and stretch her arms and then do some bends to relax her knees.

Hazel repeated Magrew's name.

"No," said Esther, "it does not tell me anything."

"What did you expect it to tell you?"

"That I knew him a long time ago. His face is familiar but the name is not."

"Where did you think you knew him?"

"Oh, it is so silly. I'm sorry I bothered you."

Hazel shrugged, got up, and walked away. Most of the company were on their feet and doing a variety of limbering-up exercises. Meditating in the lotus position, Hazel decided, could also bring on paralysis. Nina looked as though she was enjoying flattery from Don Magrew. Villon was talking to Jim Mallory. Hazel looked back at Esther. There was something bothering the woman. Hazel went to Villon and Mallory.

"Boys, there's something interesting going on with Esther Pincus."

"I'm listening," said Villon.

"It's about Don Magrew. She asked me who he was. I told her. But the name Magrew wasn't familiar. I think she thinks she knew him in years past under another identity."

"You're spooking yourself, Hazel."

That irritated Hazel. "I am not. If anything, it's Esther who's spooking me. I think she knew him in Europe."

"It would have to be Europe because she's never been out of L.A. since settling here with her husband."

Hazel said warmly, "Oh, I'm so glad she's married. I had this kind of sad picture of her going home every night to a bowl of chopped vegetables and sour cream and a glass of buttermilk."

"Her husband's dead," said Villon.

"Oh. Then I've probably got the menu right."

Herb was silent briefly. "CIA boys get around a lot. I know Magrew has had assignments in Europe and Asia. I'm going to have a chat with Esther. You two stay here and you," he warned Hazel, "don't drum up an excuse to come over and stick your nose in."

"I never do any such thing," said Hazel defensively. Villon left her in midsentence and walked slowly to Esther Pincus, who was studying Hermes Pan's notations, but with her mind too preoccupied to absorb much. Herb passed Nina and Magrew, Nina fingering her whistle while presumably flirting with Magrew. Villon decided it was an act on both their parts. They must have met on the tour prior to coming to Los Angeles. Besides, when on assignment, CIA operatives were warned not to fool around with the opposite sex, unless it was for a purpose other than having a wingding. Magrew caught Villon's eye and winked. He's big on winking, thought Villon. Nina smiled at Villon while making an exaggerated show of the whistle. Esther played a few chords and as Herb reached her he said, "That's very nice."

"Oh yes, Khrennikov is very schmaltzy. He hasn't the pure lines of Shostakovich or the bravado of Prokofiev, but he is serviceable."

Villon dived right in. "Hazel Dickson tells me you think you recognized Don Magrew from another time in your life."

Esther was nervous. She missed a few notes and rubbed her hands together by way of making her fingers behave. "My hands are cold."

From fear? wondered Villon. He said, "It's not cold in the hall."

"I suffer from poor circulation. A family curse. I'll be fine in a few minutes."

Villon realized he had frightened the woman but said nothing about it. "Magrew is with the CIA."

"Yes."

"They usually assign someone to ride herd on foreign groups."

"I know. Especially Russian troupes. I am Russian too, but I am a citizen of the United States."

"Miss Pincus, just out of curiosity, could you tell me for sure if you've known this man before?"

Esther looked at Magrew and Nina and then looked into Villon's face. Such a nice face, she thought, despite the tired eyes and the tiny lines around the mouth. She asked Villon, "Is it so important? I don't think it's very important. Until I came to this city, I never knew important people. I think Miss Dickson has made, as you say, a mountain out of a molehill." Villon could see she was improvising, she was frightened, she probably wished she had not asked about Magrew. Esther continued, "This is terribly unsettling. I'm sorry I asked about him. I'm probably mistaken. I'm always thinking I've met people before and then it turns out I am wrong." She turned her attention to Hermes Pan's notations and played several chords by way of dismissing Villon. He saw no future in pressing her, commented that the music was lovely, and excused himself. In the center of the hall, Fred was busy rehearsing several members of the corps who represented the czar's retinue. Hermes Pan counted to twenty and then signaled Ginger. Ginger raised her hands above her head with what she hoped was a soulful expression on her face and then came plowing into the midst of the dancers, clattering away with a pair of castanets attached to her fingers.

Mae Frohman was somewhat bewildered. She said to Sol Hurok, "I think Fred has his royal courts confused."

"No no no," said Hurok, "the queen loved the music of Spain and had taken lessons in dancing to the music of both Spain and Portugal. From Portugal she learned the *fada*."

"Ah yes," said Mae Knowledgeable, "life with *fada*."

At the piano, Esther was growing restless. Fred and Hermes were notorious among dancers for dispensing with the piano for long periods during rehearsal; it had something to do with the dancers learning the music in their heads or some such idiosyncrasy. She kept her eyes on Hermes Pan, who might signal her at any moment to start playing. Now she carefully followed his notations, at last understanding where he wanted the piano silent and where he wanted the music to resume. She wanted more coffee but didn't dare risk leaving the piano. God was on her side; Fred called a break and Esther made it to the coffee urn.

Villon told Mallory and Hazel that Pincus had clammed up. "I think she's positive she's met Magrew before and isn't quite sure of under what name she knew him, but I'll give odds she knew him somewhere in Europe."

Hazel suggested, "Maybe it's not his past that has her frightened, maybe it's her own. She's a good-looking broad even at her age. . . ."

"And what age is that?" asked Villon.

"Strikes me she's reluctantly pushing fifty. They might have had a toss in the hay in the past. Maybe a very fascinating one-night stand."

"Fascinating or not, who can remember a one-night stand of years gone by?" Villon was looking at Hazel. Hazel had what Villon considered to be a very silly smile on her face and regretted asking the question.

Ginger had arrived minus the castanets and said to Mallory, "Cigarette me, big boy," a line she had delivered piquantly in her first feature film, *Young Man of Manhattan*, which brought her to the attention of critics and public alike. Mallory lit her cigarette and Ginger then asked, "Any comments on the castanets?"

"I think it's kind of an exotic touch," said Hazel.

"I won't get away with it and neither will Fred. For crying out loud, great Spanish dancers like Argentinita and Carmen Amaya—I mean castanets to them are like two more fingers, and it's all I can do to maneuver my ten fingers. I've got to talk to Esther Pincus. She'll be a help. Hey Esther! I'm on my way!" She breezed off toward Esther and Villon marveled at the woman's energy.

Mallory had been focused on Nina Valgorski, who using Fred's arm for ballast, was standing on point and gracefully extended a leg. Fred smiled and nodded, apparently pleased he'd gotten a much desired movement from Nina. "Herb," said Mallory.

"What?"

"She's wearing the whistle."

"I saw it."

"She's very attached to that whistle," said Mallory.

"I know."

"What's with the whistle?" asked Hazel. "Is it really a whistle?"

Ginger sat next to Esther, an arm around the pianist's shoulders as Esther showed her some of Hermes Pan's notations on the sheet music. "Here Fred will lift you," said Esther.

"While I'm clicking those damn castanets?"

"Some of the corps will be wearing castanets too and Fred said the orchestra will interpolate some of de Falla's *Three-Cornered Hat*. Fred will then lower you to the floor and break into a flamenco."

"While I break into a rash," Ginger said forlornly. "Why couldn't he do a ballet of something classically Russian like *Uncle Vanya?*"

"What?"

"Why, Esther, I didn't mean to startle you. *Vanya,* you know, Chekhov."

"Yes, yes. At first I thought you said something else. Vanoff."

"Oh baby, we're not back to Vanoff again!"

Her voice carried and reached Don Magrew, who was standing nearby with Hurok and Mae Frohman. His eyes moved to Ginger and Esther. Esther's face was an interesting study. She looked at her wristwatch, wondering how soon Fred would want the music to resume.

Ginger, studying the score, said, "This section coming up is awfully rinky-dink, you know, like that weird French composer, George Somebody."

"Antheil," said Esther.

"Right!" said Ginger. "Did you ever meet him?"

Esther was now calm and collected, as though, while piloting a plane in bad weather, she had suddenly encountered a most welcome break in the clouds. "Yes, I met George Antheil. I met him in Paris. We were introduced by a mutual friend. I remember it as though it was yesterday. It was in a café on the Left Bank, a popular hangout for musicians and composers and Russian émigrés. The woman who ran it was quite unique. She was big and very homely but cooked and baked like an angel."

"Malke Movitz!" Ginger said, "What a coincidence! Don't you know she's here in Beverly Hills? She's been here for years!" Esther stared at Ginger, digesting everything Ginger told her, listening like a child whose mother was rewarding her with a bedtime story. "Don't you read the papers? She was Dr. Romanov's housekeeper!"

"The doctor who was murdered?"

"Poisoned. Very nasty."

"Poisoned," echoed Esther.

"It's getting very crowded around here," said Ginger. Members of the corps were helping themselves to coffee and pastries, leading Ginger to comment that ballet dancers had trencherman appetites. Esther, anxious to hear more from Ginger, didn't notice that her container of coffee had been replaced with a container of fresh brew and urged Ginger back to Malke and Romanov. Ginger didn't need much urging. In every spare moment, and she didn't have all that many, she had been running the scenario of Romanov's murder through her mind, wondering if somewhere in the scenario there was a clue that had been so obscure it was being overlooked. She then asked Esther if she'd heard of Nikolai Vanoff, Romanov's poisoning bringing to mind the same method used by Nikolai Vanoff to slay his parents.

"Every Russian has heard of Nikolai Vanoff," said Esther. "He was a very important man in the Soviet Union. He was practically Stalin's right arm. He was also murdered." She drank some of her coffee.

Ginger said, "I think that no-good brother of his, the one who pulled a disappearing act, vanished into thin air, I think he killed Nikolai." She made a shoving motion with both her hands. "Pushed him out of the window of Nina Valgorski's apartment."

Esther said to her, "That is a very . . ." She blinked her eyes quickly as though trying to clear away a cobweb. ". . . logical . . . deduction. . . ."

"Esther? Don't you feel well?"

Esther grabbed Ginger's hand. "Villon . . ."

"Yes?"

"The detective . . ."

"What about him?" My God, thought Ginger, is she putting the finger on Villon? Esther was damp with perspiration. Ginger was frightened. Esther's grip was very tight on her hand. Panicked, Ginger shouted, "Herb! Herb!"

Mae Frohman, who had been getting coffee for Hurok, heard Ginger, recognized the urgency in her voice, handed the coffee to a male dancer, saying, "Here, take a bath," and then hurried to Villon, who was chatting with Nina and Mikhail Bochno, the *régisseur général*. She grabbed Villon's arm. "Quick! There's trouble! Ginger's yelling for you!"

Villon followed Mae back to the piano, behind them Nina and Bochno. Fred saw the procession and sensed there was trouble. He hurried after them. Ginger had sent a dancer for a doctor and someone handed her a container of water for Esther. Villon was kneeling at Esther's side. Her eyes opened, and she recognized him.

"I've sent for a doctor," Ginger told Villon, who now held Esther in his arms. Ginger was dipping a handkerchief into the container of water and trying to moisten Esther's lips.

Fred knelt next to Villon and Esther. "What's wrong with Esther?"

Ginger said almost hysterically, "We were talking about the Vanoffs."

Villon said, "The Vanoffs?" Esther was trying to tell him something. Villon yelled for quiet. The dancers were buzzing among themselves as only dancers can, very cacophonous. Villon moved his head, his ear near Esther's mouth. Only Ginger and Fred were able to hear what she said. They both stared at Villon. Villon yelled for Mallory, unaware he was standing behind him.

"I'm here," said Mallory.

"Help me carry her to that couch." The couch was against the wall near the exit. Villon held Esther under her arms and Mallory held her feet, wondering why the chore hadn't been assigned to a pair of muscular dancers. As they carried her, Villon said to Hazel who was walking alongside them and fearing the worst for Esther, "Call the precinct. Get an ambulance and back up and hurry!"

Sol Hurok sat on a chair, with Mae holding a vial of smelling salts under his nose. "Take another whiff, Mr. Hurok. It's not the end of the world. The show will go on."

"A pianist," he bellowed, "we need another pianist."

"Mr. Hurok," said Mae, "I don't think either Vladimir Horowitz or José Iturbi are in town."

Ginger was slapping Esther's wrists and wishing Lela, her mother, was there. She thrived on emergencies. She would know what to do until a doctor came. The rehearsal hall's official doctor couldn't be reached but Hazel had gotten through to the precinct. She told Villon help was on the way—an ambulance and additional detectives. She didn't tell him she had given the news to the Associated Press and that Esther's collapse would be carried on the TV and radio news programs. Hot on the heels of Romanov's murder at a gala for the ballet, the collapse of the ballet's rehearsal pianist was now even bigger news, especially if it turned out she also was murdered.

And murder was on everyone's mind. Villon felt for Esther's pulse but there was no longer a beat. Her eyes were partially open but Villon could tell from experience they were sightless. He looked at Fred and Ginger and could see they sensed the woman was dead. And now they heard sirens. Ginger stifled a sob. Fred put his arms around her to console her and a very surprised and startled Ginger would never stop telling this in the days and weeks that followed. Fred consoling her! Not yelling "That's the wrong move!" or "Ginger, no more goddamn feathers on the dress," but consoling her!

Villon was standing and with hands upraised exhorted the dancers to move back to clear a path for the ambulance attendants. He was surprised to see the coroner, Edgar Rowe, heading toward him. "Edgar, how the hell did you know she'd be dead?"

"I didn't! I assumed she was dead when the call came in to the precinct."

Herb asked Hazel, "Did you say Esther was dead?"

"Oh, I think I said that she looked like she was dying. Well, that's how she looked to me!"

Rowe was examining the body. "She's dead all right. Good show, Hazel. It saved time and here I am, Edgar on the spot." He lifted her eyelids, studied them and made weird noises, then used a wooden probe to force her mouth open. He looked up at Villon. "I think it's the same stuff that finished Romanov."

"Cadmium?"

"If that's what it was, that's what it is."

Nina Valgorski seemed hypnotized by Esther Pincus's body. Esther looked so calm, so serene, so at peace. Nina clutched the whistle dangling from the chain around her neck. She heard a familiar voice asking Nina if he might examine the whistle. Nina looked up into Villon's face. She detached the whistle. She pressed the tip and the top opened. Nina lifted the whistle to her mouth.

"Stop!" shouted Villon. But he was too late. Nina smiled at Villon.

"There is still some left. It is very, very good slivovitz." She handed the whistle to Villon, who sniffed it. It was undoubtedly a liqueur he smelled. He returned the whistle to Nina, who asked, "Would a person under suspicion of poisoning be stupid enough to use the same method again under the watchful eye of the detective who thinks she might have poisoned Romanov? Mr. Villon, why do you continue to forget I am a student of criminology?"

"I guess it's because I have so much to think about."

It was Hermes Pan who could use some consoling. His eyes were moist. He blew his nose. He watched the attendants wrap and strap Esther's body to a stretcher. Villon asked him, "Is there any next of kin?"

"Just a couple of hundred dancers, singers, and choreographers who will now not know how to get along without her." Fred Astaire whispered something to Villon and he gave Fred a friendly clap on the back. Edgar Rowe said to Villon, "Where do we send the body after the autopsy?"

Fred Astaire told him to deliver Esther to the Forest Lawn mortician, the cemetery where so many celebrities lay in their final resting places. Ginger said to Fred, "I suspect you've told them you'll pay for her funeral." Fred shrugged, embarrassed. "I'll pay for half," said Ginger.

"Oh, that's not necessary," remonstrated Fred.

Ginger wagged a finger at him. "Now Fred Austerlitz"—reverting to his real name as she always did when she wanted to make a point—"don't we always go Dutch?"

Hermes Pan assured Hurok he would procure an excellent pianist for the next day's rehearsals. Mae Frohman was holding the smelling salts under her own nose.

Outside the ambulance attendants braved the phalanx of newspaper photographers as they carried Esther to the ambulance. Several reporters were on hand and were in the rehearsal hall shouting questions at Villon, and the photographers now began to descend on Fred and Ginger. Mallory and some detectives soon cleared them out of the hall.

Edgar Rowe had not yet gone and was busy soliciting Fred and Ginger's autographs while softly singing to them "They Can't Take That Away From Me."

"My God," said Ginger to Fred, "a musical coroner."

A detective shouted to the coroner that his driver was impatient and Edgar Rowe shouted back something nasty and then finally made his exit. "Strange little man," said Fred to Villon, who smiled.

"City officials in this town are noted for their idiosyncrasies."

It was quiet in the rehearsal hall. The dancers had gone and Varonsky and Bochno were at one side of the room conferring with Hurok and Mae Frohman. The subject was Fred's ballet and Hurok was refusing to substitute it with a ballet from the Baronovitch's repertoire.

Mae Frohman found herself wandering to the other side of the room where Villon sat with Fred, Ginger, Jim Mallory, and Hazel Dickson. Ginger suddenly stood up and went to the piano. "Herb! Come here, please." Herb hurried to her. She pointed to the container of coffee Esther Pincus had sipped from. "It's Esther's. I'll bet that's how she was poisoned. Well, it was mob rule around here when Esther and I were talking. Anyone could have placed the container there. Now that I think of it, out of the corner of my eye I saw somebody's hand holding that container and putting it on the piano." She went on, "Esther took a swig and the next thing, she's not feeling well."

Fred said, "Poor baby. No slow death for Esther."

"No," agreed Villon, "no slow death for Esther. Someone was in a very big hurry to get rid of her."

Hermes Pan had come back to the rehearsal hall from the men's room, where he had gone to have a quiet cry. He joined the group with Villon in time to hear why Esther was dispatched with such seeming haste. He asked angrily, "Why the hell would anybody want to kill Esther?"

"Esther whispered a name to me. It took what little strength she had left," said Villon.

"Whose name?" demanded Fred.

"Feodor Vanoff." Only Hermes Pan didn't recognize the name. He didn't know the Vanoff story.

Ginger asked with astonishment. "Here? In this room? Feodor Vanoff? Herb? Did she tell you who Feodor Vanoff was?"

"No, but I can guess." He looked around the room. "Anybody see Don Magrew leave?"

Seventeen

The designer told Villon, "Mr. Magrew left with Nina a few minutes ago!" He stamped his foot and for several seconds spewed anger in Russian. Then reverting to English he said to Fred, "She was to discuss her costumes with me! She did not like what I had done. She wanted different costumes. On one she wanted feathers!"

"Feathers!" said Ginger with delight.

"Feathers!" echoed Fred ominously through clenched teeth. He said to Ginger, "Did you put her up to feathers?"

Ginger ignored him while snapping her fingers. "That's it! That's got to be it! Magrew is Feodor Vanoff. And Nina's his girl-friend! She's been his girlfriend for years!" Fred's face had lighted up.

Fred said, "She must have pushed Nikolai to his death from her apartment."

Ginger asked, "What about her alibi? No, Fred, Feodor murdered his brother in retaliation for Nikolai having murdered their parents. What a screwed-up family!" She saw Villon rushing from the ballroom with Jim Mallory and Hazel Dickson. "Where do you suppose they're going?"

"After Magrew and Nina. Come on, let's follow them. I want to be in on this finish!"

Ginger was running after Fred, who was hot in pursuit of Villon. "Where are we going?" shouted Ginger.

"To Romanov's!"

As Villon emerged from the rehearsal hall with Jim Mallory and Hazel Dickson, a detective told Villon he'd been trying to get through to the Romanov house but the line was continuously busy.

"Keep trying!" shouted Villon.

"Hey, Herb!" Fred shouted, "we'll be right behind you!"

Fred and Ginger were not the backup Villon had asked for, but he knew it was no use trying to discourage them. Jim Mallory was behind the wheel of his unmarked police car and as soon as Mallory and Hazel piled in, he took off. Hazel asked Villon, "What was that whistle bit all about?"

Villon was busy making sure Mallory remembered the way to Romanov's place. Mallory assured him he did while wondering where the turnoff to Beverly Hills was. Villon asked Hazel, "What did you ask me?"

"The whistle!" cried an exasperated Hazel. "The one around Nina's neck."

"It held slivovitz," said Herb. "It was the wrong whistle."

"Herb, stop confusing me!"

He told her about visiting Nina in her suite that morning, and the scene with the whistle which Villon was almost positive had contained the final fatal dose of cadmium.

"Smart lady," said Hazel, "rinsing it clean."

"She didn't rinse it clean," said Herb. "There's another whistle." He yelled at Mallory. "Make a right! Make a right! This is the turnoff!" Wheels screeched as Mallory worked the steering wheel and the car swerved sharply, almost throwing Hazel, in the backseat, to the floor.

"For crying out loud!" shouted Hazel, "you trying to cripple me?"

Herb was back with the whistles. "There's the slivovitz whistle and there's the cadmium whistle. Nina didn't have to switch them last night because they weren't suspect then."

"She couldn't have had a second whistle on her last night. That gown was form-fitting, she'd have had a bulge," reasoned Hazel.

"Magrew had the second whistle on him," said Villon. "His suit wasn't form-fitting."

"A very expensive suit," said Jim Mallory, hunched over the wheel as though participating in a race at Indianapolis.

"I know," said Villon. "You don't afford that suit on a CIA salary."

"Maybe he takes in washing," suggested Hazel.

They heard Mallory say, "There's a car up ahead tearing hell out of the asphalt."

"Sure," said Hazel, "and not a motorcycle cop in sight. If it was me I'd be ticketed within seconds."

"I hope it's Magrew and Nina," said Mallory, "and not some crazy kids from Hollywood High out joy riding."

"It's some crazy kids," said Villon, "but not from Hollywood High."

In Fred Astaire's car, speeding at eighty miles an hour, Ginger wished her heart wasn't in her mouth so she could say something. Fred had been theorizing about the murders and Ginger was fascinated at how unusually knowledgeable he seemed. He had gleaned information from Villon, but better yet Hermes Pan had known about Esther's life in Paris firsthand from Esther. "Esther met Feodor Vanoff at Malke Movitz's restaurant and apparently found him irresistible. She thought he was a handsome American student who smoked a pipe, and when he got around to asking 'Your place or mine,' it had to be his because she lived with her aunt and didn't know or want to know auntie's reaction to her entertaining a young man in her boudoir."

Ginger asked, "Did she know him as Feodor Vanoff?"

"He was now Don Magrew, and being trained by our CIA in Paris to be one of them. He painstakingly lost his Russian accent and, cliché of clichés, acquired a pipe, and was very quickly indispensable. And when he was ready to be assigned to the U.S., he did a quick disappearing act."

"But Esther reacted to Vanoff just before she was killed."

"I suspect that's because the Vanoff case had been a red hot scandal and probably discussed in Malke's restaurant. Maybe Esther had a suspicion or two and planned to get around to asking Magrew some questions, like how come he was hanging out so much in Malke's place when most Americans spent their time and money in the Café des Deux-Magots, Le Boeuf sur le Toit, or Ben Benjamin's Jazz Club on the Right Bank. Ben still runs the place. He's an old friend of my sister Adele. Or maybe at some point Malke slipped up, as could very well be expected, and referred to him as Feodor, you know, the way you occasionally call me Fred Austerlitz . . ."

"And you occasionally call me Virginia McMath." She added wistfully, "I still get those days when I miss Virginia McMath." She was looking ahead out the windshield at the unmarked police car and said, "Mallory's driving like a maniac! Look at him!"

"He's probably got Magrew and Nina in front of him!"

In Magrew's car, Nina Valgorski was shouting, "Feodor! Feodor! Not so fast! We are not pursued by wolves!"

"Oh yes we are, two-footed ones."

She suddenly turned dramatic. "This wasn't supposed to turn out this way! I am ruined! We will be tried and found guilty and shot as spies." Thinking quickly, she said, "I shall throw myself on the mercy of the court! I shall convince them I was a poor innocent young girl duped into espionage!"

"You might have been poor but you were never innocent. You knew exactly what you were getting into, my little pirogen . . .

"Pirogen!" she exclaimed, "how I wish I had some! I am starving to death!"

"That's not the way you'll die if we're caught and you cooperate with the authorities."

"You are threatening me!"

"You are beginning to panic and panic is dangerous. There are many routes set up for us to escape the CIA. When I was ordered to eliminate Malke Movitz and her nephew I was assured by the one person I can trust that we will be safely rescued and spirited out of this country to any place we desire."

"Not the Soviet Union?" asked a wide-eyed Nina.

Magrew's laugh was far from a hearty one. "Feodor Vanoff can never set foot in the Soviet Union again."

Nina stormed with indignation. "And why not? You have served your country faithfully! You have murdered those you were ordered to murder. Could they be so ungrateful?"

"Nina baby," said Magrew, "you don't know the half of it."

Back in Sol Hurok's suite at the Ambassador Hotel, a council of war was underway, the participants being Hurok, Mae Frohman, Theodore Varonsky, and Mikhail Bochno. Hurok was pacing the floor and punctuating the air with a hand that held a very expensive cigar. Mae was busy refilling glasses with strong tea and wishing she could go to a movie. Any movie but a Russian movie. Hurok and the executives of the Baronovitch Ballet were conversing in Russian, and Mae understood very little. Occasionally Hurok paused to give Mae a quick translation of what had been said, but Mae didn't give a damn. Murder and espionage had never been her dish, but the forced feeding she'd been getting lately gave her something worse than acid indigestion. Under discussion now was Fred Astaire's ballet and the executives were all for canceling it. They hadn't seen much of Fred's choreography, but what they had seen was totally discouraging.

Castanets!

Mikhail Bochno hid his face in his hands and moaned. Varonsky murmured soothing words but Bochno continued to rock back and forth in pain. He associated castanets with Generalissimo Franco of Spain, and Franco during the war had given aid and comfort to Hitler, Hitler the archenemy who had betrayed a peace pact with Stalin. Mae was thinking the Soviets had conveniently short memories. Hurok was busy badgering the men and Mae's money was on her boss, who suddenly reverted to broken

English. "You must not break faith with me. I will not let you!" Mae waved away cigar smoke that threatened to both choke and blind her. "To break faith with me would be worse than a doctor betraying the hypocritic oath!"

"Hippocratic," corrected Mae despite a coughing fit.

In the unmarked police car, the Romanov inheritance was under discussion. Hazel asked, "Who do you suppose gets the loot if Magrew wipes out the heirs?"

"I'm sure Snyder the lawyer has that all worked out. I suspect he'll be a very rich man."

Villon said with assurance, "Magrew won't wipe out all the heirs."

"But if they're in the house with Malke," insisted Hazel.

"They're not," said Villon.

He was annoying Hazel. "Now how the hell do you know?"

"Alida and Mordecai just passed us in a limousine going in the opposite direction."

"You're kidding!" Hazel turned to look out the rear window and saw a limousine racing past Fred Astaire's car.

In his car, Fred asked Ginger, "Did you notice the two in the limousine heading back to town?"

"What limousine?" Ginger was trying to figure out what lay in store for them at Romanov's. A suspicion was growing in her mind and she decided it was worthwhile to nurture and cultivate it, a suspicion that there might be more to Malke Movitz then met the eye.

"Malke's nephew was driving Alida Rimsky back to town."

"Oh, the poor dears," said Ginger. "Probably driving to the rehearsal, Mordecai to see his Luba Nafka and Alida to see her husband, and how are they to know Esther was murdered and the rehearsal's been canceled."

"Ginger," said Fred patiently, "it's probably been on the radio by now!"

Ginger snapped her fingers. "Of course! Malke is addicted to the radio. She has it going in the kitchen all day!" She paused and then said, "Fred?"

"What?"

"Malke Movitz."

"What about her?"

"Why do I suspect she's more important than we think she is?"

"Because she's more important than we think she is."

"How do you know?"

"Because Russians work in pairs and Romanov had to be one half of a pair and who more likely to be his secret sharer then Malke Movitz?"

"That's exactly what I've figured out." She folded her arms and wished they'd get to Romanov's.

Fred smiled to himself while thinking, Dear Ginger, a threat only to fiction's Nancy Drew, girl detective.

At the wheel of the Romanov limousine, Mordecai worried aloud to Alida. "But who would want to murder a rehearsal pianist? If she is inadequate, you replace her, you don't kill her." Alida said nothing. She was preoccupied with how this second murder would affect her and Varonsky. The police aren't fools. Like all police forces the world over, they harbored a certain percentage of idiots, and Villon and his partner Jim Mallory did not come across as idiots. Mallory was slow and plodding, but no idiot. Villon was slow and plotting and would soon come up with the necessary logic that would lead to the revelation of how and why Romanov was murdered, and by whom. She had to discuss this with Varonsky. She had tied up the Romanov phone for almost an hour but her husband couldn't be found. The hotel had not been apprised of the council of war in Hurok's suite.

Mordecai said anxiously, "Alida, you are not listening."

"Not to you, but to myself. Drive faster, Mordecai. I must find my husband."

"You think he is in danger too?"

"Mordecai, you dear innocent lamb, we are all in danger." Her statement was followed by a sigh so heavy that had it fallen in Mikhail's lap it might have fractured his knee.

In Villon's car, Hazel asked, "Herb? How long since you began suspecting Magrew wasn't all that kosher?"

"The time he spent on tour with the ballet and didn't come up with anything all that feasible. But it wasn't until he began reeling off who participated in Romanov's poisoning, I knew he wasn't what he wanted us to think he was."

"Herb, I'm confused."

A frequent state for Hazel to be in, but Villon didn't mention that. "Magrew listed three participants. He left out the fourth. He accused Malke, Mordecai, and Alida. But not a mention of Nina. And he knew she'd brought the glass of soda to Romanov with plenty of opportunity to doctor it with the cadmium. That whistle carried a heavy dose, the way the other whistle carried a heavy helping of slivovitz. When Nina took a swig of the alternate whistle, there was at least another healthy swig left. They ended up doing what they had so cleverly, they thought, avoided to suspend suspicion. Death in small doses. The Dr. Crippen bit." He explained, "A classic case of slow poisoning in England a lot of years ago. Look it up. It's fascinating. That's Romanov's place on the right. Hazel, you wait a few minutes before coming in."

"Herb"—there was suspicion in her voice—"you think there's more to this than you're letting us in on."

"If God is good, it'll all fall into place and all will be right with the world again."

Inside the house, Malke was in the library with Don Magrew and Nina Valgorski. Magrew held a gun in his right hand. Malke's hands were at her sides, fists clenched, defiance in her face. "Do not menace me, Feodor Vanoff, you should remember I am impervious to threats."

"The papers, Malke. Romanov's papers. They incriminate us. They are dangerous."

"Go ahead and search. Look in his desk, in his safe, under the rug—wherever you suspect they are secreted. I do not have any papers."

"Where are they?" persisted Magrew while Nina wondered where the kitchen was located and, if she could get there, what culinary delights the refrigerator would yield. But she stood frozen next to Magrew, admiring Malke's courage in facing the prospect of imminent death.

"All of Romanov's papers are in Morris Snyder's office. You know he was Romanov's lawyer." Their eyes locked. His were anxious, hers were defiant and unafraid. "Go to Snyder's office. And if you choose not to go there, then go to hell."

"If you lead the way," said Magrew blithely.

Neither he nor Nina heard the door opening behind them. Malke's face showed nothing as Villon and Mallory slipped into the room with guns drawn. Villon said smartly, "Magrew, my gun is bigger than yours." Magrew spun about but before he could pull the trigger of his gun, Villon sent a slug into his shoulder. Nina screamed and backed away from Magrew, hand at her mouth looking like a distressed silent screen heroine. Magrew dropped his gun, staggered back, and fell into Malke's sturdy arms. "Nice catch," said Villon.

Mallory thought he meant the three they had rounded up. Hazel came running into the library followed by Fred and Ginger. Hazel yelled, "Herb! Herb! Are you all right?"

"I'm just dandy," he said over his shoulder while Mallory was at the phone dialing the precinct for backup. Malke helped Magrew into a chair as Fred said to Ginger triumphantly, "What did I tell you? Magrew is Feodor Vanoff! How about that!" Ginger patted him on the back and knew he'd be dining off the story for months into the future.

Nina stood over Magrew, holding out a whistle. "Here is slivovitz for you." Villon grabbed the whistle, which annoyed Nina. She said with a haughty toss of her head, "It is positively slivovitz, Mr. Villon." Villon had pushed the trick bottom of the whistle and the top popped open. He sniffed. His eyes widened in amazement. "I'll be damned, it's slivovitz."

Ginger marveled at the woman's audacity as Nina slunk over to Villon and patted his cheek. "My dear, dear detective. There is no need to poison Vanoff. He has nothing to fear just as I have nothing to fear." She crossed to Malke and snapped her fingers under the older woman's nose. "Malke has nothing to fear. All of us involved in this bungled mission have nothing to fear." Villon, the gun steady and aimed at Magrew, said something to Mallory that Hazel strained to hear but didn't catch. She suspected Villon was up to something when he backed away from Magrew to speak to Mallory.

Ginger said to Nina, "Honey, you have nothing to fear but fear itself. Now where did I hear that one? Roosevelt or Churchill?" Nobody told her because nobody was sure.

Nina faced Ginger. "My dear movie star, Nina Valgorski fears nothing and nobody. Nina Valgorski did not fear the beast Lavrenti Beria and she did not fear the monster Stalin. You have made a great capture, Mr. Detective. You have Feodor Vanoff, who defected from Russia with classified information that he sold along with himself to the highest bidder, in his case, the United States. He has not been forgiven. The Soviets are anxious to have him back."

Ginger interrupted. "And it was *your* job to bring him back alive." She said to Fred, "You know, like 'Bring Them Back Alive' Frank Buck who makes those wild animal movies."

Fred said with a smile, "I like those."

Nina reclaimed the spotlight, looking at Magrew. "The Soviets shall have him. Unless America thinks he is important enough to be retained and tried as the poisoner of Esther Pincus."

"Shut up!" cried Magrew.

"Why should I shut up? Speak now and then they won't have to beat the truth out of you." She elaborated to the others. "We have seen those brutal films of yours where a suspect sits on a stool under a solitary overhead lamp and the policemen beat the suspect with rubber hoses. Very sadistic."

Mallory relinquished the phone to Hazel, who was reveling in the glory that she was scooping every newshound in the city. Oh what a tidy sum it would bring her!

Fred was standing next to Villon, anxious to ask him something but there was no quieting Nina Valgorski, who was now zeroing in on Malke Movitz. They heard sirens coming closer. While watching Villon's eyes afire with expectation, Fred said to himself, Here comes the grand finale. He's going to unveil the big surprise. I hope he makes the most of it. He realized Herb was smiling at him. Herb was possibly realizing what Fred was thinking. Ginger was thinking Fred and Herb looked like a pair of gays in a bar making time with each other. In this town, nothing would surprise Ginger.

Nina said, "And now Malke, after fifteen good years in America, it is now back to the salt mines." She said to the others, "Did you guess Malke was much more than a mere housekeeper?"

"Oh yes we did, Miss Smarty Pants. Malke was Romanov's partner! She's as guilty of espionage as he was, right, Malke?"

To Ginger's amazement, the woman's eyes were misting. "Almost right, Miss Rogers. I gave the orders. I saw that everything that had to be done was carried out. I did everything I was instructed to do; and I have no regrets." She said to Villon. "Sir, my nephew, he is innocent. He had nothing to do with poisoning Romanov or anyone else. He is very gifted. He dances beautifully and he sings like a nightingale. Ask him to sing for you 'Chickory Chick Chelah Chelah Checklearomy in the Bananaga.' It will melt your heart."

I can't wait, thought Fred. The sirens had reached the house.

Villon asked Malke, "Malke? Isn't there anything else you want to tell me?"

"What else could there be? What else you need to know I'm sure you will learn from Morris Snyder. Vanoff thought that by removing poor Esther Pincus who knew him in Paris he was erasing the threat of his true identity."

Fred asked her, "Did she know in Paris he was Feodor Vanoff?"

Malke said, "I always feared after too much to drink, Vanoff might have given himself away. But you see, he had nothing to fear. Most of us in Paris chose pseudonyms, to protect our families and friends still trapped in the Soviet Union. Esther knew this."

"No kidding!" exclaimed Ginger, "Well, Malke? What's your real name?"

Malke laughed. It was the first time they had heard her laugh. The sound was surprising. It wasn't lusty or booming. It was a mellifluous contralto. "My real name? My real name is Pollyanna, the glad girl," and she continued laughing.

Villon's additional detectives had arrived. There were four of them and they entered the library followed by two ambulance attendants and Edgar Rowe, the coroner.

Ginger gushed, "Oh, here's the adorable coroner who worships me and Fred!"

"Well, where is the body?" asked Edgar Rowe as Malke's laughter dwindled away, as though for lack of oxygen. Rowe was staring at Don Magrew. He said sternly, "You are supposed to be dead." An ambulance attendant was examining Magrew's shoulder wound.

Ginger said to Fred, "Who's playing games around here?" She was pointing at Edgar Rowe. "I saw cutey pie here whispering something to him"—she pointed at Magrew—"as he left the rehearsal hall. Sayyyyy . . . he's not mixed up in this, is he?"

Eighteen

$\mathcal{E}$dgar Roe smiled at Herb Villon, while whistling through his teeth another Astaire and Rogers oldie, "The Way You Look Tonight." "Why, Herb Villon, you had me completely fooled. I thought I had covered all my tracks."

"Edgar, to borrow from Ginger, you were just too cute to be true. Let's go back to your so-called breakdown after your wife's death." Hazel had abandoned the phone and now stood mesmerized listening to Herb.

"What do you mean so-called? I was a nervous wreck. I thought there'd be an autopsy revealing I poisoned the bitch. It was either that or suffer arrest. I didn't relish the thought of jail." He added softly, "I still don't."

"Your trip to Europe, presumably to visit cemeteries and all that crap. You went to Moscow under an assumed name and a false passport. That was for a refresher course."

"Yes, Beria thought I was falling down on the job. And I must admit I was. I was unnerved by the HUAC investigations and the fear my beloved wife had turned over some of my papers to the CIA. She hadn't. But she was leaving me. And since she wanted to go, I thought it best to help her. I was quite wrong about an autopsy. After all, she was the coroner's wife. I explained she had suffered a seizure while watching television. It was a Sunday night. We watched Ed Sullivan's *Toast of the Town* religiously. My word was good, so I got away with it." He smiled again at Villon, of whom he was genuinely fond. "And don't ask that dreadful cliché, 'But why are you telling me all this?' "

Ginger said, "I saw you whisper something to him," pointing at Magrew, "as you left the rehearsal hall. You were instructing him to kill Malke, weren't you!"

"You clever dancing darling! Not just Malke. He was told to make a clean sweep of the household and then disappear to Mexico with the ballerina."

"The ballerina has a name," said Nina ominously.

"Indeed she does," said Rowe, "but not to be repeated in polite company."

Villon spoke. "Your biggest mistake was jumping the gun this afternoon at rehearsal. Arriving with the ambulance while Esther Pincus had not yet died."

"Mother always told me, haste makes waste. But when Magrew a.k.a. Vanoff phoned from the rehearsal to tell me he feared Esther might expose him, I told him to blow the whistle on her. Forgive my poor little joke, but there has been so little laughter in my life since my dear wife Sybil took her leave. She could be a very funny lady when she wasn't threatening to unmask me." He said to Villon, "You know, Herb, ever since I was a young man in college and was seduced into joining the Young Communists League, I did truly believe that in communism lay the promise of the future."

Ginger said to the room, "The promise of my future lies in Leland Hayward. He's my agent," adding grimly, "and he got me mixed up in this mess."

"Why just think, Ginger," said Fred, "if Leland hadn't, you might never have gotten to meet Edgar Rowe."

With one leg stretched in front of him and his arms raised overhead, Rowe cried, "Ta-da!"

Half an hour later in the Polo Lounge of the Beverly Hills Hotel, one of Hollywood's most popular watering holes, Fred and Ginger sat with Villon, Hazel, and Jim Mallory. Ginger asked Villon, "What happens to this bunch? A trial? Firing squad? Jail? What?"

"Why, Ginger, don't you read magazines like *Time*?" asked Herb.

"I can never find the time." Fred's eyes rolled up in his head and then returned while he reached for his glass of red wine.

Herb said to Ginger, "They'll be swapped."

"Swapped? What do you mean swapped?"

Fred said, "Swapped, sweetheart, like baseball cards."

She was astonished. "You mean they'll be traded?"

"That's right," said Herb, "We'll give them back their spies and they'll give us back ours."

"You mean the Russkies have some of our guys behind bars?" Ginger couldn't believe it.

Fred said, "Ginger, they take as many of our people prisoner as possible. They hold them in reserve, just for emergencies like this. We do the same thing with their guys. But like Nina says, someone like Magrew isn't looking forward to going back. I kind of feel sorry for Varonsky and his wife. They wanted so badly to stay here once Varonsky defected."

"They'll be all right," Villon assured Fred. "Varonsky will defect successfully. He has a lot to tell the boys in Washington and he'll make a deal that includes getting Alida free of the charges against her, aiding and abetting in poisoning Romanov."

"Oh Romanov," wailed Ginger.

Fred patted her hand, "He's probably quite content in that great Psychiatric Clinic in the Sky."

"Or playing piano on cloud nine," said Hazel.

"Well, folks, I'm going to phone Sol Hurok. He's probably having a series of fits." Fred asked a waiter for a phone, which was brought promptly. A few minutes later he was hearing Hurok cry, "Where did you and Ginger disappear to? You left me historical!"

"Hysterical," corrected Mae.

The show, of course, went on. Sol Hurok would not have it any other way. There was no *Rasputin* ballet; instead Fred substituted a reprise of several numbers identified with him and Ginger and it proved to be much more satisfying than Fred tapping with a matted beard covering his face and Ginger coping with castanets and flamenco foot stomping. Luba Nafka was elevated for the night to Nina's former position as prima ballerina and convinced Hurok to let Mikhail Pfenov partner her in a *pas de deux* which they performed quite satisfactorily. The guest viewing room at NBC was filled with VIPs, including Hurok, Mae Frohman, Villon, Jim Mallory, Hazel Dickson, and Lela Rogers, who was entranced by her daughter in the closing number with Fred. There were four television screens and Fred and Ginger dominated all of them.

The number opened with Ginger singing *"They all warned me not to spy on, Mr. and Mrs. Backburner's charming scion. Now I've got a table to eat my humble pie on . . .'"* and then Fred sang, *" 'But what you really need, Is a shoulder to cry on . . .'"*

"Oh, it's adorable," said Lela Rogers while trying to figure out what percentage of the company were "commies." Hazel shushed her and immediately became suspect in Lela's eyes.

Ginger sang, *" 'So I'm singing a very sad medley, The consequences have turned quite deadly, Because I let all the things he said be, As dangerous as a lion . . .'"*

" 'You need a shoulder to cry on!'" sang Fred.

Mae Frohman was glad she and Hurok were returning to New York the next afternoon. She needed the peace and quiet of her apartment on West End Avenue to settle her nerves. Imagine the coroner being a master spy! Incredible! And he committed suicide by drinking poison from a trick hollow whistle! A whistle!

Ginger was twirling in a spin guided by Fred, who was trying to fight off the multicolored feathers flying from Ginger's gown as she sang, *" 'Ohhhh! Why can't I ever trust, A member of the upper crust!'"*

Herb Villon was sneaking looks at a happy Hurok who three

weeks ago was in despair at the scandal embroiling the Baronovitch Ballet, but now was singing with joy at the realization that nothing boosted a show's ratings like the scandal the company was involved in.

Fred was singing, " 'Now I guess she'll go get high on, Some dry martinis that she'll fly on . . .' "

Ginger sang, " 'And lots of makeup I'll apply on . . .' "

Fred added with feeling, " 'Your beautiful face . . .' "

He ad-libbed the lyric and saw Ginger was beginning to choke up she was so touched, so he joined her, singing " 'But what I really need to do, Is find a shoulder to cry on!' "

Despite misting eyes, Ginger fell into Fred's arms and didn't miss a beat as they tapped before a simple white back curtain that featured twinkling stars of all colors. They danced splendidly, realizing this might be the last time they would ever appear together.

Hurok said to Mae Frohman, "There will never be a pair like them ever again."

Mae agreed. And she didn't have to correct Hurok.